STILL
LAKE

ANNE STUART
STILL LAKE

MIRA®

MIRA®

ISBN 0-7394-2783-0

STILL LAKE

Printed in U.S.A.

STILL
LAKE

Prologue

Summer, 1982
Colby, Vermont

When he awoke there was blood on his hands. The sheets were tangled around his sweating, naked body, his mouth tasted like copper, and there was blood on his hands.

He sat up, cursing, pushed his long dark hair away from his face and looked blearily out into the morning sunshine. It was early—he hated waking up before noon.

And he sure as hell hated waking up covered in blood.

He stumbled out of bed, heading toward the back door to take a leak. He looked down and saw he had streaks of blood on his body. He leaned against the door and closed his eyes, groaning.

He slept in one of the tumbledown cabins by the lake, but it didn't have a shower, and there was no way in hell he was going up to the big house like this. No way in hell he was going to stand around with some animal's blood on him. He must have hit a deer last night, driving home, though for the life of him he couldn't remember a goddamned thing.

He pulled on a pair of paint-spattered cutoffs and headed down to the lake, as fast as his pounding head would let him. He'd smoked too much, drunk too much, the night before, and he needed it to wear off, fast. The cold lake water would clear his head, bring his memory back. When he got back to his room he'd finish packing and get the hell out of there. He'd had enough of small-town Vermont.

Even in August the lake was icy cold, shocking the hell out of him. He let out a shriek as he dived beneath the surface, but he kept going, letting the frigid water flow around him, washing the blood from his hands, from his long hair, from his thick beard.

He surfaced twenty yards from shore, tossing his long wet hair over his shoulder, and squinted into the sunlight. There were more people than usual up at the inn—Peggy Niles must be in seventh heaven. She'd be wanting him to fetch and carry, even though he'd told her he was leaving. Maybe he'd just skirt around the back of his place, grab his stuff and get the hell out of there before he could change his mind. Lorelei had told him to get lost, and he wasn't the kind of man who stayed in one place for too long. Winter was coming, jobs would be opening up in Colorado, and he was ready for the life of a ski bum.

He dove back under the water, heading toward shore with long, easy strokes, circling around past the small sandy beach and the long wooden dock he'd built a few months back.

When he surfaced again, he saw a pile of clothes floating at the edge of the water, among the cattails that he'd spent half the summer trying to get rid of. He recognized the garish striped shirt that was one of his favorites, and he wondered who the hell had taken his suitcase and thrown it in the lake. Probably Lorelei—she'd been pissed off big time when he told her he was leaving, but then, she hadn't given him one good reason to stay. Not that he could even imagine one.

He moved closer, squinting. He was slightly near-sighted, but he never wore glasses except for his prescription sunglasses, and God knew where they were back in the mess of his room. The clothes were floating, half in, half out of the water, but he didn't recognize the white shirt. He didn't own any long-sleeved shirts.

He stopped moving, waist deep in the chilly water, and his skin froze. And then he moved, fast, running through the water till he reached her side, turning her over to see her pale, dead face, and the sliced throat, like a jester's grin, curving beneath her jaw.

They loomed over him, coming out of nowhere, waiting for him, and he couldn't move, frozen in the chilly water with Lorelei's body in his arms.

"Thomas Ingram Griffin, alias Gram Thomas,

alias Billy Gram, you're under arrest for the willful murder of Alice Calderwood, Valette King and Lorelei Johnson. Anything you say..."

He didn't listen to the words. He looked down at the girl in his arms, the girl he'd held last night, the girl whose blood had stained his hands.

And he began to cry.

1

There was only one major problem with trying to save the world, Sophie Davis decided as she stuffed half a blueberry muffin in her mouth. No one wanted her help.

The kitchen at Stonegate Farm was deserted, and Sophie perched on one of the stools, hiking her flowing chintz skirt around her legs as she devoured the rest of the muffin, no mean feat since it was one of those wickedly oversize ones, with enough fat to clog the arteries of a family of four. She was a firm believer in the tenet that calories consumed in private didn't count. There had been three muffins left from breakfast. She reached for the second one.

It wasn't as if anyone else wanted them. Her mother, Grace, barely ate enough to keep alive, and when her half sister, Marty, finally dragged herself out into the daylight she'd refuse everything but coffee and cigarettes.

Sophie could sympathize with the cigarettes. She'd given them up four months ago, and in return she'd added fifteen pounds to her already generous frame. And she never spent a day without thinking longingly of one last smoke.

She broke the second muffin in half, putting the rest back on the English stoneware plate in the vain hope she wouldn't succumb to temptation. Sugar and butter were an entirely satisfactory substitute for nicotine, but unfortunately she could see what they were doing to her body. The cigarettes had been turning her lungs black, but no one was looking at her lungs. If she kept on at this rate she'd be out of size twelves before long and into fourteens. She took the second half of the muffin and shoved it into her mouth.

She needed to get her life back under control. The first year of a new business was always bound to be a bit shaky, but Stonegate Farm was the perfect location for a country inn, and Sophie had energy and enthusiasm to spare. For years most of her decorating and baking had been only in theory, research for the syndicated column she wrote while she lived in a small apartment in New York. Marty called her the poor woman's Martha Stewart, which Sophie would have taken as a compliment if Marty hadn't been sneering when she said it.

And now she had this early nineteenth-century farmhouse on the edge of the Northeast Kingdom of Vermont, a dream location for a dream profession. It was a huge, rambling old house, with half a dozen bedrooms and an extra wing off the back that might be salvaged and eventually turned into even more guest rooms. Everything had seemed so simple when she'd mortgaged her life and her soul to bring Marty and Grace up here.

Not that Grace was particularly thrilled. She'd never been the bucolic type, but her last bout with breast cancer had left her surprisingly weak, and for the first time she admitted she needed help. She'd accompanied them, reluctantly, insisting that as soon as she regained her strength she'd be off on her endless travels. Four months later Sophie knew she wasn't going anywhere.

This time it wasn't the cancer. As far as she could tell Grace had made it through this second reoccurrence with flying colors. But in the past few months her mother had gotten more and more forgetful. Grace had never been much of a deep thinker—Marty and Sophie's mutual father had called her Spacey Gracey with equal parts malice and affection. But her current situation was serious enough that Sophie had gotten worried.

Not that there was anything she could do about it. Doc had been her best friend and confidant since she arrived there, and he'd basically shaken his head. "I don't know whether she's having tiny strokes or if it's early-onset Alzheimer's disease," he'd said. Grace had flatly refused to go into the hospital for testing, and Doc had told her there'd be time enough if things progressed.

Marty, with typical teenage charm, resented everything about the inn, including the fact she was expected to help out. She resented her older sister even more, but then, that was nothing new. And Grace was getting more and more forgetful, so that she drifted through their lives like a ghostly stranger, old before her time. Which suited Marty just fine. It was bad enough that Sophie had dragged her to the back end of beyond—why did she have to bring the old lady along, as well? Wasn't this torture enough? she'd demanded.

Sophie eyed the last muffin. If she ate three of them she'd feel sick, not immediately, but soon enough. It didn't matter, she wanted that muffin, and no one was around to watch her.

She was just about to reach for it when she heard someone outside the kitchen, and she pulled her hand back guiltily.

Grace wandered into the room, her gaunt figure dressed in mismatched clothing, the buttons on the raveling sweater awry. Grace, who'd always been so particular about her designer clothing and her hair. She looked twenty years older than her actual age of sixty. Marty came in behind her, not looking particularly pleased.

"I made muffins," Sophie said cheerfully, ignoring the fact that only one remained.

"How nice, love," Grace said in her soft voice. She had made a vain attempt at putting her long, graying hair in a bun, but strands of it stuck out at strange angles, and Sophie knew it would come down in a matter of minutes, leaving Grace looking even more disheveled. "I think I'll just have some coffee."

"You need to eat, Mama," Sophie said. "You know what Doc said."

Grace stopped to look at her, an odd expression in her hazy blue eyes. "Don't believe everything everybody tells you, Sophie. People aren't always what they seem."

"I'm not..." Sophie began, used to Grace's increasing paranoia, but her mother had already poured herself a mug of black coffee and wandered off, leaving Sophie alone with her sister.

Marty headed straight for the coffeemaker without a word.

"Good morning to you, too," Sophie said, then could have slapped herself. Sarcasm didn't make anything better.

Marty didn't even bother glancing at her. She poured her coffee and took a deep gulp of it, studiously ignoring her.

"Did you put the new towels in the closet?" Sophie tried to keep her voice light and nonconfrontational. God knows Marty could find something to take offense at in the most innocuous of conversations, but Sophie did her best to avoid conflict whenever she could.

Marty kept her head buried in the crossword puzzle she was perusing. This week her short-cropped, spiky hair was black, tinged with fuchsia at the tips. She'd need to bleach it again when she went to her next phase. Sooner or later she wouldn't have any hair at all, a prospect that Sophie regarded with mixed feelings. At least she could hope that not too many incipient bad boys would want to impregnate a bald-headed seventeen-year old. "You told me to, didn't you?" Marty said in a hostile voice.

Sophie sighed, controlling her frustration. "I need your help, Marty. You need to contribute your share to the running of this place if we're going to make a go of it. It's nearing the end of summer, and you know we need to open by foliage season if we're going to recover some of the renovation costs. I've already got reservations for September...."

"Why should I care? It was your idea to drag me off into the middle of nowhere, away from my friends. I'm not interested in running a bed-and-breakfast, I'm not interested in being locked up in the country with you and that crazy old bat, and I'm not interested in helping you."

It was a good thing she hadn't gone for that third muffin, Sophie thought—the second one was already doing a number on her stomach. "That crazy old bat is my mother," she said. "I know she's not yours, but I have a responsibility to her. Do we have to go over this every single day, Marty? Why don't you go find someone else to harass?''

"I don't have a problem with anyone but you, and I'll keep after you until you listen.''

"I listen," she said patiently. "I know you miss your friends, but, Marty, those people are no friends to you.''

"How would you know? I haven't noticed anyone flocking around you. Face it, Sophie, you don't know how to make friends and you're jealous that I have so many.''

"Your so-called friends are nothing but trouble.'' Another mistake, Sophie thought the moment the words were out. It just gave Marty more reason to fight back. How did her little sister always manage to get her back up?

Marty gave her a sour smile. "Then I fit right in with them, don't I?''

"Please, Marty…''

"The goddamned towels are in the goddamned linen closet. Teal and beige and ivory and lavender and every other damned color you seem to think is necessary," she snapped. "All set for your goddamned guests. Now, leave me alone.''

She slammed out of the room, taking her coffee and the paper with her. Sophie watched her go, a tight hand clamping around her heart. She reached for the third muffin.

It didn't look as if things were going to get any

better in the near future. Marty had been sullen and depressed for the last few months, ever since they'd arrived in Colby. Sophie had hoped and prayed that getting her away from the city would give her a new start. That sunshine and country air and hard work would start to make the difference.

So far things hadn't improved noticeably. While Sophie did her best to manage a strained smile and ignore Marty's sullen hostility, she wasn't really made for sainthood. Tough love, she reminded herself, like a litany.

They were a mismatched family, the three of them. Grace had divorced her stodgy, Midwestern husband when Sophie was just nine, put her only child in boarding school and taken off for parts unknown. Sophie's father, Morris, had quickly remarried, sired another daughter, Marty, providing a stifled, antiseptic existence for Sophie on her vacations. All that had changed when Marty was nine and her parents died in a car accident. Family was family, and Sophie, fresh out of Columbia, had taken her sister under her wing and provided a home for her in Grace's rambling old apartment on East Sixty-sixth Street. Losing her parents at a young age had been bound to have an effect on Marty, but globe-trotting Grace and stay-at-home Sophie had done their best to fill that void, and succeeded marginally well. Until the last year and a half, when Marty had gone from one disastrous incident to a worse one, and Grace had been diagnosed with a recurrence of breast cancer. It had been downhill from there.

She finished the muffin, then pushed away from the table before she could go searching for more comfort food. She'd been working nonstop for the last few months. Stonegate Farm hadn't been run as an inn since the early 1980s and the entire place had been abandoned for the last five years. Just clearing out the debris had been a massive undertaking, and the decorating and painting—not to mention structural repairs that had taken what little money Sophie had left—were a Herculean effort. She'd finished the main building, but the wing off the back was outright dangerous, and she'd boarded it up until she could decide whether to try to salvage it or to tear it down completely.

For the time being she had enough on her plate with the main part of the farm. She couldn't afford much help—and Grace was too scattered and Marty was almost more trouble than she was worth to be of much use. The inn was close to being ready for its grand opening, and Sophie's nerves were stretched to the breaking point. Every room was booked for the foliage season, and if she managed to carry this off then her worries would be over. Wouldn't they?

She moved to the multipaned window over the

sink, glancing down to the lake. The cool stillness of it called to her, and she tried to resist.

She ought to get to work, she knew it, but for some reason she couldn't quite manage to exert herself. It was a beautiful morning in late summer—the windows were open, letting in a soft breeze, and overhead the sugar maples stirred and whispered. She'd been working so damned hard in the six months they'd been in Vermont—surely she deserved a day off? A day where she could lie around and do crossword puzzles and smoke cigarettes as Marty spent her days when Sophie wasn't hassling her.

Scratch that, no more cigarettes. And she'd really rather curl up in a hammock with a stack of cookbooks and another muffin....

She'd eaten the last one, without even realizing it. It was a good thing she favored loose-fitting clothing that covered a multitude of dietary sins. Unlike her skinny sister, who liked to show as much skin as she could.

Lazing in a hammock on a warm summer day wasn't for the likes of her, not this summer. Maybe by next year, when the inn was flourishing and she could afford to hire more help, she could take the occasional day off and enjoy the peaceful country existence she'd been fantasizing about all her life. In the meantime, there was work to be done if she was ever going to get the place ready for the invasion of guests in two weeks' time. Not only that, but she had a column due on Friday, and she hadn't even started it.

She probably ought to give up the writing, but she couldn't bring herself to do it. *Letters from Stonegate Farm,* the column she wrote for the small Long Island magazine, kept her grounded, reminded her that she was living her dream. After years of telling bored women how to make their own pasta, how to turn empty milk jugs into elegant plant containers, how to turn a tract home into a rural charmer or a fairy-tale palace, she was finally able to put it all into practice. And before long she'd have an appreciative audience, instead of a moody teenage sister and a mother who didn't seem to notice anything at all.

The day was going to be unseasonably warm for mid-August. The sun was already bright overhead, and Sophie pushed the sleeves of her dress up past her elbows. Maybe she'd take just a short walk, down to the edge of the lake, soak up the last bit of quiet. Here, at the north end of Still Lake it was relatively secluded, even at the height of summer. The only other house nearby was the old Whitten cottage, and it had been closed up and deserted for years. Sophie owned the rest of the area, as well as the outbuildings, which included the sagging barn and the old cabins. Those were past saving, and when she could afford it she'd have them torn down.

Eventually this place would be pristine and perfect, teeming with paying customers. For now it was a silent oasis amid the summer bustle.

Whether or not she actually wanted crowds of people here was something she didn't allow herself to consider. It was the only way she could afford to live here, and she always tried hard to be a realist. If taking care of hordes of strangers meant she could live in the country, then she'd accept the price, willingly. Besides, it would be nice to have an appreciative audience for a change.

She pushed open the door, heading down the sloping lawn to the lake, feeling momentarily peaceful. The water was still and dark, seemingly untouched by the frenzied activity at the busy south end. Still Lake was a large, meandering body of water, and if one came upon the north end one might think the peacefulness of Whitten's Cove was all that existed. It wasn't until you got near the end that you saw the wide fingers of water that stretched off toward the west and the south, out of sight of Sophie's quiet expanse of lakefront.

This was the least populated area around Colby. Years ago Stonegate Farm had been a prosperous dairy concern, but no cows had grazed on the wide green fields for forty years now. She'd bought the place from the last of Peggy Niles's drunken sons, who seemed more than happy to get rid of it. It didn't take her long to figure out why. Most people weren't attracted to the site of a famous murder.

Then again, the Niles family had always been a shiftless lot, according to Marge Averill, her good friend. The husband had run off, the drunken sons had bled their mother dry, selling off pieces of the old place while their mother tried to make a go of it, renting rooms to the summer people. She made a decent living until the murders.

It was almost unbelievable that this perfect New England village had been witness to such violence, but Sophie wasn't that naive. Any old town with a long history would have violent stories attached to it, and the Northeast Kingdom murders were far from the most colorful. A tragedy, of course, that three teenage girls had been murdered, but the case had been solved, a drugged-out teenage drifter had been convicted and sent off to jail, and if, twenty years later, some parents still mourned their lost daughters, then that was only to be expected. The very thought of losing Marty was enough to send Sophie into a mindless panic, no matter how determinedly obnoxious she was. Reality must be so much worse.

But the town of Colby had gotten over it, and it no longer mattered that one of the girls had been found down by the lake, the other two close by, or that all three girls had helped out Peggy Niles at the inn. Doc had even suggested, with ghoulish humor, that Sophie could capitalize on the inn's morbid history and advertise it as haunted.

She could never do that, not in such a small town. And Doc Henley hadn't been serious. He was the essence of a kindly, old-fashioned GP—he'd brought half the town, including the three murdered girls, into the world, and he'd pronounced a goodly number of them dead when their time had come.

Sophie sat down on one of the Adirondack chairs, resting her feet against a large boulder as she looked out over the stillness. Waiting for that elusive sense of peace to envelop her.

Something wasn't right.

She heard the car on the graveled driveway, so attuned to the sounds of Vermont that she even recognized the irregular rhythm of Marge Averill's aging Saab. She waved a lazy hand, not bothering to rise. Marge was middle-aged, friendly, with a ruthless streak beneath her sturdy exterior, and she'd been particularly solicitous to Sophie since she'd sold her the old Niles farm and its various decrepit outbuildings, probably because, Sophie suspected, she'd paid too much.

"Glorious morning!" she greeted Sophie, striding toward the edge of the lake with her usual determination. "How's your mother doing?"

"Fine," Sophie said. This was one of the real estate agent's busiest times of year, and she wasn't the sort who came calling if she didn't have a damned good reason. "What brings you out here?"

"You're not going to like it," Marge said flatly, throwing herself down on another chair and shoving her gray hair away from her flushed face.

Sophie groaned. "What did Marty do this time?"

"Absolutely nothing, as far as I know," Marge said, momentarily distracted. "No, it's something I did, I'm afraid. I rented out the Whitten place."

Sophie swiveled around, squinting in the bright sunlight across the shallow cove. That's what was different. The old house was no longer deserted. The shutters were open, and so was the front door, even though there wasn't a vehicle or a person in sight.

"Damn," she said.

"You can't blame me. We haven't had any interest in the place for half a dozen years, and then suddenly the lawyers handling the estate call to tell me they've rented the place out from under me, and he might be wanting to buy. I couldn't very well come back with a higher offer from you without talking to you, and there was no keeping the guy from showing up."

"I'm not in any position to buy it right now and you know it," Sophie said. The third muffin was sitting like a rock in the pit of her stomach. "Everything I have is tied up in Stonegate Farm."

"Look, chances are this deal will fall through. No one has stayed on at the Whitten house for more than a few weeks, and there's no reason this man will be any different. Just be patient. He'll hear about the murders and get spooked.''

''I didn't,'' Sophie said.

''And we both know that women are much tougher than men,'' Marge replied. She squinted into the bright sunlight toward the old house. ''Look at it this way—you can't even see the Whitten house unless you're down here by the lake. And besides, he's not bad-looking, to put it mildly. We don't get that many single men around here over the age of thirty.''

Sophie followed her gaze. In the dazzling sunlight she could now see someone moving around at the side of the old house, but he was too far away to get a good look. Besides, he was the enemy. She wanted the Whitten house, almost more than she'd wanted Stonegate Farm. It was part of her plan, to turn the north end of Still Lake into a serene little enclave that would soothe the body and soul. She didn't want strangers around, getting in the way of her plans. She most particularly didn't want ostensibly good-looking male strangers, not when she had a vulnerable younger sister around.

She turned back, frowning. ''Who is he?''

''He says his name is John Smith, believe it or not. Someone thought he might be a computer nerd, planning on setting up business around here. Someone else thought he might be some kind of financial consultant. That should last about six months, max. No one can make a living around here unless they're independently wealthy.''

"I'm planning to."

"That's different," Marge said blithely. "You and I live off the tourist industry. We'll make out just fine. Now, if Mr. Smith were a carpenter or a plumber it would be a different matter. Not that we haven't got more than our share of carpenters around here. Anyway, I wanted to warn you in case you decided to go wandering around the place. He's got a year's lease with an option to buy, but I bet he'll be out once the snow flies. Or once he hears about the murders.''

He'd disappeared behind the old house, leaving Sophie to look after him thoughtfully. "Maybe," she said. "Or maybe he already knows."

"What's that supposed to mean?"

Sophie shrugged. "I don't know. It just seems funny he'd rent at this end of the lake, when you've told me there are several places open around the south end, including some places that haven't been abandoned for years. Why would someone want to come to a decrepit old cottage, sight unseen?"

"Beats me. I just take the rent check," Marge said. She rose, brushing a stray leaf off her twill pants. "Tell you what, maybe I'll do a little investigating. He's too young for me, but I never let a little thing like a decade or two stand in my way, and I'm getting tired of sleeping alone. Unless you're interested.''

"No," Sophie said flatly.

"You haven't even had a good look at him."

"Not interested. I'm having a hard enough time keeping my own life under control—I don't need complications and neither does Marty.''

She didn't miss Marge's brief expression of sheer frustration. Marge had made no secret of the fact that she didn't approve of Marty or the way Sophie treated her.

"Marty can take care of herself if you'd just let her," Marge said.

"She's done a piss-poor job of it so far." She waited for Marge to tell her she'd done a piss-poor job, as well, but Marge said nothing. She knew she didn't have to.

"I gotta get back to work," Marge said, pushing herself off the bench. "Doc said he might come by later. Bet he's curious about your neighbor, even if you aren't.''

Sophie smiled reluctantly. "Doc's an old gossip and we both know it. If the man has any secrets, Doc will ferret them out."

Marge cast a final, longing look toward the old cottage. "He's a fine figure of a man, I'll say that much," she said, smacking her lips. "Let me know if there's anything I can do to help."

"Short of evicting him, I don't think so."

"Just keep Marty away and everything should be fine," Marge said. "In another few weeks you'll be too busy to worry about unwanted neighbors and so will your little sister."

"I always manage to find time to worry."

"Well, stop it," Marge ordered.

"Yes, ma'am. Maybe I'll bring Mr. Smith some muffins to welcome him to the neighborhood. That way I can see whether or not I can find out how long he really plans to stay."

"You bring him some of your muffins and he won't want to leave," Marge said blithely. "My cooking would drive him clear back to...to wherever it is he came from."

"I suppose I could poison him," Sophie said thoughtfully. "That's one way to get rid of him."

"Don't joke about murder, Sophie. Not here." There was no missing the seriousness in Marge's voice. "People have long memories."

"Do they?" She glanced back over at the Whitten house, looking for her unwanted neighbor.

He was nowhere to be seen.

2

The place hadn't changed much in almost twenty years, Griffin thought. A few more tourists crowding into the general store, fewer parking spaces on the town common. There was a gift shop in the once-deserted mill, and a new Scottish woolens store was opening up in the center of town, catering to the wealthy summer folk. And there was a new owner out at Stonegate Farm, planning to open as an inn in September, just in time for the leaf peepers.

No, it hadn't changed. They were still the same overbred, overeducated scions of Harvard and Yale and Princeton, still the same locals who smiled and waited on them and despised them behind their backs. Except there were more of them.

Why the hell had he come back here? He hated this place, with its bucolic charm and small-town nosiness. Twenty years ago it was the first place that had ever felt like home in his rootless life. He'd found out just how hospitable a place it was when he'd ended up railroaded for a murder he wouldn't believe he'd committed.

No, he didn't give a damn about Colby, Vermont,

or the people who lived there. He only cared about the truth.

He wasn't interested in running into any old acquaintances who might happen to remember him, but he'd managed to avoid almost everyone when he picked up a few necessities in town and headed out to the Whitten place. That was another change— two decades ago you couldn't walk out of Audley's General Store without being quizzed as to where you were renting, what brought you to Colby, how long you were planning to stay, and who you were related to. The summer people added where you went to college to their list of questions, and he'd had his answers primed. But they'd taken his money without even glancing at his face, and he'd left the old-fashioned country store with a six-pack of Coke and a block of Cabot cheese and no one paid the slightest bit of attention. He was almost disappointed.

The woman at the real estate office had looked flustered when she handed him the key, and he got the feeling she wasn't too happy about his renting the place. Tough shit. He knew exactly what he was doing, and he didn't give a damn if the place had been cleaned, if the water was on, or if squirrels had taken up residence in the chimney. He just wanted to get there and lock the doors behind him, so he could feel safe once more.

It was an annoying weakness, and he hated it, but

all the will in the world couldn't make it go away. He always felt that way when he came to a new place. Maybe someday he'd get over it, but for now he locked the doors and windows and kept the world at bay. It was better that way.

It didn't take him long to get settled. The road to the Whitten house was rutted and overgrown, discouraging the curious, and the house looked abandoned. He pried open the shutters, then opened the windows to the fresh mountain air. The water had been turned on, after all, and if the living room cushions showed recent evidence of mice he could live with it. He swept the place out, cleared off a dusty harvest table in the living room and carried in his laptop computer before he bothered with groceries and suitcases. At least he'd learned to keep his priorities straight in the last twenty years.

He put the Coke and the cheese in the warm refrigerator, plugged it in and went out onto the front porch. The chairs were stored in a corner, so he sat on the railing, looking down the weedy lawn to the lake. His last sight of Colby, Vermont.

He glanced up at Stonegate Farm across the stretch of water. It looked prosperous—the new owners must have put a great deal of money and energy into it. Now he had to figure out a way to get inside without arousing any suspicions.

It would have been a hell of a lot easier if he had the faintest idea what he was looking for. He didn't remember much about that night, and twenty years hadn't improved his memory.

But he'd been up at the house—he knew that much. Back in the closed-off wing that had once served as the town hospital. And he hadn't been alone.

Maybe that was the last time he'd seen Lorelei alive. Or maybe he'd been the one to kill her—cut her throat and carry her down to the water.

If so, there'd still be traces of blood somewhere. Something, anything that could tell him what happened that night. Maybe just being there would jar his stubborn memory.

Being back in Colby had done zip so far, except make him feel unsettled. If he couldn't sneak his way into the old inn he'd try talking his way in. If worse came to worst, he'd break in.

If that didn't do any good, he'd start taking a look at the rest of the town. How many of the same people still lived there? How many remembered the murders?

Sooner or later he'd find the answers he needed. The good people of Colby might think it was over and done with, the chapter closed.

It wasn't closed, and he knew it better than anyone. By the time he left there'd be answers. An ending. All the questions answered, the dead buried, the ghosts settled.

By the time he left he'd know the truth. He'd

know who killed Alice Calderwood, Lorelei Johnson and Valette King. He'd know whether or not it was him.

It was early evening when he saw the woman coming across the stretch of rough lawn beside the house, and for a moment he thought he was imagining things. He'd spent the rest of the afternoon airing out the old place, tossing mouse-eaten cushions and ancient newspapers into the trash, making a stab at the cobwebs. He'd found two chairs that managed to survive the years of storage and pulled them onto the porch, and he was sitting there, a can of Coke in one hand, his feet propped up on the railing, when she appeared out of the woods.

His emotions were mixed. On the one hand, he sure as hell didn't want people walking in, unannounced, particularly women like this one. She was pretty in a pink-and-gold sort of way, dressed in a flowery thing that was too long and too loose on her body. All she needed was a huge hat and white gloves and she'd belong at a goddamn garden party.

Except that, instead of a teacup, she carried a plate of what looked very much like muffins. And he, a man who needed nothing and nobody, decided not to scare her off. He had his priorities, and food was definitely one of them.

Besides, she was coming from the old inn. Maybe he wouldn't have to make much effort to gain access at all. Maybe the answers would be delivered, like a plate of muffins, right to his doorstep.

Griffin knew well enough he should rise from his indolent position and greet her. He hadn't had a stern mother to teach him any manners, there'd been just his father and him, moving from place to place until he was fifteen and his father died. After that he'd been on his own, but he knew what was proper, anyway. He stayed put, though, still wary, as she climbed the short flight of steps onto the front porch.

He didn't like pretty women, he liked women with character. He liked them sleek and smart like his former fiancée, Annelise. No nonsense, no sentiment. This one had stepped out of a house-and-garden magazine, smelling of flowers and fresh-baked bread, sweet and soft and warm. He just looked at her, deliberately unwelcoming.

"I'm Sophie Davis," she said, and her voice matched her dress. Light, musical, annoyingly charming. "My family and I are running the old inn—I'm afraid we're your only neighbors for the time being until the place opens up this fall. I brought you some muffins to welcome you to Colby."

He took them and set them on the railing in front of him. He needed to dredge up some semblance of charm, but something was stopping him. Maybe it was the complacent normalcy of the young woman standing there. She belonged in a different world from the rootless one he had always lived in—hers was a land of tidy homes and secure families. He was big, rough, sweaty from opening up the house. She was smaller and irritatingly perfect.

He also didn't want her thinking she could just drop in. He valued his privacy, especially when he wasn't planning on being particularly public about who he was and why he was here.

"Thanks," he said, then realized he sounded less than gracious. He glanced over at the old Niles place. "Seems like a strange time to open an inn."

"We've been working hard to get it ready. The place was abandoned for years, and it's taken us a while to get it in any kind of shape."

Empty for years, he thought. He could have had a dozen chances to come back, find the answers he was looking for. He'd been too busy trying to forget.

"Besides," she added, "autumn is the busiest time around here. Even more than summer or skiing season. We're already completely booked for September and half of October."

"When did you say you opened?"

"Two weeks."

Two weeks. Two weeks to get inside the old place before it was overrun with tourists. Two weeks to see if there were any secrets left.

She was staring at him oddly. No wonder. She was probably used to men fawning all over her. He roused himself. If he only had two weeks, then he'd better make the most of every opportunity, whether he was in the mood to or not, and it wouldn't do to rouse her suspicions.

"Can I get you something to drink, Mrs. Davis?" he asked politely, rising from his chair. He towered over her. He didn't like short women, but then, she wasn't really that short. It was just the damned sense of femininity about her that bugged him. She probably wasn't even thirty yet, but she had an old-fashioned air that annoyed him. He didn't want her staying, he hadn't had time to get acclimatized yet. But if she owned the inn then he'd be a fool to drive her away so quickly.

She didn't look too happy to be here, either—she was looking for a chance to escape. "It's Sophie," she said. "I'm not married. And I really need to get back to the inn. I just wanted to welcome you to the neighborhood. When we open you should come by for dinner."

She looked as if she'd rather eat worms than feed him. He'd failed to charm her, which was no surprise. She was looking at him as if she were Little Red Riding Hood and he, the Big Bad Wolf. She wasn't far off.

"Sure," he said. Lying. In two weeks' time he'd be gone. With or without the answers he needed. "Thanks for the muffins." It was a curt dismissal, one she couldn't fail to notice.

Her smile was brittle. "Anytime," she said, turning her back on him and heading off his porch, out of his life. Her flowered skirts flounced in the breeze.

He sat back down in his chair, watching her go, and his eyes narrowed. He didn't trust her, but then, he wasn't in the habit of trusting anyone. No one could be that squeaky clean. She said they'd been working on the place for months. What kind of secrets had she uncovered? What had she obliterated? He'd waited too damned long to face his past. He wasn't going to wait any longer, and no pink-and-pretty hausfrau was going to get in his way. No matter how tempting she was.

"Bastard," Sophie muttered beneath her breath, making her way through the overgrown path to the inn. There was nothing worse than a good-looking bastard in the bargain. Sophie had to admit Marge was right about that. He was tall, with the rangy kind of body she'd always found particularly appealing in men. His features were interesting rather than pretty—a bony nose, high cheekbones and a strong chin gave him the look of an ancient Roman bust. He was about as animated. His eyes were dark behind the wire-rimmed glasses, and his mouth would have been sexy if it had been employed in something other than a frown. His hair was too long—a tangle of gray-streaked dark curls, and he had the personality of a python.

There was a watchful stillness about him that made her nervous, and she'd never been the paranoid type. But she couldn't rid herself of the notion that John Smith was looking for trouble.

It was just as well he was unfriendly, because when it came to good-looking men Marty didn't particularly care about age differences. She'd probably take one look at Mr. Smith's elegant, classical face and fall madly in love. Sophie could only hope he was equally unwelcoming to Marty.

In the best of all possible worlds he'd provide enough distraction for Marty to cheer up. She was still mourning the loss of her latest boyfriend, an unpleasantly tattooed young man known as "Snake," and so far her seclusion at the north end of the lake had kept her away from any possible substitutes. Sophie wasn't naive enough to think country boys were any safer than city boys, but if Marty developed a harmless crush on their unwelcoming new neighbor it might manage to keep her energized and out of trouble.

Assuming Mr. Smith would be just as unwelcoming to a nubile young woman as he was to her.

Sophie had no delusions about her own charms. She was nothing above ordinary—average height, average weight verging dangerously toward plumpness, average features, ordinary hair. She'd never been one to inflame men's passions, and given Mr. Smith's reaction, that wasn't about to change.

Which was fine with her—right now she was far too busy with the inn and her motley family to be distracted by an unfriendly stranger with the face of a renaissance angel. She'd done her duty, baked him muffins, and with any luck she wouldn't have to see him again. The solitude of the Whitten place and the stories about the murders would drive him away, fast.

There was no sign of Marty when she got back to the inn, though she could hear the muffled thump of music Marty seemed to prefer. At least she was keeping the volume down so the tender musings of Limp Bizkit and company didn't spew out over the tranquillity of the lake.

Grace was sitting in her room, rocking back and forth in the old wicker chair, that too-familiar vacant expression on her face, and a new wave of guilt assailed Sophie. Her mother's deterioration had been rapid once they'd come to Vermont—she'd even stopped reading her beloved true-crime books. They lay piled in the corner, heaped on tables, and not even the newest, most gruesome entries into the field could entice Grace's once-avid mind. She simply sat and rocked, a sweet smile on her face, looking decades older than her actual years.

"You didn't eat much," Sophie said, taking a seat beside her.

Grace turned to look at her. "I wasn't hungry,

love. You shouldn't worry so much about me—I'm fine.''

"Did you take your medicine? I bought you some ginkgo biloba that's supposed to help with memory.''

"What's wrong with my memory?'' Grace asked.

Sophie bit her lip in frustration. "You've just been more forgetful recently.''

"Maybe some things are better off forgotten,'' Grace murmured. "Now, don't you worry about me, Sophie. I hear there's a gorgeous young man down at the Whitten place. You should be thinking about him.''

Her mother never failed to surprise her. "How did you hear about him?''

"Oh, there's not much I don't know about this place, even if it seems like I'm not paying attention,'' Grace said. "So why don't you put on something sexy and go welcome him to the neighborhood?''

"I already did. I just came back. I have to tell you he wasn't particularly pleased to see me.''

Grace's eyes were surprisingly critical. "You consider that something sexy?''

Sophie glanced down at her flowered skirt. "I didn't say I was going to wear something sexy— that was your idea. It's not my particular style, anyway. I like flowery, flowing stuff.''

Grace shook her head despairingly. "You'll never get a husband that way."

"Who says I want a husband?" Sophie replied. "You didn't enjoy yours much while you had him."

"You and I are very different, Sophie. You need a good-looking man to distract you from being so damned responsible all the time. You need to fall so much in love that you stop behaving yourself and go a little wild. You need children so you stop fussing over me and Marty. We'll be just fine."

"I'm not in any hurry," Sophie said, trying not to sound defensive.

"Dearie," Grace murmured in her soft, sweet voice. "You need to get laid."

Sophie tried to stifle her shocked laugh. Not that Grace had ever been shy about passion. She'd always been a free spirit, and during her years of travel she'd always been with one man or another. But with Gracey a ghost of her former vibrant self, the earthy suggestion sounded ludicrous.

"As you said, you and I are very different, Mama. I tend to keep my...libido under control."

"Straight-jacketed is more like it," Grace said with a sniff. "Are you so sure you know what you're doing?" She sounded surprisingly sharp.

"What do you mean? Doing without sex?"

"This course you've set your life on. You're not even thirty years old and you've moved to the back end of beyond to work like a dog on this old place.

There are no eligible men around, no movies, no bookstores, nothing to do but work on this old house and take care of your family. Don't you deserve a better life than that?''

"There aren't any eligible men in New York— they're all either gay or married," Sophie said. "And I think this is a very nice life, indeed. I want to take care of you, Mama."

Grace shook her head. "I'm sixty years old, Sophie. I don't need taking care of. I think you should sell this place," she said. "Go find your own life."

"I .wouldn't find a buyer—not at this point. Once I prove it's a going concern then maybe people would want to buy it, but right now I'm afraid we're stuck."

Grace's expression changed, slowly, as if a veil was being pulled over her mind. "Of course, love," she murmured in that vague tone. "Whatever you think is best."

Whatever you think is best. The words echoed in Sophie's ears as she wandered out onto the wide front porch. The moon had risen over the lake, and the night was clear and cool. The overstuffed, re-furbished glider sat in one corner, beckoning her, and she wanted to go and curl up on it, tuck her hands beneath her head and stare at the night sky.

She had paperwork to do. She had bread dough to make, so that it would rise overnight in the re-frigerator. She had laundry and menus and a column to write. She had to spend at least half an hour worrying about Grace and Marty, and she had to do it all without a cigarette.

She'd come to Vermont hoping to simplify her life. To get back to basics, to concentrate on day-to-day living. So how had it all gotten so incredibly complicated?

She looked down toward the Whitten house. From this vantage point she could barely see it in the woods, just a faint light shining through the trees. There was something about the mysterious Mr. Smith that didn't seem right. If he'd moved to Colby to set up some kind of year-round business he'd made a stupid move. There wasn't enough work to support him. And Mr. Smith didn't strike her as a particularly stupid man.

He didn't strike her as a Mr. Smith, either. There was something more going on, and unlike her mother, Sophie had never been fond of unsolved mysteries.

It was probably simple enough. He might have vacationed here when he was a child, or maybe he had a college friend who'd spent time in Colby. The small town was a closely guarded secret. Its pristine beauty depended on limiting the flow of tourists—locals had been known to jokingly suggest they put border guards on the Center Road to keep too many strangers from coming in. It had been sheer luck that

Sophie had heard about the town from a writer friend.

Somehow or other Mr. Smith had found his way to Colby, to the Whitten house. It would be easy to find out what or who had brought him to town, to her very doorstep.

And she had every intention of finding out. Then maybe she wouldn't have to waste time standing on her front porch, staring out into the darkness, thinking about him and what secrets lay behind his cool, dark eyes.

For now she needed to concentrate on getting the inn up and running, and forget about the beautiful, mysterious stranger who'd moved practically into her backyard. In a month or so he'd be gone.

And she'd be here, taking care of her guests, running her inn. Being happy. Or at least serene. Sometimes that was the best she could hope for.

3

Griffin didn't sleep well. Not that he'd expected to—being back in Colby was nerve-racking, and staring down at the lake gave him the creeps. Enough so that he couldn't quite bring himself to break into the old inn to look around while everyone slept. He was going to have to get over that, and fast, if he was going to accomplish what he needed to do.

He opened the casement windows in the bedroom under the eaves. No screens, of course, but it was long after blackfly season, and with luck the mosquitoes wouldn't be too bad. If worse came to worst he could go down to Audley's and get some screening to tack up. But he'd lived through worse than a few mosquito bites—besides, insects tended to have the sense to leave him alone. He just wished he could say the same for people.

There was no coffeepot in the ramshackle kitchen. He found a stovetop percolator, but half the innards were missing. He should have just bought a jar of instant coffee, but he never considered the powdered stuff to be worth drinking. Right now he was ready to change his mind.

He knew where he could find coffee, of course. And probably more blueberry muffins like the ones his visitor had brought over last night. It would give him the perfect excuse to get his foot in the door. Surely a neighbor would be willing to share a cup of coffee with a desperate man? Maybe he should apologize for being so unfriendly yesterday, try to worm himself into her good graces. It wouldn't hurt to try the easy way of getting inside the old building.

The only thing he could remember from the night that Lorelei died was being up at the inn. He and Lorelei used to sneak into the abandoned wing at the back and fuck like rabbits. They'd had too many close calls in the tumbledown cabin by the lake, and Peggy Niles considered it her duty to keep the girls virtuous. She'd had a fanatically religious streak, and Griffin had always figured it would be easier to just avoid her rather than arguing about his right to screw anything that would lie still long enough. He was counting on finding something—anything—in the old wing to jar his memory. If that didn't work, he'd try something else, but it was the obvious place to start. And in order to get in there, he was going to have to get into Miss Sophie Davis's good graces. Even if that was the last thing he wanted to do.

He didn't like the thought of going up there without caffeine already fortifying his system, but he didn't have much choice. It was that or head into the next town over to the old diner, and he wasn't in the mood for grease and canned coffee. Two weeks until the place opened, she'd said. He hadn't come for a vacation—he might as well start now.

The path between the houses was narrower than he remembered, overgrown in places. He tried not to think about the last time he'd walked the footpath, and who'd been with him. It was more than twenty years ago—why couldn't he pick and choose what he remembered and what he forgot? He would have been perfectly happy not to remember Lorelei clinging to his arm, laughing up at him, stumbling along beside him. He would have given anything to remember what happened that final night in Colby, when he woke up and found himself covered in blood.

He'd forgotten the smell of the countryside, the clean, fresh scent of the lake, the sweet resin of the pine trees, the incense of growing things. He'd loved it here once—stayed here longer than he'd stayed anywhere after his father died and he'd been tall enough to pass himself off as an adult. In fact, he'd been much better off without dear old Dad, who'd been a little too fond of the bottle and belt. The old man spent his time either belligerent or mournful. Or passed out. Still, he'd been the only family Griffin had ever known with his mother long gone, and he'd loved him, anyway.

But it was easier to find work, a dry place to sleep, decent food, when you didn't have an old boozer trailing after you.

Funny thing was, he couldn't remember where his father was buried. His mother was buried with her family in Minnesota, but he couldn't remember where he'd ended up laying the old man to rest. That bothered him.

His father had died in Kansas or Nebraska. One of those big, flat states, in a small town, and Griffin had just managed to beg, borrow and steal the money for the funeral expenses. He never could afford a stone, but it didn't matter. He was never going back.

He hated returning to places, especially this particular one. There'd been one point when he was fool enough to think he could spend the rest of his life in Colby. He'd been young, with just a trace of innocence left. The Vermont legal system had knocked that out of him, fast.

Of course, that was before he and Lorelei had gotten involved. Back then he'd never had much sense when it came to women. Lorelei was trouble from the word go. She was thin, lithe and sexually voracious. So voracious, in fact, that one man hadn't been enough for her, and probably not two, either. He'd known he was sharing her, and he'd told himself he didn't mind. He would have liked to know where she went on the nights she didn't creep into the decrepit cottage down by the lake, but she wouldn't tell him and he stopped asking. He didn't want to care enough to feel jealous, but he'd been a kid, and sooner or later it had all boiled over.

He remembered that much. Remembered the screaming fight they'd had, which too many people had overheard. But he couldn't remember anything else. If she told him who else she was seeing. If she'd said anything that would lead him to the truth.

And he couldn't remember if, in his adolescent outrage, he'd put his hands on her and killed her.

That's what a jury had believed, no matter what he'd said. That he'd killed her, and his so-called blackout was only a convenient ploy to get off the hook. But no one knew he'd been in the old wing that night. Hell, even he hadn't remembered until five years later, and by then all he wanted to do was forget.

Now he was ready to remember, ready for the truth. No matter how ugly.

He'd had no reason to kill the other two girls. He'd barely known them, just managed to flirt with them at the Wednesday night square dances. Well, there had been a one-night stand with Valette, but that hadn't amounted to anything, and most people didn't even know about it. Valette had certainly managed to forget it in short order.

In the end the police hadn't even bothered trying to pin the other two murders on him, satisfied that they could tie him to Lorelei and put him away for the rest of his life. They'd been found far enough away—Valette in a cornfield and Alice by the side of the road. The police never bothered to wonder how unlikely it would be to have two killers in a town the size of Colby. Two who preyed on pretty teenage girls. They'd been happy enough to railroad Thomas Ingram Griffin. It was just a good thing the death penalty was outlawed in Vermont. And there hadn't been enough energy for a lynch mob.

He'd worried someone would recognize him once he came back, but he decided they probably wouldn't. It had been easy enough to track down the twenty-year-old newspapers, to look at the grainy photograph of the boy he once was. Hair past his shoulders, a beard covering half his face, a James Dean kind of squint that obscured the fact that he needed glasses. The picture they'd regularly run was a doozy—taken when they'd slapped handcuffs on him at the edge of the lake. He was wearing cutoffs, and you could see his tattoo quite clearly if you bothered to look. He was going to have to remember to keep his shirt on. The snake coiling over one hip would be a dead giveaway.

Without that, no one would be likely to connect the reclusive, bespectacled Mr. Smith with the murdering teenage vagrant. He wore khakis and cotton now, without rips. His beard, something he'd cultivated quite assiduously to hide his too-pretty face, was long gone, and the face that was now exposed was too full of character to be called angelic. His hair was shorter, with streaks of premature gray, and if anyone could still remember the troubled kid they'd locked up, they'd see only a passing resemblance in the face of Mr. Smith. If they bothered to look at all.

He was counting on them to not look. And to not remember. Over the years he'd discovered that people pretty much saw what they wanted to see, and no one would be looking for the lost soul of a once-convicted murderer in a well-heeled tourist.

Stonegate Farm had improved in the last twenty years, though he found that hard to believe. The peeling white clapboard had been painted a cheerful yellow, and baskets of flowering plants, not too many, not too few, hung from the porch. The windows were spotless, shining in the sunlight, the once-wild lawn was tamed into obedience, and even the old barn looked like it was being worked on. The old wing stretched out back, spruced up with a fresh coat of paint, but he couldn't see past the smoky windows. It looked boarded up, impregnable, a mixed blessing. At least the new owner hadn't gotten around to messing with that part of the place, thank God. There was still a chance he might find something that could lead him to the answers he needed to find.

Someone was sitting on the porch, watching him,

and he saw a pair of long, bare legs swinging back and forth.

"Who are you?" It was a teenage girl, probably not much older than Lorelei when she died. She had fuchsia-streaked black hair, a ring through her eyebrow, a skimpy bathing suit showing off a too-thin body, and a belligerent expression on her face. Presumably this was Sophie Davis's sister. No wonder the older sister looked worn out.

"John Smith. I'm renting the house in the woods." He deliberately didn't call it the old Whitten place—there was no reason a stranger would know its name. "I wondered if you happened to have a spare cup of coffee?"

The girl shrugged her thin shoulders. "Sophie usually makes a pot—go on in and help yourself. I'm Marthe. With an *e*. Like the French."

"You sure your sister wouldn't mind?"

The girl's eyes narrowed in suspicion. "How do you know she's my sister?"

"Logic," he said, climbing up onto the porch. The decking had been painted a fresh gray, while the porch ceiling was sky blue with fleecy white clouds stenciled on it. "She told me she was living here with her mother and her sister, and I'm assuming if you were hired help to run the bed-and-breakfast you wouldn't be sitting on your butt."

"Maybe I'm taking a break. You don't happen to have a cigarette, do you?"

"I gave them up. How old are you?"

"Twenty-one."

"Yeah, sure."

"Eighteen," she said.

"Uh-huh."

"Next January."

"Sorry, I'm not about to contribute to your bad habits."

She leaned back, surveying him slowly. "Oh, I can think of much better ways for you to lead me astray."

He laughed, without humor. "Honey, I'm much too old for you."

"I'm willing to overlook a few drawbacks," she said in a sultry voice. "How'd you meet my sister?"

"She brought me some muffins to welcome me to the neighborhood."

The girl's laugh was mirthless. "Watch your back. She wants the Whitten place, and she doesn't care how she gets it. You don't want to end up floating facedown in the lake."

The macabre suggestion was like a blow to the stomach, but Sophie's sister seemed blissfully unaware of the effect she'd had on him. Or the imperfect memories she'd resurrected, of another body floating facedown in Still Lake.

"She doesn't strike me as the murderous type," he said carefully, leaning against the porch railing.

"Things aren't always what they seem," the girl

said cheerfully. "For instance, does this place look like the scene of a savage murder? Not likely. You'd be more likely to die of boredom than having your throat cut. Perfect peace and quiet."

"That's what I'm looking for."

"You wouldn't have found it twenty years ago," she said with ghoulish enthusiasm. "There was a serial killer around here, and he murdered three teenage girls. Raped them and cut apart their bodies. It was really gruesome."

"It sounds it," he said in a bored voice. His memory wasn't that bad—there'd been no rape, and only Alice had been mutilated, though the autopsy had revealed that all three girls had had sexual relations within twenty-four hours prior to their deaths. "Did they ever find the guy who did it?"

"How'd you know it was a guy?" Marthe said suspiciously.

"Most serial killers are men. Besides, you said they were raped."

Marthe shrugged her thin shoulders. "Gracey would know the details—there's nothing she loves more than true-crime thrillers. Of course, she's gotten so addled she doesn't even remember her own name, but if you're curious maybe she might come up with some details."

"Not particularly," he said, lying. "I was more interested in coffee."

The girl hopped up from her perch on the railing,

twitching her flat little rump in what she obviously hoped was a provocative fashion. "I'll show you," she offered. "We'll just have to hope we can avoid Sophie."

The kitchen of the old place had been completely redone. The painted cabinets had been stripped back to bare oak, the floor was a rough-hewn tile, the stove was one of those huge restaurant-style-things, and the countertops were butcher block and granite. A far cry from Peggy Niles's fanatically clean surroundings—he always thought her kitchen was like an operating room. Spotless and scrubbed, even the homey smells of cooking hadn't dared linger in its pristine environs. Only the door to the old hospital wing remained the same. Locked, probably nailed shut as it had been back then, albeit it was covered with a fresh coat of paint.

This room was far more welcoming than its original incarnation. Or maybe it was just the smell of fresh coffee and muffins that gave him a deceptive sense of peace. Smells were one thing that could always betray you, make you vulnerable to old emotions. He'd fought against them all his life.

There was no sign of Sophie Davis, and he didn't know whether that was a consolation or a regret. She wouldn't like her nubile little sister twitching her underclad butt around him, and he wasn't any too fond of it, either. He was as healthy as the next man, but Miss Marthe Davis left him completely cold.

Maybe because he'd never been particularly interested in teenagers.

"So what are you doing today, John?" she asked in an artless voice.

Like a fool, it took him a moment to remember that was the name he'd given her. "Cleaning up the house I rented. I didn't give them any warning when I was coming, and the place is a mess."

"I could help. If there's one thing I know how to do nowadays, it's clean houses," she said with a moue. "I'm sure you could do with a little company."

"Actually I'm fine...." he began, but she'd already twitched her way out of the kitchen.

"I'll just go put something on," she called back to him. "I know Sophie wouldn't miss me."

"Hell," he muttered. There were hand-thrown pottery mugs on the counter, and he took one, filling it with coffee. He drank it black, and he almost snarled when he took his first sip. He should have known that Sophie Davis would make the kind of coffee most men would die for.

He should have poured the rest out, left the deserted kitchen and headed straight for Audley's General Store and the instant coffee section. He didn't usually succumb to temptation, but for some reason being back in the place where he'd let his appetites run wild seemed to be doing a number on his iron self-control. The least he could do was drain the

mug and get the hell out of there, before Martha
Stewart found him.

Too late. Just outside the kitchen, he heard footsteps coming from the old hallway, and he froze.

The last thing Sophie Davis expected to see when
she walked into her kitchen was the enigmatic Mr.
Smith. He was leaning against the kitchen counter,
his long, elegant fingers wrapped around a huge mug
of coffee, and the dark eyes behind his wire-rimmed
glasses were cool and assessing.

"What are you doing here?" she demanded, too
startled to remember her manners.

"Your sister offered me a cup of coffee," he said.
She didn't like his voice. It was slow and deep and
sexy, at complete odds with his cool manner. And
then his words sank in.

"You met Marty?" She tried to keep the note of
suspicion and worry out of her voice. For a brief
moment she'd thought Mr. Smith would provide a
harmless distraction for her younger sister. In the
full light of day, in her bright and airy kitchen, she
knew instinctively that Mr. Smith was far more dangerous than she'd ever imagined.

"Yes," he said, giving nothing away. He seemed
entirely at ease, drinking her coffee and watching
her.

"She's not even eighteen years old, Mr. Smith,"
she said sternly.

"So she told me. Not that I was interested. Nubile nymphets aren't exactly my style."

She wasn't sure she believed him. "What is your style, Mr. Smith?"

He cocked his head. "Is your interest personal or academic?"

The question startled her, but she met his gaze stonily. "I'm trying to look out for my little sister."

"And who looks out for you?"

No one at all, she wanted to say, but she kept her mouth shut. If this was John Smith's idea of making small talk she preferred his taciturn persona. "I don't mean to be rude, but I have a lot of work to do today, and I don't have time to spend socializing."

"Is that what we're doing?" he said. There was an undercurrent of amusement in his rough voice. She didn't like it when men found her amusing.

"I'll be happy to send you home with a thermos of coffee. We're set up to offer them to our guests."

"You mean you'll be happy to send me home and you don't care what you have to do to get me there," he corrected her. "Trust me, Ms. Davis, I'm absolutely harmless."

"Sure you are," she muttered. "You underestimate the effect of those brooding Byronic looks on an impressionable teenager."

"Brooding Byronic looks?" he echoed, his horror unfeigned.

"I'm ready!" Marty appeared in the kitchen door, dressed in a micro skirt and tube top.

"Ready for what?" Sophie demanded.

"I'm going to help John open up the house," she said with sunny ingenuousness. It was almost enough to make Sophie waver—there were times when she thought she'd do anything if Marty would just smile.

But that didn't include sending her off with a good-looking stranger. "No, you're not," she said flatly. "I need your help around here, and I'm sure Mr. Smith is entirely capable of handling the Whitten house on his own. If he needs any help I can give him the names of a couple of people who work out of the village."

"I don't need help..." he began, but Marty broke in, stamping her foot like a spoiled child.

"You're always trying to stop me from doing anything I want. You don't want me to have any fun! You'd just as soon lock me up in a convent and throw away the key."

Sophie took a deep breath. "When did you decide that cleaning old houses was fun? You've been complaining since the day we got here—why in heaven's name would you want to volunteer to do any more than you've grudgingly agreed to do here?"

"Maybe because I want to?"

"And what's a convent got to do with it? Were

you planning on helping him open the house or having sex with him?''

Smith choked on his coffee.

''You hate me!'' Marty cried in a fury. ''Well, I hate you, too!'' And she stormed out of the kitchen, slamming the door behind her.

Sophie didn't want to face her unwelcome guest. She should have gotten used to Marty's scenes by now, but she hadn't slept well the night before, and for some reason Mr. Smith made her uncomfortable. ''I'm sorry about that,'' she said, heading for the coffee and pouring herself a mug, determined not to look at him. ''My sister is at a difficult age. She's got a lot of problems to work through.''

''Does she? She seems fairly typical to me. All teenagers are a pain in the butt.''

She glanced over at him. ''You're a father, Mr. Smith?''

''No. I just remember what it was like. Don't you?''

''Not particularly. I was too busy being responsible to behave like a selfish adolescent. I didn't have time to rebel.''

''Maybe you should try it when you get a chance,'' he said evenly.

''I'm just as happy to have skipped that part of growing up.'' She glanced out the kitchen window toward the lake, not wanting to look at him any longer.

"I've found that you can't really skip parts of the process. Sooner or later they catch up with you and you have to go through them, anyway."

"Let's just hope I'm immune to that particular theory. I don't have the time or the inclination to act like a giddy, lovesick brat."

"Maybe you don't know what you're missing," the man said, setting his empty coffee mug down on the counter. He'd chosen her favorite mug—the teal blue one shaped like a bean pot. She had the gloomy feeling that she'd never be able to drink from it again without picturing his long, elegant fingers wrapped around it. His mouth on it. There was no way around it, the man had the sexiest mouth she'd ever seen.

"I'm better off that way," she said. Wondering why the hell she was even discussing this with him. She knew he was watching her out of his cool, dark eyes, even though she was determined not to meet his gaze.

"Maybe," he said. "In the meantime, since your sister's otherwise occupied, would you consider coming over to the house and taking a look? Give me some idea what kind of help I'll need, maybe give me a few names?"

She stared at him in shock. Yesterday afternoon he'd looked as if he'd be more welcoming to a horde of Vikings rather than his neighbor. Now he was suddenly being relatively pleasant, asking her for help.

The problem was, she didn't trust him. "I can give you the names, anyway...."

"Do I bother you, Ms. Davis?"

She had no choice but to meet his gaze. He was taunting her, and she was half tempted to tell him just how much he bothered her. And why.

But that would be stupid. There was no question at all that the man was extremely attractive, with just the sort of romantic looks that would appeal to an angry, vulnerable teenage girl. If Sophie was to keep Marty safe from temptation, she needed to know her enemy, and Mr. Smith was giving her the perfect opportunity. She couldn't quite figure out why, but she'd be a fool to miss it.

"I told you, call me Sophie. And no, you don't bother me," she added with deceptive breeziness. "I'll be happy to come back to the Whitten place and help you figure out what kind of work you're going to need to have done. I believe in being a good neighbor."

"Oh, me too," he said, and Sophie wondered whether or not she imagined the faint note of amusement in his voice.

"Just let me check on my mother and tell Marty where I'm going."

"You sure that's a good idea? Your sister was already pretty pissed at you."

"Marty's always mad at me," Sophie said with a sigh. "I'm used to it. Why don't you wait for me out on the porch and I'll be with you in a minute? Things seem pretty quiet around here for now."

He glanced toward the door that Marty had slammed on her way out. "All right," he said, and headed out into the morning sunshine.

But Sophie had the firm belief that the mysterious Mr. Smith wasn't nearly as agreeable as he was trying to make her think he was.

And she wondered if she was making a big mistake.

4

Two people were sitting down by the lake, talking in low voices, the freshly painted Adirondack chairs glistening in the August sunlight. Griffin should have stayed on the porch—Sophie Davis wasn't going to be pleased with him for not following orders, but he'd never been the dutiful sort. Besides, the couple sitting down by the lake looked old enough to remember what had happened twenty years ago. Assuming they weren't part of the massive influx of newcomers that had crowded Colby's once-pristine confines.

He walked down the lawn at a leisurely pace. He was playing with fire—what if they took one look at his face and recognized him? It would stop his investigation cold. Anyone who cared enough about the case would know his conviction had been overturned after five years and he'd been released, but that didn't mean they wouldn't raise holy hell if they realized he'd come back.

But he hadn't returned to Still Lake to play it safe. If it had been up to him he never would have come back here at all. He'd made a perfectly comfortable life for himself, and the huge, yawning question had been easy enough to ignore.

Not for Annelise, his law partner and ex-fiancée. It was time for them to get married, she'd announced in her cool, emotionless tones. She was ready to have children, she'd informed him, and all he could think of was a hen getting ready to hatch. He'd had the wisdom not to share that particular image with her.

After all, she was smart, she was gorgeous, she was sophisticated. She was sexually adept. They knew each other well, appreciated their better qualities and ignored their worse ones. But Annelise had no intention of breeding with a murderer.

"You've got to find out what really happened back then," she'd told him in no uncertain terms. "There's no way we can concentrate on the future without settling the past."

He wasn't particularly interested in the future, any more than he cared about his sordid past. One day at a time was more his style, but Annelise was a woman with plans, and very talented at getting what she wanted. This time her wants coincided with his. Twenty years had passed—it was time to find out what really happened. Time to put the past to bed.

And then Annelise had broken the engagement. His cool, practical bed partner had fallen ridiculously in love with one of their clients, and by the time she chose to inform him she had already been married for two days.

Not that he was pining for her. As a matter of fact, what really bothered him was how little he cared. That and the faint note of relief that she hadn't made the mistake of falling in love with him. The very thought made him shiver.

Onward and upward, he reminded himself, drawing closer to the lake and the two old people watching him with unabashed interest. He'd never seen the woman before—he was sure of that, though he certainly hadn't been paying much attention to older women during his previous sojourn in Colby. She was thin, oddly dressed, with flyaway gray hair and a slightly vacant look to her. She could have been anywhere between seventy and ninety, though he suspected she might be younger. And then he met her eyes, and found himself drawn by the surprisingly sharp gaze in their blue depths.

A moment later they seemed to glaze over. "Who are you?" she demanded, not rudely, but like a young child. "Doc, who is he?"

Shit, he thought, as he realized who her companion was. Doc Henley was one person he'd just as soon avoid, at least for the time being. It was Doc who'd stitched up the cut running up his thigh, the result of his careless use of a scythe. It was Doc who'd checked him over while he waited in jail, to see whether the blood that still smeared his body was his own or somebody else's. It was Doc who'd brought the three murder victims into the world, and Doc who'd pronounced them dead.

He hadn't changed much in the years between fifty and seventy. The white hair was thinner, the face had more lines, but the mouth was just as firm beneath his salt-and-pepper mustache. He still had wise, kind eyes, but they met Griffin's without recognition, and he rose, holding out a hand in welcome. A welcome that would be quickly withdrawn if he'd known who he was.

"Must be your new neighbor, Gracey," he said easily. "I'm Richard Henley, but most folks around here call me Doc. And this is Mrs. Grace Davis. Welcome to Colby."

Griffin took his hand. There was still a lot of strength in the old man, and not a trace of a tremor. He was only slightly stooped from age, and he could look Griffin in the eye. "John Smith," Griffin introduced himself. He really should have picked a more interesting alias—John Smith was just too damned plain to be believed.

Gracey didn't seem to have any doubts. "How nice," she said in her soft, fluty voice. "What brings you to Colby, Mr. Smith? To this end of the lake in particular?"

He didn't know whether or not he'd imagined the intelligence in her eyes—it was at sharp odds with her wispy voice and manner. If she was Sophie's mother she couldn't be much older than her mid-sixties, maybe even younger. She looked more like a candidate for a nursing home.

"Looking for peace and quiet, Mrs. Davis," he said. "I thought this seemed like a nice, boring place to spend a few months."

"The snow will fly in three months' time," Gracey said in a singsong voice. "I don't think you'll want to be here then."

"Why not? I'm not afraid of a little snow."

"Probably because the old Whitten place isn't really winterized," Doc said in his genial voice. "If you're planning to stay on past the frost you'll need to find someplace a little more habitable—you surely wouldn't want to put that kind of money into a rented house. Though I can't imagine why you would want to stay—jobs are scarce around here in the off-season. Most folks have to commute to Montpelier or Burlington."

Griffin smiled faintly, not about to offer any more information despite Doc's careful prying. "I'll deal with that when I have to," he said easily. "In the meantime I'm just here for the serenity."

Doc turned to look out over the lake, his eyes narrowing in the sunlight. "Looks can be deceptive, my boy. This town isn't nearly as quiet as it seems. Most places aren't."

It was a perfect opportunity, and he'd be a fool to let it pass him by. "What do you mean?"

"Murders," Gracey announced with ghoulish delight, pushing her flyaway gray hair away from her face. "Lots of unsolved crimes in the Northeast Kingdom, including peaceful little Colby."

Griffin shrugged. "You mean the teenage girls who were murdered twenty-five years ago? Someone mentioned it to me. But they told me they caught the killer."

"Twenty years ago," Doc corrected him. Griffin knew exactly how long it had been since Lorelei, Valette and Alice died. To the day. "And they caught the boy, all right. Sent him to jail, but he got out a few years later on a technicality. There are some who say he wasn't the killer, anyway—that he got railroaded."

That was the first Griffin had heard of it—it had seemed as if the town was out for his blood. He was lucky the Northeast Kingdom didn't go in for lynching, or he wouldn't be here right now. "Really?"

"Then there are others who believe he killed those three girls and more besides, and sooner or later he'll come back here, to finish up what he started," Doc said.

Griffin didn't even blink. "Well, what's taking him so long? He's probably dead himself by now."

"Not that boy," Doc said. "He's a survivor. Nothing was gonna get that boy down, not prison, not nothing."

"Do you think he did it?" Griffin asked. The moment the words were out of his mouth he realized it was a mistake.

Doc focused his pale blue eyes on him for a long, unsettling moment. "I don't know. There were times when I thought that boy was pure evil. Then there were other times when I thought he was just a lost soul. I suppose he could have killed them. But I think he would have had to have been out of his mind on drugs or something to have done it."

Not much help, Griffin thought grimly. And now Doc was staring at him with an odd expression on his face, as if he could see past the wire-rimmed glasses and the curly hair and the clean-shaven face, see past twenty years into the face of a boy who might be a killer.

Doc shook his head. "One of life's little mysteries, I guess. Just like Sara Ann Whitten."

"Whitten?" Griffin echoed uneasily.

"Seventeen-year-old daughter of the folks who owned the place you're renting," Doc explained. "She took off a couple of years after the murders. Just up and disappeared one day, and no one's ever found a trace of her. If it weren't for that boy being locked up they would have thought she'd been murdered, as well."

"But you said some people didn't think he did it," Griffin said.

Doc just looked sorrowful. "No one knows what happened. Whether the boy was a mass murderer or just a jealous lover. Or maybe just an innocent caught up in a mess bigger than he could handle. It doesn't matter—it was long ago, and folks around here don't like to think about it. Let the past rest in peace.''

Griffin said nothing. The past wasn't resting peacefully, it was haunting him. And he wasn't going to stop until he laid it to rest himself. No matter what the price.

Sophie didn't plan to waste any time—the sooner she got him off the property and away from Marty the happier she'd be. Not that Mr. Smith was Marty's type—her sister tended to go for young and buff and brainless. Smith had gray in his hair, for heaven's sake, and he wore wire-rimmed glasses. Hardly the stuff teenage dreams were made of.

And yet Sophie knew with a gut-sure instinct that Mr. John Smith would be just about irresistible to any impressionable young woman. Even she, armored and totally, determinedly uninterested, could feel the inevitable pull. All that mysterious, brooding beauty, even the hint of danger, was ridiculously tempting. Fortunately she wasn't the sort to be tempted.

He hadn't waited for her on the porch, which didn't surprise her in the least. He'd wandered down the lawn to the edge of the lake, and he was staring across the shimmering blue expanse toward the unseen village, his back straight and tall. And he was no longer alone.

At least it wasn't Marty this time, though the alternative wasn't much more reassuring. Gracey was looking up at him, her gray hair tumbling to her shoulders, her mismatched clothing drooping around her too-thin body. Doc was there, as well, a small buffer, but Sophie almost took a header off the wide front porch in her haste to get down to the water's edge.

"You didn't tell me we had a new neighbor," Gracey said as she approached.

Sophie bit her lip in frustration. "Yes, I did, Mama. We already discussed this yesterday, remember?"

Gracey's eyes brightened for a moment. "Oh, yes, love," she said. "I remember now. I told you you needed to get laid."

Mr. Smith's choking sound didn't make the hideous situation any better. Doc had jumped in quickly, taking Gracey's thin hand. "Now, Gracey, you know you're not supposed to say things like that."

"But it's true. Sex is very healthy for a young woman like Sophie. Besides, he's very attractive. Isn't he, Sophie?"

Sophie tried not to cringe. "He's not my type, Mama. Why don't you go back to the house with Doc and..."

"What do you mean, he's not your type? You're too picky." She swung her wicked gaze to the silent stranger. "Tell me, Mr. Smith, are you married?"

"No."

"Involved? Gay?"

"No," he said. The monosyllable was delivered entirely without inflection, and Sophie refused to look at him to see his reaction to her mother's outrageousness.

"You see!" her mother said triumphantly. "He'd be perfect. You go off and have sex with him and I'll look after the inn. Marty can help me."

"Come along, Gracey," Doc said kindly. "I'll make you a cup of tea."

Sophie didn't wait any longer. She headed toward the narrow path through the woods, not stopping to see if John Smith was following. If he wasn't, just as well. She'd keep going, hike out to the main road and circle back to the inn.

He was close behind her—there was no escape. He waited until they were out of sight of the inn, almost at the edge of the Whitten place, before he spoke.

"Why are the women in your family so interested in my sex life?" He sounded no more than vaguely curious, but Sophie wasn't fooled.

It was now or never. She stopped, turning to look at him. He was closer than she'd realized, and she had to look up. He was the kind of man you'd need to wear high heels around, so as not to let his height intimidate you. "What do you mean?"

"Well, you think I want to have sex with your seventeen-year-old sister, your mother thinks I ought to have sex with you, and I imagine Marthe probably has ideas of her own."

"Well, you can just ignore any ideas Marty might have. She's an impressionable teenager. And ignore my mother, as well—surely you can see she's got some kind of senile dementia."

"Maybe," he said. "But I think she's a lot sharper than she pretends to be."

"And you base that on what? Five minutes in her company? Or the absurd notion that I would want to go to bed with you?"

"See? Obsessed with sex," Mr. Smith said in a calm voice.

"I'm not! We're not." She took a deep breath. "I have no interest in you at all, Mr. Smith, except to help out a neighbor in need."

"And to keep your sister away from me."

It would be foolish to deny it. "There's that, too."

He nodded. "As long as you're honest," he said. "I don't like lying."

"Neither do I, Mr. Smith." Another man might have missed her slight emphasis on his anonymous name. He didn't.

His faint smile was self-deprecating, but he didn't

say a word. He just moved past her down the path to the derelict old house.

A weaker woman would have simply turned and headed back home. Sophie squared her shoulders and followed him, pushing the tall grass out of her way as she kept his back firmly in her view. Not that she would have had any trouble finding her way. She'd explored the property around the abandoned Whitten house not long after they moved to Colby, and whenever things were overwhelming at the inn she'd disappear for a few hours, sit on the porch and watch the quiet glide of the water as it moved past the rocky point of land just beyond the house.

She took her time, and he was waiting for her on the porch when she got there. "Did you know I've got an option to buy this place?" he asked abruptly.

She doubted she could keep the stricken expression off her face. "Why?"

"I like it here. The peace and quiet. The remoteness."

"The house is a mess. I doubt it could be winterized, and there's no way to earn a living year round..."

"Maybe I could turn it into a bed-and-breakfast."

She stared at him in horror. "What?"

His slight smile was far from reassuring. "I'm kidding," he said. "Do I strike you as the hospitable type? I'm not sure I even like sharing this end of the lake with anyone, much less my house.''

She took a deep breath. ''No wonder you're un-attached.''

''Are we back to sex again?''

''No!'' She moved past him, pushing open the torn and rickety screen door and walking into the old cottage. She'd never been inside before, only peered through the windows, but it looked and smelled just as she'd imagined it. The furniture was old and solid—a mission oak sofa and table that had probably been built at the same time as the house; a couple of sturdy rocking chairs; a wide table and chairs. The fieldstone fireplace held nothing but ashes, the bookshelves were crammed with the detritus of vacationers over the years—*Reader's Digest* condensed books and paperback mysteries. The floor creaked beneath her feet, and the mice had gotten into the braided rug. And if the so-called Mr. Smith bought this old wreck out from under her she'd kill him.

If there'd been any way to turn this place into a bed-and-breakfast she would have bought it in a snap. The Niles homestead was bigger, with more lake frontage and the good-size wing in back for when she wanted to expand. But the Whitten house called to her soul, a hidden little jewel in the forest by the lake.

"What do you think?" he asked, oblivious to her covetous thoughts.

"I think you need an army of people to come in and shovel out this place," she said frankly. "The screens are torn, the chimney probably needs cleaning, the cushions have been chewed by animals. What's the roof like?"

"I haven't the faintest idea," he said wryly.

Without thinking she started up the long, narrow stairs to the second floor. There were four bedrooms and a bath off the center hallway. The claw-footed bathtub was stained with rust, the old linoleum on the floor was cracked and torn. Three of the bedrooms were abandoned, smelling of mice and mildew, the fourth was relatively more habitable.

It had a fireplace, as well, probably connected to the same sorry chimney. The old iron bed was high and wide, covered with quilts and a myriad of pillows that had somehow survived the mice. The casement windows stood open to the lake, and an old wicker chair had been drawn up close. There was a book open on the floor beside it, and she moved closer, curious. Then she realized that Mr. Smith had followed her up the stairs and was leaning in the doorway, watching her while she poked around his bedroom.

"Looks like the roof needs replacing," she said calmly. "Or at least mending."

"Oh, really?"

The man was very annoying. He either said too much or too little. "Look at the watermarks on the ceiling by the fireplace," she said. "The flashing needs fixing. And there are some stains near the window. Maybe ice dams, but since this house isn't used in the winter that's probably not it. No one shovels the roof in the winter, so it's most likely weakened from the weight of the snow. You need someone to come and check it out or the whole thing might collapse on you while you're lying in bed."

Damn, why had she said the word *bed?* she thought hastily. Without thinking they both turned to contemplate the bed. "We wouldn't want that, now would we?" Mr. Smith said. "Who do I call?"

She was still curious about that thick tome by the side of his chair, and she had no intention of leaving the room until she read the title. "Hank Maynard fixes chimneys. Zebulon King does carpentry, and you can probably get his wife and son to come in and clean the place if they're not too busy working for the other summer people. They're a little odd, but good workers."

"Summer people? Is that what I am?" He sounded amused at the notion.

"Those are the people who come in the summer and leave when it gets cold. You're a summer person."

"What makes you think I'll be leaving?"

She ignored that. "How's the plumbing?"

"Aren't you going to check?" he asked. "You're very thorough."

She refused to blink. "I'll take your word for it."

"The water's rusty, but the pipes seem to work."

She moved around the chair, too damned close to the bed, ostensibly to look at the casement windows. The framing seemed in good shape, and the glass was still intact. She glanced down at the book, then stepped back hastily.

"Finished?" he asked pleasantly.

"Finished. I'll write down those names and phone numbers for you. The first rush of summer business is over, so they should be able to help you. I imagine Marge Averill can send the bills to whoever still owns this place." She looked up at him. "You really ought to find a more comfortable place to rent. This place is in lousy condition—anyone would be a fool to buy it."

"What makes you think I'm interested in buying it?"

A wave of relief washed over Sophie. "Silly of me. No one would want to buy this place...."

"Except you, obviously. Don't worry, Sophie. I'm not here permanently. You'll have your privacy back before long."

She still didn't trust him. "In the meantime I'm not sure how safe this place is. Maybe you ought to see about renting the Wilson place on Black's Point—"

"I like it right here." He moved out of the doorway, just enough to let her pass. She had to brush against him in the narrow, dark space, and she didn't like it. She found she was holding her breath until she got past him.

She was sitting at the table, scribbling down notes, when he came up behind her. She concentrated on her list, ignoring him, until he spoke.

"So what happened to the Whitten girl?"

She glanced up at him. "I imagine she just got bored with the place and took off. Just because there were murders here a long time ago doesn't mean that it will happen again. Most young women need a little more adventure than Colby can offer."

"Don't you?"

"I've never cared much for adventure," she said in a calm voice.

"When did she disappear? Before or after the killer got out of jail?"

She turned to face him. "You seem awfully interested in our old murders, Mr. Smith."

He shrugged. "Just curious."

"Curious enough to be reading a book called *Encyclopedia of Serial Killers?*" she shot back. "You're as bad as my mother."

"Your mother likes to read about serial killers? How very interesting."

"She used to like true-crime books. Now she doesn't read much of anything." She rose from the

table. "Those names should get you started. That is, if you've decided to stay."

"Oh, I've decided. Nothing could make me leave here until I'm good and ready to go."

It was far from the best news she'd ever heard. There also wasn't a damned thing she could do about it. "I need to get back to the inn," she said.

"Of course you do. You've been very... neighborly."

She didn't glare at him, as much as she wanted to. She headed toward the door, uncomfortably aware of his eyes on her. She paused. "I wouldn't drink the water from the tap if I were you. Buy some bottled stuff at Audley's. I think they get the water straight from the lake here."

"I don't mind a little gasoline."

"That would be the least of your worries. I'd hate to think of how sick you'd be if you picked up something organic. Stomach bugs can be downright nasty around here."

"Now, why do I have trouble believing you care?" he murmured.

"If you were doubled over in your bathroom you'd be out of reach of my sister, but I don't think I could in good conscience let that happen," she said in her coolest voice.

"It's not your sister I'm interested in."

She almost thought she'd misunderstood him. She

stared at him across the room, but he didn't even blink. Finally, she gave in to her cowardice, letting the screen door slam behind her as she made her escape down the path.

5

Why the hell had he said that? Griffin picked up the sheet of paper and squinted at the names, then took off his glasses to get a better look. Instead he found himself analyzing her handwriting. He would have thought she'd have a tight-fisted, crabbed style of writing. That, or something with too many curlicues and even smiley faces over the *I*s. Instead she had a bold, slashing script, a little hard to read, but strong. He glanced up at the screen door, half expecting her to still be there. She was long gone.

Not his type, he reminded himself. He liked his women skinny and sophisticated, with short skirts and long legs and no emotion. He wasn't interested in a chintz-wearing domestic goddess who viewed him as the Big Bad Wolf come to chow down on her little sister. Particularly when Sophie Davis was much more succulent.

The thought was unbidden and quickly dismissed. He didn't have the time or the inclination to spend thinking about getting beneath his neighbor's flowered, ruffled skirts, even though he was obscurely tempted. He needed to find out what he wanted to know and then get the hell out of there. Telling her he was thinking of buying the Whitten place was just a bluff, to see her reaction. There was no way he'd tie himself to a town like Colby, not with his history. No matter how much it called to him. It was nostalgia, not destiny. Hell, he didn't even believe in destiny, or much of anything at all.

In the meantime, though, he was going to have to make himself more comfortable, and getting rid of mouse turds and being able to make a decent cup of coffee were two major requirements. Not to mention making sure the roof didn't fall in on him while he was lying in bed with...

Lying in bed alone, he reminded himself sharply.

Shit, maybe it was the air around Colby. Maybe he hadn't just been a randy young drifter, maybe the air had an aphrodisiac quality. Because truth to tell, he'd been hard ever since he'd seen Sophie Davis look at his rumpled bed, and he knew better than that.

Get in, do the job and get out. It had always been his mantra in life, and this situation was no different. He needed to concentrate on finding out what happened twenty years ago, not waste his time being distracted by animal instincts he'd long outgrown.

He leaned back in the old chair, looking at the decrepit cottage with new eyes. So Sara Ann Whitten had disappeared some time while he'd been in prison? He tried to remember her but came up blank.

The Whittens had been an older couple, and their daughter must have been too young to catch Griffin's predatory eye at the time.

He glanced around the room. In the wake of Colby's burgeoning revival as an exclusive vacation spot, this place would be worth a fortune. Instead it sat by the lake, abandoned, for years on end. According to the real estate agent the title on the old house was murky. The parents were dead, and the daughter had been missing for years. There was no one around to care enough to have the girl declared dead, no one who cared enough to see to the old house. The town fathers had finally decided to rent it to cover some of the unpaid taxes, but sooner or later it would be sold at auction.

What would make a young girl run away? Granted, northern Vermont was about as far off the beaten track as you could get, but to never return, never tell anyone where you were going, seemed unlikely. Particularly when a murderer had roamed that very area.

Too bad for Sara Ann Whitten, but he really wanted to believe she was murdered, her body buried somewhere. Because that would prove without a doubt that he hadn't killed anyone, that there'd been a serial killer loose who happened to prey on the young women of Colby's year-round community. Or at least it would prove it enough to give him peace of mind.

He reached for his notebook, shoved the list of names inside, then started writing. Number one, get into the hospital wing and see if anything jarred his memory. Number two, find out anything he could about Sara Ann Whitten. When she disappeared, who she was involved with at the time, what people thought happened. See if she had any friends still around who might have heard from her.

Number three, search the Whitten house for anything that might suggest what happened to her.

Number four, find out if any of the murdered girls' families still lived in Colby, and figure out whether or not he could talk to them without them realizing who he was.

Number five. Keep away from Sophie Davis and her randy sister and her gaga mother with the too-sharp eyes. And try to avoid Doc Henley, as well.

And all that would only be a start. He figured he'd give it a couple of weeks if he was lucky, maybe less if the weather turned cold early. He couldn't spend too much of his life looking for answers that he might not find. He'd already lost five years he wasn't going to get back. Finding the truth would simply enable him to let go of it and get on with things. Maybe.

No time like the present to get to work. He pulled out his cell phone and punched in numbers before he realized there was no signal. Nada.

He flipped the paper over to Sophie's side, and

wrote beneath her list, *Get the goddamned telephone turned on.* Then he shoved his cell phone back in his pocket.

"He's a reporter."

"I beg your pardon?" Marge gave her a strange look. "Who is?"

"John Smith. If that's even his name. He's doing research on serial killers, he's got law books and medical books and case studies all over his bedroom."

"His bedroom?" Marge said blankly. "How the hell did he get you in his bedroom so fast? I thought you were the Virgin Mary."

Sophie gave her an irritated look. "I was helping him out."

"Sure you were."

"He wanted my advice on what needed to be done around the Whitten camp, so I showed him. I told him to have it done and have them send the bills to you."

"Like hell you did," Marge said in horror.

"Like hell I did," Sophie agreed placidly. "Whenever the town finally decides to sell the old place you'll get the money back. In the meantime it can come out of the rent."

"The town's garnishing the rent for back taxes."

"Then tell them to sell it to me."

"You can't afford it right now."

"Good point," Sophie said morosely, stabbing her slice of peach pie. The two women sat on the porch. "And that man probably can. He said he wasn't interested in buying it, but I don't believe a word he said. There's no way a stranger would just show up here toting a bunch of books on serial killers if he didn't have some kind of agenda. And why the hell would he want to buy it? He was just trying to scare me. Though why would he want to scare me?"

"He told you he's really a reporter?" Marge broke in on her rattled musings.

"Of course not. And I could be wrong—instead of a reporter he could be writing the kind of true-crime thrillers my mother used to devour. I bet if I look through her stacks of books I'll find one with his picture on the back cover."

"As long as it's the back cover and not the front," Marge said. "You know, it seems to me that you're the one whose imagination has gone into overdrive. Lots of people read about serial killers."

"Then he's probably a very rich writer," Sophie said grimly. "Which means he can afford to buy the house out from under me."

"I think you need to take a deep breath and calm down," Marge said, pushing her empty plate away from her. "And you need to stop feeding me your food. I've gained fifteen pounds since you moved here."

"So have I," Sophie said mournfully. "And I can't afford it."

"Tell you what. Get your mother and sister to help with the cooking. That way no one will be tempted to eat much."

Sophie made a face. "Great idea. Then I'll be flat broke in a matter of weeks."

"I thought you were already flat broke."

"Close to it."

"So why are you wasting your time worrying about the Whitten place and your Mr. Smith?" Marge asked, practical as always.

"Not *my* Mr. Smith!" she protested. "And maybe I just want to be distracted from my problems."

"And maybe you're more interested in Mr. Smith than you want to admit. There's no question he's a very attractive man if you like that sort."

"What sort? Tall, dark and loathsome?"

Marge grinned. "Yeah, you keep on thinking that way, missy. If you ask me, the man's hot, and you'd be a fool not to do something about it."

"The only thing I'm about to do is check on my mother and sister. Mr. Smith can snoop around all he wants—I'm planning to ignore him."

"As you've ignored him so far? Good luck, babe," Marge said lazily. "If you're really not interested in him I'll have a crack at him. He's too young for me but I can be open-minded."

Sophie opened her mouth to protest, then shut it

again. Marge was baiting her, and the awful truth was, Sophie was rising to it. She didn't want Marge sleeping with her mysterious neighbor. She didn't want anyone having him. She wanted him to simply disappear, as Sara Ann Whitten had so long ago, so she could concentrate on important things like her family and her extremely shaky business venture. She didn't have the time or energy to waste on a stranger with a hidden agenda.

"Feel free," Sophie said breezily. "Just don't say I didn't warn you. He's probably only here to research a new book on the Colby murders, and he doesn't care who he uses."

"I think you've got one hell of an imagination yourself, Sophie. You ought to start writing fiction instead of columns on the perfect strawberry jam and how to turn your lawn mower into a planter."

"I plead guilty to the first, but not the second. And speaking of which, I need someone to help with the garden and the mowing. Jeff Pritchard went back to college early. Can you think of anyone?"

"I'll send Patrick Laflamme over," Marge said, sounding amused at the notion. "He's the only one I can think of who's strong enough to resist Marty's siren lures."

"Is he old and ugly? Anything less would be too dangerous."

"Sorry, he's young and cute. He's also tough enough to ignore Marty. Don't worry about him—

he's got good old-fashioned Yankee values and a mother who'd put the fear of God into anyone. He won't lead your sister astray.''

''I'm more worried about the other way around,'' Sophie said grimly.

It was late afternoon by the time Sophie got back to her kitchen. The weeds in the perennial garden couldn't be ignored any longer, and then there was laundry to do and Marty to harass into eating something. Sophie was always terrified that Marty was going to become anorexic, but in fact she ate enough. Her reed-thin body just never showed it. Which just went to show how unfair heredity was. Sophie's mother Grace had always been slender and willowy, while Marty's mother had constantly battled her weight. Sophie should have been the one to inherit a skinny metabolism.

She was planning on making another peach pie, a dire mistake since she'd end up eating most of it, but she couldn't let all those wonderful peaches go to waste. Marty had left her dishes in the sink, as usual, and she was lying down by the lake, courting skin cancer at an early age. Sophie just shook her head and put the dishes in the dishwasher, then reached for the earthenware crock she kept her flour in when she noticed the yellowed newspaper on the counter.

At first she thought it was some kind of flyer, but as she looked closer she realized it was an actual copy of the *Northeast Kingdom Gazette* from long ago. Twenty years ago, in fact. And the headline read "Murder in the Kingdom."

Sophie's appetite for peach pie vanished. She poured herself a cup of coffee, shuddering slightly at its strength, and picked up the newspaper with careful hands. Tucking it under her arm, she went out onto the side porch, setting her coffee down on the windowsill behind her and curling up on the hanging glider. It was a beautiful day—a soft breeze was blowing across the lake, bringing with it the scent of pine resin and cool water, and the sun was bright overhead. Sophie stared down at the newspaper, at the grainy pictures, and started to read.

The account was relatively straightforward, devoid of conjecture and sensationalism, which wasn't surprising, considering the reporters and owners of the paper had lived in Colby for generations and knew all of the families involved. It was one thing to splash murder pictures all over the front page when you didn't know the helpless victims, another when they were your neighbors and friends.

There was a photo of the killer. Alleged killer, as they referred to him, and in fact, he might still be alleged since apparently he'd gotten off years later. Thomas Ingram Griffin looked like almost any drifter from twenty years ago. Long hair and beard, dazed but defiant expression on his face. The photo was faded from age, and it hadn't been the best of quality in the first place, but for some reason he looked vaguely familiar. Sophie shrugged. The man would look completely different twenty years later. He'd be clean shaven, clean cut, probably forty pounds heavier. If he was even still alive.

The three victims had been found over a two-day period. Alice Calderwood had been strangled and dumped by the side of North Road, Valette King had been stabbed to death—her killer had used his knife with savage fury. Her body had been left in a cornfield. And Lorelei Johnson had been found floating in Still Lake, near the cattails by the old Niles place, her throat cut.

Only Lorelei had a connection to Thomas Griffin. The paper didn't come right out and say it, but clearly they'd been lovers. And it didn't sound as if any of the three victims had been overly circumspect in their personal lives. The hinting was delicate, due to the sensibilities of the girls' grieving parents, but it was fairly clear that the three girls had been wild ones.

But then, wasn't everyone when they were in their late teens, early twenties? Sophie thought. Everyone except her, of course. She'd never had the chance to be particularly wild and wicked—she'd been too busy working, too busy trying to look out for her mother and her baby sister. Gracey's lifestyle had been a warning note, and she'd been too busy in college to think about boys, much to her mother's dismay. And when she'd graduated, ready to start making a full life, there was Marty on her doorstep, orphaned and miserable, and Sophie had ignored any passing hormonal flutterings to concentrate on her family.

There were times when she wanted to just toss everything to the winds, fling off her responsibilities and run wild.

But she hadn't, and if the result of sowing wild oats was to have your throat cut, then she was very happy the way she was, thank you very much. The only thirty-year-old virgin on the face of the planet.

That wasn't particularly something she liked to waste her time thinking about, but the oblique tragedy of Colby's wild daughters made it unavoidable. She glanced down at the lake, to her sister's skinny, bikini-clad form soaking up the northern Vermont sunshine. Maybe she was being too hard on Marty. Maybe her surliness was only normal.

She looked past her, to the calm, clean crescent of the beach, and then to the cattails beyond. That's where they'd found Lorelei. Where Thomas Griffin had found her, in fact. He was holding her body in his arms when they'd arrested him, and her blood had stained his body.

Sophie shivered, putting the paper down again. Where in the world had this come from, anyway? She didn't particularly want to dwell in the past, or even think about the tragedies that had occurred long ago. She wanted the bucolic peace that Colby offered, not the memories of murders disturbing her peaceful afternoon.

But then, Mr. Smith had arrived on her doorstep and suddenly the past was alive. If Grace had been her old self Sophie would have asked her about it. Grace devoured true-crime stories as if they were delicate canapés—she would have known the details of the Still Lake murders, and if anyone had written a book about them, Grace would have read it.

But Grace had lost interest in everything. She was almost a caricature of senility, sitting in her rocking chair, humming softly, that dreamy expression in her eyes. At least out here they could keep an eye on her, make sure she didn't wander into trouble. And if Sophie had errands, she could always count on Doc to stop in and make sure Grace was all right.

Richard Henley had been a gift from God. Colby was his town, and he knew each and every one of the year-round residents and most of the summer people, and he took care of all of them, as well as his quiet, unassuming wife, Rima.

Sophie glanced down at the crumbling yellow newspaper beside her. Maybe Doc had left it, in hopes that it might revive Grace's fascination with old crimes. Even a morbid interest was better than no interest at all.

He would have known all of them. He was even quoted extensively in the article, describing the causes of death in unemotional terms, adding gentle words of comfort for the grieving parents and the whole town. His kind, wise presence was probably the main reason such an awful tragedy hadn't pulled the entire town apart. That, and the fact that the murderer had been caught so swiftly.

Sophie picked up the paper again, flipping it over, but there was nothing else. No follow-up. She needed to know what had happened. Why had the killer's conviction been overturned?

She set it down. Not what she wanted to be thinking about on a beautiful late summer day, when she had more important things on her mind, like the future of her sister, the safety of her mother, the financial viability of running a bed-and-breakfast, and expecting it to support the three of them. She was worried enough—she didn't want death and horror intruding on her perfect future, her every thought. But she couldn't dismiss it.

Because if the killer wasn't really the killer, then who had murdered three teenage girls some twenty years ago, one at her very doorstep? And who was to say he wouldn't kill again? Now that another teenage girl had taken up residence. Marty had the sense of a white rabbit—like most teenagers she considered herself invulnerable and immortal. She wouldn't listen to warnings, especially vague, unfounded ones.

If they were unfounded.

Hell, she was borrowing trouble. She wasn't going to brood on old murders—peach pie was a much better concern on a hot summer day. Even if she did end up eating it all.

Better to concentrate on peach pie than murder. And better to think of peach pie than the man next door with his dark eyes and his enigmatic face. She didn't like him. She didn't trust him. When it came right down to it, she was even a tiny bit scared of him, though she wasn't sure why.

But there was one more nasty complication to John Smith's presence at the edge of her property. Not the fact that her sister might be attracted to him—that was presumably only a minor worry.

No, the nasty complication was that Sophie couldn't stop thinking about him. She was fascinated, drawn to him, when she was much too smart for that.

She wished to God that she hadn't chosen that year to give up smoking.

He could feel it rising again. The deep, powerful need that started small and spread throughout his body like a holy fire. He thought his work was done here, but the Lord had other plans. It had been three years since he'd worked God's vengeance. Three years since he'd crushed the life from that wicked child of Satan. He'd atoned, of course. He knew what he did was wrong—it was part of his punishment. To mete out God's justice, and to repent for his part in it.

It was calling to him. Calling to him in the shape of that girl, that sinful child who painted her face and exposed her body and was just looking for a way to glorify Satan.

He would save her. He would cleanse her of the wickedness that threatened her. The wickedness would be burned from her sinful body.

And she would die at his hands, a pure soul.

6

The crash woke him up. It was pitch black outside, and the quiet sounds of the lake had lulled Griffin into a deep sleep, but something had broken through his dreams, jarring him awake. He squinted at his watch—one-thirty in the morning. He knew he was alone in the house, but he'd definitely heard a thump downstairs.

He sat up, reaching for his jeans. Whoever it was didn't seem to be making much of an effort to cover their presence, but he still dressed as quietly as he could so as not to frighten off whoever was there.

Of course it might be something as simple as one of the mice he'd evicted. That, or a nosy raccoon, or even, God help him, a skunk.

He moved toward the door, trying to be as quiet as he could so he wouldn't scare away his intruder, but the old house wasn't made for stealth, and the floorboards creaked beneath his weight. He paused, half expecting his unexpected guest to go crashing out of the house, but the quiet thumps continued, undeterred by the sound of his approach.

Someone had turned on a couple of the lights. The

living room was filled with shadows when he reached the bottom of the stairs, but he could see something moving in the kitchen. He switched on the bright overhead light, but whoever it was didn't react.

It took him a moment to recognize her. The crazy old lady from next door had wandered into his house, into his kitchen, and she was rummaging around, singing beneath her breath, totally at home.

"Mrs...." Shit, he couldn't remember her name. "Grace?"

She looked up at him with those disarmingly vague eyes. She was dressed in a bathrobe, and her feet were muddy and bare. "Hello there," she said gaily. "I'm so glad you've come back. I've missed you."

He felt a frisson of horror run down his spine, and then he remembered who he was talking to. "This is the first time I've been here, Grace," he corrected her patiently.

She frowned. "Is it? I didn't realize. Do you want some ice cream?"

"No, thanks," he said. As a matter of fact, he didn't have any ice cream in the house, not even Vermont's own Ben & Jerry's. "Were you looking for something in particular?"

"Oh, no. I just thought I'd come visit." She let out a cry of triumph and emerged from the refrigerator with a can of Coke. "You don't mind, do you?"

"I don't mind," he said. "But don't you think your daughters will be worried about you?"

"Daughter," Grace corrected him amiably, handing him a can of soda as she waltzed past him. "Marty's mother is that wretched club woman Morris married after I left him. I don't blame the girl for rebelling against Eloise, though in the end they were fine parents. A tragedy they died, but Marty dealt with it quite well. I just wish Sophie wouldn't worry so much. She'll be fine."

She'd lost him. "Who will be?"

"Both of them," Grace said firmly. "I won't have it any other way. So tell me, young man," she continued with one of her rapid shifts of conversation, "why did you come here? It's the murders, isn't it?"

She'd ensconced herself on the old sofa, her fluttery garments draped around her, giving him time to school his answer.

"What murders?"

Grace's cackle verged on the macabre. "You know as well as I do what murders. You saw him."

"Saw who?"

"Saw whom," she corrected him, sounding like his seventh-grade English teacher. "The killer. You saw him."

"What makes you think it was a him?"

"He," she corrected him again in her daft, cordial voice. "Semen."

He blinked. "I beg your pardon?"

"Semen. The girls had just had sex. Women don't produce semen." She smiled sweetly.

"No, they don't," he agreed, rattled. "Grace, it's the middle of the night. I really think I ought to take you back home."

"Oh, would you? That would be so kind. I'm sure Sophie is terribly worried about me. She does worry, poor girl. She needs a man." She eyed him speculatively. "I'm not sure you'd do, though."

"I wasn't offering."

"You don't need to," Grace said. "You're an intelligent man—I can tell as much from a glance, and any intelligent man would find my Sophie worth the effort."

"Effort?"

"But I don't think you'll do. I think perhaps you should go away."

He struggled to follow her line of reasoning. "Why?"

"Because you saw him," she said with a touch of asperity. "And he'll have to kill you. Go away."

"Who will? Who would have to kill me?" He should have known better than to ask her. She looked and sounded perfectly reasonable, sitting there in the middle of the night in her bathrobe and flyaway gray hair, but she jumped from one subject to another the way a hummingbird sampled flowers.

Grace rose, suddenly majestic. "Take me home, young man. It's getting late. Sophie will be quite cross with you for keeping me out so long."

Griffin sighed. "With any luck your daughter will never know you've been out wandering. Let's just hope she's asleep when we get back there."

"I wasn't out wandering. I was paying a social call." Grace rose, smoothing her skirt as if it were layers of crinoline. "You shouldn't underestimate me. I know exactly what I'm doing."

He looked into her soft, hazy blue eyes, and for a moment he thought he saw the sharp glint of intelligence there. It must have been a trick of the shadows. Or was it? Was Spacey Gracey really as spacey as she wanted people to believe?

"Maybe you do," he said.

She was a little woman, much smaller than her luscious daughter, and the look she cast up at him was almost coquettish. "I'd tell you to button your shirt but I'm rather hoping you'll distract Sophie with that nice chest of yours."

Shit. He began buttoning the soft flannel shirt he'd grabbed. He hadn't even been thinking about the tattoo, but Grace would have been hard put to see it with the shirt over him. The snake coiled over his left hip, usually hidden by clothing, but he wasn't wearing a belt and the jeans hung low on his hips. If he'd moved the wrong way the shirt could have exposed the tattoo. Not at all what he wanted. He looked completely different from the man who'd been dragged away for murder twenty years ago. But the tattoo was still the same.

He should have had it removed. Would have, too, except that Annelise had always hated it, and it had become a matter of principle. Besides, he had a sort of affection for it. The tattoo was part of who he was, who he had been, and you couldn't escape from the past. It made you who you were today.

He wasn't sure how pleased he was with the kind of man he'd grown into. But he wasn't ready to wipe out the rebellious young drifter completely with a bit of laser surgery. Not until he found out the answers to the questions that haunted him.

His life had always been dogged by luck, both good and bad. Bad luck to have been in the wrong place at the wrong time, with the body of a murdered woman found nearby and blood staining his body. Good luck that some fool in the prosecutor's office had been so sure he was guilty that he'd been ridiculously sloppy in his paperwork. So sloppy, in fact, that by the time Griffin had spent three years of his jail time studying the law he'd known it would be a relatively simple matter to get his conviction overturned. Everything they had on him was circumstantial, and most of it had been gained illegally. All he'd had to do was find the right lawyer.

It had taken another couple of years, but Bill Cragen had taken to the case with enthusiasm, and taken Griffin under his wing when he got out, supporting him through law school and his fledgling career. Anyone as smart as he was shouldn't waste his life as a ski bum, Bill had said. Besides, why not put those years of study to good use? And by the time Bill died of cancer, Griffin had earned his degree, joined Bill's practice and become engaged to Bill's daughter, Annelise. Stalwart, upstanding, with a snake tattooed across his hip and a dark night hidden deep in his soul.

Grace cackled. "She's probably called the police by now. Or at least that nice doctor. Maybe I should go back by myself. We wouldn't want people to get the wrong idea."

He was half tempted to let her. The thought of walking up to that house to a crowd of police brought back too many ugly memories, and not the ones he was searching for. But he couldn't let the old lady wander alone at night down that overgrown path so near the lake—he was a ruthless shit, but he still had that much decency left in him. He wasn't convinced she was as loony as she appeared to be, but he couldn't really take any chances.

"A gentleman always sees a lady to her door," he said. Not that anyone ever taught him that. Griffin had pretty much raised himself, and he'd picked up manners from reading, not from example. "And we

don't want to worry your daughter, now do we?''
he said.

Grace tucked her arm in his and gave him a companionable smile as they started out onto the porch.
"You didn't kill her, did you?" she asked in her sweet voice.

She must have felt the involuntary jerk in his body, a dead giveaway. "Who?"

"I don't remember. I just know someone was killed. I don't think it was Sophie, but I can't be sure. You didn't kill Sophie, did you, young man?"

He didn't answer. There was nothing he could say, even if he knew the truth.

But Grace wasn't waiting for an answer that would never come. "Of course you didn't, love," she said, patting his arm in a vague, soothing manner. "Do you think I'd be wandering around in the night with you if you were a murderer?"

He looked down at her. He still wasn't sure what to make of her—whether she was pulling an elaborate prank with her dotty-old-lady act, or whether she was really senile. She couldn't be that old if she was Sophie's mother, but she was so frail. He wasn't in the habit of taking things at face value. Maybe she was playing a game, or maybe not. Maybe her mind was so addled she just picked up on things other people didn't. Or maybe she asked everyone if they were murderers.

She'd run into trouble if she did, he thought

coolly. Because someone *had* killed the three girls. And unless that someone was him, the killer might strike again.

His vain hope that Sophie might be unaware of her mother's wanderings was dashed when they came through the end of the pathway. The main building of the old Niles homestead was ablaze with lights, and he thought he could see her standing on the porch, peering out into the darkness. At least there were no police cars parked there. No cars at all except for the late-model Subaru that belonged to Sophie.

"Yoo-hoo, dearie, I'm back!" Grace called out in a cheerful voice. "And wait till you see who I've brought with me."

"I'll head back now," Griffin said, trying to disentangle his arm from her surprisingly strong grip. "Your daughter will take it from here."

"I'm not sure I can make it to the house," Grace said in a quavering voice, suddenly sounding frail. "I'm very, very tired." As if to convince him she started to sag, and he had no choice but to put his arm around her fragile body and help her up the small slope to the porch, cursing inwardly.

"What the hell have you done with my mother?" Sophie looked like an avenging angel there on the porch. She was wearing some kind of white lace nightgown that looked more like an Edwardian wedding dress than something to sleep in, and her hair was down. He hadn't realized how long her hair was. It looked rich and warm in the overhead light, and he wanted to touch it. Her feet were bare, and she had a shawl wrapped around her shoulders.

"Brought your wandering lamb home," he said. "I found her in my kitchen half an hour ago."

"Don't you think it might have been a good idea to call me and tell me where she was before I got completely frantic?"

"Considering that I don't know your phone number, my telephone isn't hooked up, and my god-damned cell phone doesn't work at the back end of beyond, I couldn't very well call you, though I think it would have been an excellent idea. That way you could have come and gotten her instead of me having to traipse out in the middle of the night."

Grace seemed to have mysteriously regained her strength, and she abandoned him, scampering up onto the porch with all the energy of her teenage stepdaughter. "I'm going to bed now, Sophie," she said. "Don't let me sleep too late—I've got things to do."

"What things?"

"Oh, many, many interesting things," she said. "And he didn't kill anyone. He told me so."

"Who did?" Sophie said sharply, but Grace had already wandered back into the house, humming happily.

"Me. She asked me if I was a murderer and I told

her no." He should leave, go back to bed, but for some reason he wanted to stand in the moonlight and look at Sophie in her ridiculous nightgown. Just for a moment.

And for some reason Sophie didn't disappear into the house, chasing after her errant mother. She was looking at him warily, as if she'd accidentally come across a wild bear, but she didn't back down. "I'm afraid that's a remnant of when she was still..." She glossed over the word. "She loves to read true-crime books. I thought she'd stopped, but when I checked on her this evening she was reading one of her old ones. She probably can't tell the difference between reality and what's in the books."

"Not the kind of fantasy world I'd choose," he said. What the hell was he doing, standing there in the moonlight, talking to her? He had better things to do—Sophie Davis couldn't help him with his search for the truth. She hadn't even known of Colby, Vermont, twenty years ago. He needed to make his excuses, get the hell away from her. From inexplicable temptation.

"No, I like mine better."

It was enough to stop his excuses. "Your fantasy world?"

She gestured toward the moonlit house. "Victorian values. Edwardian simplicity. Flower arranging and antique lace and wonderful food and everything just as it should be. I'm no fool, Mr. Smith. I know perfectly well I create my reality to suit myself, and it has nothing to do with the way most people live. I just happen to prefer it.''

"Prefer living in a dream world?''

"Dreams are usually much better than the real world.''

The wind had come up, blowing the long, lacy nightgown against her body. A good body, nicely rounded, just a bit plump, he couldn't help but notice. An old-fashioned woman with hair that drifted away from her face in the soft breeze.

Not his type, he reminded himself. But for a brief, irresistible moment he wished she was. Wished he was the kind of man who could embrace this kind of life, instead of always living in the darkness. Wished he could simply climb up the steps to the wide front porch and pick her up in his arms, carry her to some fluffy, old-fashioned bed and strip that ridiculous nightgown from her lush body.

He wasn't about to do any such thing, and he dismissed the brief fantasy automatically. "Dreams turn into nightmares,'' he said. "And they can't be shared.''

"You look like you know more about *having* nightmares than sharing them,'' she said.

It was an odd conversation to be having with her, but she seemed unaware of it. A light in the house turned off, and he assumed Grace had finally gone back to bed. The bright half moon bathed the sloping lawn in silvery light. What would she do if he came closer? Would she turn and run?

Of course she would. And he wasn't about to move any closer, to put his hands on her skin and see if it was as soft and cool as he thought it would be. He wasn't going to see if she tasted of honey and fresh bread and wild clover. Even if he wanted to. He'd lost his innocence long, long ago and he'd never had a taste for it in bed. And as illogical as it was, he sensed that hardheaded Sophie Davis was, at heart, as innocent as a lamb.

He wasn't in the mood to play hungry wolf, no matter how tempting.

"I should let you get some sleep," he said, turning to go.

"I can't."

The quiet tone of desperation in her voice stopped him. He turned back. "Can't what?"

"Can't sleep," she said with a rueful shrug. "For some reason I can't sleep. Too worried, I guess. I've just been lying in bed, tossing and turning."

Innocent, indeed. In another woman, in Annelise, for example, that would have been a come-on, pure and simple. *Sure, darling, I'll take care of you, wear you out so you can fall asleep. You just need a good man and a good fuck.*

"They say worry is a waste of the imagination." *Go away,* he told himself. *Don't stand here talking in the moonlight.*

"Then I've definitely got too strong an imagination. Do you want a cup of coffee or something?"

He closed his eyes in exasperation for a moment. Maybe he was wrong, maybe he'd misread her, let that virginal nightgown convince him she was something she wasn't. And maybe he wasn't interested in fighting temptation, after all.

"If you drink coffee at this hour it's no wonder you can't sleep," he said. "Or was that your subtle way of asking me to go to bed with you?"

Victorian virgin, all right. She reacted as if he'd slapped her, with shock and outrage. "You really do have delusions, don't you, Mr. Smith?" she said, her voice icy. "I'm not interested in sex." The moment the words were out of her mouth she stumbled. "Not with you, I mean. Someone else, maybe, at another time. I'm perfectly healthy, but I'm not the slightest bit interested..."

"Don't tie yourself in knots, Sophie. I figured as much, but by the way you were acting I thought I might have been mistaken. Let me give you a little hint. Don't stand on the porch in the middle of the night wearing only your nightgown, especially when the light behind makes the damned thing just about transparent, and don't invite strange men in for coffee at two in the morning unless you're wanting something else. People might get the wrong idea."

Her mouth opened to say something, but she bit

the words back. Nice mouth, he realized with belated regret. Very nice mouth, indeed.

"Go ahead and say it, Sophie," he said. "You
know you want to, and you're not going to shock
me."

"Fuck you." No hesitation this time. She was
furious, and he told himself he should be sorry he'd
goaded her. He knew he wasn't.

"I'll come back when you mean it," he said. If
he'd been closer he would have kissed her, just to
see how she reacted. Just to taste her mouth.

But she was too far away, up on the porch, and
by the time he reached her she would have locked
herself back in her inn, well out of reach, and he'd
feel frustrated and foolish.

He hadn't come here to waste his time with an
uptight Victorian throwback. So he simply turned
and walked back toward the lake path, half expecting her to hurl something at his departing head.

All he heard was the slam of the door behind him.
And he had no choice but to admit he was damned
sorry he wasn't on the other side of that door, drinking her coffee, drinking her mouth.

He gathered his tools with the care and delibera-
tion of a master craftsman. He prided himself on his
work, and on the variety of his approach. It was part
of his divine mission, given to him as a way to finish
his task in this world of sin and grievous sexuality.

He never killed the same way twice, and there were infinite ways to snuff out an undeserving life.

He had stabbed, slashed, garroted. Poisoned, beaten with his fists, hanged and drowned. Never the same, and the police had no way to track him down. The corrupt officials of the law had no idea how many women had died by his hand, their lives of filth and wickedness wiped out before they could ensnare another innocent.

He was running out of ideas, and he was a man who didn't like to repeat himself. He'd thought he had finished with his quest, until the newcomers arrived at the old inn. And he knew he had one more task.

Flames, he thought. A purifying fire to cleanse the body, the soul and the spirit. The old Niles place would go up like tinder, and by the time the volunteer fire departments arrived from the neighboring towns it would be too late. No one would ever know it wasn't the result of an old firetrap and an accidental cigarette from that young harlot. And if others died in the conflagration—well, there were always casualties in a holy war.

He'd pray for their souls.

7

Marty opened her eyes to the glaring sunlight, cursing. It was well before noon, and outside her open window the sun was hideously bright, enough to give her a headache. A great, growling noise had shaken her awake, the insistent buzz like some giant dentist's drill, and she fumbled on the bedside table for her pack of cigarettes. Sophie had forbidden her to smoke in the inn, so Marty did her best to do so every chance she got. She encountered only an empty, crumpled package.

She shoved the covers away and stepped out onto the shiny wood floor. Everything was its usual blur—she pulled her glasses from the drawer and planted them on her nose, breathing an unexpected sigh of relief when the room came into focus. If Sophie would only let her have laser surgery to correct her eyes then she wouldn't have to bother with her damned contacts. At least extended wear would have been an improvement, but she'd never been able to get used to them, so each morning she had to wear glasses until she was ready to emerge from her room. There was no way she was letting anyone see her without her contacts.

The horrible buzzing noise grew even louder, and she headed straight for the windows overlooking the side lawn. She grabbed the window frame, ready to slam it down to shut out the noise, when she saw the young man.

He was stripped to the waist, wielding a chain saw with deliberate power. For a moment she stared at him, mesmerized by the play of muscles beneath his tanned skin, the controlled strength of his movements, and she couldn't breathe.

He must have felt her watching him. He looked up, but she couldn't see his face beneath the shadow of the protective helmet he wore. She only knew he was looking straight at her as she stood in the window, dressed in nothing more than a baggy T-shirt, her hair sticking up, her glasses perched on her nose.

She jumped back, away from the window, just as the roar of the chain saw sputtered to a stop. There was no way she would edge back up to that window. For one thing, she wasn't going to risk having anyone see her in her glasses, and if she took them off she wouldn't be able to see a damned thing.

Where the hell was the plain, gawky boy who usually did the mowing and the gardening? He'd been of no interest whatsoever, and she'd decided she was doomed to an empty summer. Doubtlessly one reason Sophie had dragged her up here was the complete and total lack of good-looking boys. It wasn't as if she was a sex fiend or anything. She just liked boys. A lot.

Things were definitely beginning to look up, judging by the muscular torso of the man outside. If only his face matched the body. She had friends who would have told her it didn't matter, but she hadn't gotten quite so jaded that she didn't appreciate a pretty face. But she was working on it.

There were times when it seemed like Sophie had hired the most homely people in northern Vermont to renovate the old inn. This was the first decent possibility she'd seen in months, and she wasn't about to let him get away until she got a good look at his face. Maybe he had cigarettes. Otherwise she was going to have a hell of a time getting new ones—Audley's was very strict about selling to minors, and she hadn't yet found someone to buy for her on a regular basis. People were so judgmental up here. It wasn't as if they all hadn't smoked when they were younger. Even her paragon of a sister.

Still, things were looking up. She passed Sophie in the hall on her way to the shower, and for once she didn't growl when her sister wished her a good morning. Maybe, just maybe, Colby, Vermont, wouldn't be so bad, after all. Maybe she wouldn't need to run away.

Sophie opened the door as quietly as she could. Gracey lay sound asleep, tangled in her soft covers, her face oddly youthful in repose. It was no wonder—after her late-night excursion she must be exhausted.

What in God's name had sent her to the old Whitten house? She'd never shown any interest in it before now. She'd shown no sign of wandering in the past—it was all Doc could do to tempt her to have dinner with him and his wife in their little village home. Normally she kept to her room or the front porch, staring vacantly, humming beneath her breath.

It would be an absolute disaster if her mother started taking off. The money was so tight that Sophie didn't know where she could find enough to pay for a baby-sitter, and she couldn't add anything to her already overwhelming responsibilities. She could ask Marty, but chances were Marty would agree sullenly and then forget all about it. And Sophie couldn't bear the thought of her mother getting lost in the woods that circled the pristine lake.

Gracey was snoring softly—more like a faint purring sound than an all-out snore. There were books piled beneath her bed, and one lay open on the plain white coverlet. Sophie didn't have to look closer to know it was one of those lurid true-crime books—the blurry photograph on the cover was unmistakable in the genre. She supposed she should be glad. It was the first time in months that Gracey had shown interest in anything at all. Even the gloomy and macabre were preferable to the dazed dream-world she was floating in.

She'd have to tell Doc. He'd be very pleased—he was always telling her that Gracey needed to find new interests. In this case she was simply returning to her old ones, but at least she was reading, using her mind for something other than staring vacantly at the cool, clear lake.

Gracey stirred again, muttering something in her sleep, and Sophie turned and closed the door behind her, careful not to make any noise. At least while she slept Grace would be safe. But after last night's wandering, she doubted she herself would ever get a good night's sleep again.

She took her mug of coffee out onto the front porch, propping her skirted legs up on the railing as she looked out over the lake. There were early morning fishermen, and over near the Whitten place some wild ducks swam peacefully. No sound of the loons yet, and no sound of motorboats and jet skis. For now all was peaceful and quiet, just the birds and the fishermen and the occasional kayaker slicing through the stillness of the lake. Gracey was safe in bed, and even Marty had been marginally pleasant this morning, a welcome change. For now she could just drink in the peace and quiet, safe and serene.

She closed her eyes, letting the scent and sounds

wash over her. Then her eyes shot open again, as she realized what book Gracey had been reading.

Murder in the Northeast Kingdom. A lurid, sensationalized account of the Colby murders by a famous true-crime writer. Sophie hadn't bothered to read it herself—Doc and the others in town held it in contempt as a lurid, inaccurate piece of trash. Obviously Gracey didn't have any such compunctions.

Odd, though. When Gracey's mind had begun to slip, soon after they moved to Colby, Sophie had gone into her room and taken the book out of her huge stack of paperbacks, planning to read it until Doc told her not to bother. Anything she wanted to know, he'd tell her, he'd said. Without the melodrama and emotion and the purple prose. So Sophie had dumped the book in the trash, and presumably it had been incinerated with all the other garbage.

So what was a copy doing back in Gracey's possession? How could she possibly have gotten it, when nowadays she was only just capable of seeing to her own physical needs and not much more?

She should set down her coffee and sneak back into Gracey's room to get the book. Her mother would never miss it—she probably didn't even realize it took place in the same town, some of it in the same house. Or if she did, it was only on some subconscious level.

Maybe the so-called Mr. Smith had given it to her. She still couldn't rid herself of the firm belief that he was something other than what he said he was. No tourist immured himself in a falling-down house in the middle of nowhere, no matter how beautiful it was. Colby and Still Lake were well-kept secrets, and almost everyone who ended up here could trace their arrival to a long-time resident. Mr. Smith had appeared out of nowhere, and she didn't trust him.

She was still stuck on the idea of him being a reporter, someone doing an update on the unsolved Colby murders. He was probably asking Gracey all sorts of questions, confusing her even more than she already was, sending her scurrying back to her dreamworld of serial killers and innocent victims.

Sophie was going to have to have a word with him. Order him to leave her mother the hell alone. Gracey had enough problems without having some blood-sucking journalist confusing her even further.

She'd make cookies, that's what she'd do. Three-ginger cookies, and take them down to her reluctant neighbor. They could sit on his decrepit porch and she'd tell him, very politely, to keep away from her vulnerable mother. And at the same time, maybe she could find out for sure who he was and what the hell he was doing there.

For heaven's sake, it wasn't as if she was truly scared of the man. She didn't let people intimidate her, and if Mr. Tall Dark and Brooding wanted to be standoffish, that was just fine with her. As long as he left her family alone, they'd get along just fine.

No, she'd face him, whether she wanted to or not, whether he frightened her or not. For some reason the notion was bizarrely irresistible, and she didn't want to stop and consider why. To think about why the necessity of bearding the lion in his den was so appealing. Unless, at the advanced age of thirty, she'd developed a taste for lions.

Vermonters woke too damned early, and they started work at an obscene time of day. Griffin hadn't slept well—for some reason he kept thinking about Sophie Davis's bare feet beneath that silly nightgown. He'd drifted off sometime around dawn, and it was only a couple of hours later that the barely muffled sound of the chain saw rasped through his sleep.

He put one of the limp feather pillows over his head and groaned. He could have closed the window, but that would have meant getting up, and if he got up he might as well stay up. So he shut his eyes and his mind and willed himself back to sleep.

Only to be jarred awake by the thunderous pounding on the front door below his bedroom. He cursed, loudly, distinctly, and hauled his ass out of bed. He ignored the fact that that peremptory pounding sounded like the police. He had nothing to fear from the police, hadn't in years. He was a lawyer, for

Christ's sake, and unlike Annelise he didn't even skirt the limits of the law. It was his own special challenge to get what he wanted within the confines of the system that had put him in a maximum-security prison for five years for a crime he didn't commit.

By the time he stumbled down the stairs he half expected to see old Zeke waiting there to arrest him. Behind the grimy lace curtains he could see several people standing on the porch, and he yanked the door open with a snarl.

For a moment he thought they were some kind of religious fanatics on a door-to-door mission for Christ. The tall man at the front of the delegation looked like Abraham Lincoln without a sense of humor—a long, narrow, disapproving face framed with a gray beard; beady, disapproving dark eyes; a thin, cold mouth; and an expression of deep wariness on his leathery face. He looked like something out of a Stephen King novel, and if he was going to talk about being saved then Griffin was going to be very pissed off, indeed.

"You Mr. Smith?" The question was terse, couched in the kind of thick Vermont accent that was rarely heard outside the Northeast Kingdom.

"Yeah. Who wants to know?" He could be just as surly as his unwanted visitor. He could see a small elderly woman standing just behind the man, but neither of them were carrying a Bible, so maybe he was jumping to the wrong conclusion. Someone else hovered behind them, just off the porch.

"Zebulon King," he said. "That's my wife and my boy. Marge Averill sent us out to work on the place. Seems you had some complaints."

Shit. He wasn't sure anymore if he wanted locals prowling around his domain. And then something clicked in his brain—Zeb King was the father of one of the murdered girls. He'd testified at his trial some twenty years ago, all hearsay evidence that had been struck from the record but had done its share of damage, nonetheless. He remembered the man's daughter, as well. Valette King had rebelled against her parents' strict religious upbringing and slept with anything in pants. He'd spent a couple of nights with her, but she'd been too voracious even for his strong appetites, and he'd hooked up with the more pliant Lorelei. Valette hadn't liked it, not one tiny bit, and even her father had known there was bad blood between them. And so he'd testified at the trial.

It was twenty years ago, and Griffin hadn't even recognized the man. He was in his sixties now, with that leathery, ageless look that came from working long, hard hours in the sun, buoyed by an unswerving, rigid faith in right and wrong. There was no way Zeb King could recognize him. But he still hesitated.

"You gonna let us get to work?" King said, impatient. "We waited till a decent hour to come over here, but time's awasting."

Griffin glanced at his watch. He'd traded his Rolex for a cheap Timex as part of his cover. Zebulon King considered eight o'clock in the morning a decent hour.

Griffin unlatched the screen door and pushed it open. If he had any sense he would have sent them away, but the opportunity was too good to miss. Two people intimately connected with the murders had shown up on his doorstep, the only surviving relatives still in Colby. How could he refuse such an offering from the gods?

Zebulon King strode into the living room, an old-fashioned wooden toolbox in one huge hand. His wife scurried after him, head down, dressed in some kind of faded dress with an equally faded apron covering her lumpish body. The apron was crisply starched.

"You start in the kitchen, Addy," Zebulon ordered. "Perley and I will see what's up with the roof. Miz Averill says there might be water damage." He made it sound like the plague had struck.

Griffin didn't bother to enlighten him. He'd spent the last truly free summer of his life doing carpentry and yard work for Peggy Niles—he knew one end of a hammer from another and knew just how bad the water damage was. Nothing that a skilled carpenter couldn't fix in a day or so.

He'd spent the first year in prison in the wood shop, as well. At one point he'd been good, damned good. He'd built a picnic table and a fanciful gazebo for Peggy just before he'd been arrested, and it had been some of his best pieces—more art than lawn furniture. The day he got out of jail he turned his back on woodworking and never picked up a hammer again. It was too deeply ingrained in the nightmare that had been his life.

There were times when he missed it. Since he'd taken up residence in the ramshackle Whitten house he'd been itching to work on it—to replace a rotting windowsill, reglaze the windows before the panes of glass fell out. He hadn't touched anything, though. He could hire people to do those things nowadays—he didn't have to do them himself. And he didn't want to remember the boy who'd found satisfaction and pleasure from the feel of tools in his hands.

"Suit yourself," he said. Zeb's "boy" moved past him into the house, thirty-five if he was a day, looking just as grim and not nearly as smart as his father. "Just keep out of the bedroom for now. I've got work laid out and I don't want anyone messing with it."

"We ain't interested in your work," Zeb said. "We're just here to fix the place. And you keep away from my woman."

At that point Addy rushed into the kitchen. The woman was in her sixties, built like a sack of po-

tatoes, with iron-gray hair tucked in tight little pin-
curls that had probably never been in fashion in her
entire lifetime. "I'll resist temptation," Griffin said
dryly.

Zebulon King wasn't the sort to find humor in a
situation. "See that you do."

The woman jumped a mile when he walked into
the kitchen. She had already begun scrubbing the
oilcloth-covered table, and she looked at him as if
he were a hound from hell. Or the man who murdered her daughter.

He had no idea whether she'd been at his trial.
He hadn't owned any glasses besides his shades, and
his court-appointed, totally incompetent lawyer
frowned on a teenage malcontent wearing sunglasses
on the witness stand. For all he knew Addy King
could have been sitting there glaring at him, memorizing his features and branding them into her soul
with a fiery hatred.

She looked too beaten down for anything that energetic. She focused on scrubbing the table while he
started a pot of coffee for himself.

"Gonna need new oilcloth," she muttered in a
barely audible voice.

"Do they even sell oilcloth nowadays?" He made
an effort to sound pleasant and unthreatening.

She didn't look up. "Audley's does. Audley's
sells everything."

"How about a new life?" he muttered to himself.

"What?" Her head jerked up. "I'm hard of hearing."

"Just talking to myself," he said, leaning against the sink and staring out at the lake as it glistened through the trees. It looked deceptively peaceful, as if it had never held the blood-soaked body of his murdered girlfriend. Looking at it didn't remind him of death and despair—it had a curiously tranquil effect on him. But he still hadn't talked himself into actually swimming in it.

He looked at the timid little woman. Her dour husband wouldn't have been much comfort when she lost her daughter, he thought. She looked as if she'd never had much comfort in her life.

He racked his brain, trying to remember what he knew about the King family. They'd been in Colby since the 1700s, but the blood had grown pretty th' by the twentieth century. "Lived here long?" asked casually.

"My husband said I wasn't to talk to yo' woman muttered, still scrubbing. The oilc' beneath her fierce handling, and she let ou' ful cry.

"There's no harm in talking, Mrs. K' "And don't worry about the coverir it needs replacing."

She looked up at him, with ev deep sorrow that for a momer' himself. Only a moment. "I '

Mr. Smith. I don't trust them. I've lived in Colby all my life, and I know everyone I need to know.''

"Yes, ma'am," he said meekly. The coffee was ready, and he poured himself a mug, black the way he liked it. She was a tough one, and he didn't expect he'd get very far with her. He might just as well head out to the porch and drink his coffee in relative peace, despite the hammering that had started from behind the house, joining in with the distant buzz of the chain saw.

He tried one more time. "That's a fine son you have, Mrs. King," he said, heading toward the screen door that was barely attached to its hinges. "It must be nice to have your children close to home when they grow up. You have any other kids?"

Her reaction reminded him what a bastard he really was. Her tired face crumpled for a moment and her milky blue eyes filled with tears. "He's the only one we were blessed with," she said.

He couldn't bring himself to push her any further. He'd always been considered rapacious in court— he could destroy a witness in a matter of minutes, no matter how carefully they'd been coached or how firmly they believed in their particular truth. But he just couldn't do it to a tired old woman who'd had enough pain. He wasn't that much of a bastard, at least on this peaceful August morning. Maybe later. In the meantime he'd better make sure that any-thing incriminating in his bedroom was out of sight

in case King or his son wandered up there. It wouldn't do to have them find a pile of books connected to serial killers in general and the Colby murders in particular.

He set his mug of coffee on the newel post and took the steps two at a time.

For a moment he thought the upstairs was deserted, and he breathed a sigh of relief. Only to see Perley King standing in the middle of the room, peering at the notebook Griffin had left on the bed, a confused expression on his face.

Shit, Griffin thought. I am totally screwed. And he cleared his throat, racking his brain for a plausible explanation.

8

"What are you doing?" Griffin said, and the man turned bright red, dropping the notebook on the bed.

"I d-didn't mean no harm," he stammered. "I was just checking the water leaks by the chimney like my pa told me to do."

"By reading my private notes?"

"Can't," the man mumbled.

"Can't what?"

"Can't read," he said in a slow, expressionless voice. "Never had much call for it, I guess. Pa says I do just fine without. I can write my name."

"I'm sure you can," Griffin said, crossing the room and picking up the notebook. It was opened to his list from the day before, written in his dark scrawl. Perley King seemed unperturbed, and Griffin had no choice but to believe him. If he'd understood the words on the notepad he wouldn't have the pleasantly vacant expression on his face.

He'd already upset a battered-down, grieving mother, Griffin thought. Why not move on to someone mentally impaired for good measure? Just so he could feel really good about himself on this warm summer morning.

"You like living here, Perley?" What the hell kind of name was Perley, Griffin thought absently. The tall, shambling man/boy hardly seemed pearl-like.

Perley squatted down by the chimney, poking at the wood with a screwdriver, checking for rot. "It's okay," he muttered. "Kind of lonely, though, since Valette's been gone."

It shouldn't be that easy, Griffin thought. He moved to the dresser, making a show of looking through the drawers. "Who's Valette?"

"My sister. She was real pretty. She went away a long time ago. Satan took her."

"Satan?"

"She was a sinner, Pa said. We aren't to speak her name ever again. But I miss her. She used to get after Pa when he beat me. Made him stop. But then when she was gone, Pa was saved and gave up liquor and he didn't take the belt to me no more, nor to Ma, either, so I guess things are all right. She was pretty as a picture, Valette was."

"What happened to her?"

Perley had given up stabbing at the floor and was now attacking the ceiling around the chimney. Sooner or later he was going to come upon the soft spot in the back, but Griffin wasn't in any hurry to enlighten him.

"I told you, Satan took her," Perley said with great patience. "Mama said God wanted another angel in heaven, but Pa said it was Satan, and Pa's always right. Still an' all, I woulda thought Satan had enough to keep him company with them other ones.''

Bingo. "Other ones?'' Griffin prompted.

"I'm not supposed to talk about it,'' Perley muttered. "That was long ago, and we didn't have nothing to do with it. Pa says it's nobody's business.'' He stabbed at the wood, a steady, methodical jabbing motion. Was Valette the one who'd been stabbed to death? Griffin watched the rhythmic plunge of the long screwdriver with a kind of sick fascination.

"It sounds very sad,'' Griffin said, his voice noncommittal.

"I go to her grave sometimes. Pa beat me when he caught me, even without the liquor, so now I go when he's off on business. I'm not the only one who goes there. *He* does, too.''

"He? Your father?''

Perley shook his head slowly. "Nope. Satan. He goes to visit those girls and he leaves flowers on their graves. He was real sorry to take them, I know he was. He leaves them on other graves, too. That's how I know which ones were taken by Satan and which ones by the Almighty.''

Griffin managed to keep the excitement out of his voice. "So someone leaves flowers on the graves of the three murdered girls?''

Perley didn't stop his stabbing, didn't stop to wonder how a stranger would know about the three girls. "More'n three. He took them," Perley said patiently. "I didn't say he killed them. And he leaves flowers on their graves. All of them. By the lake, in the village. I seen him there, sometimes, in the dawn, when he thinks no one is around."

A cold shiver ran across Griffin. "What does he look like?"

Perley's long screwdriver sank deep into the rotten ceiling, and he let out a visceral grunt of satisfaction. "Found it," he muttered. He moved to the casement windows and called out. "Pa, I found the rot!"

"Coming, boy!" Zeb King was already on his way up the stairs, and it wouldn't do for him to catch Griffin interrogating his slow-witted son. But he couldn't just leave without getting the answer to his question.

"What does Satan look like, Perley?" he asked again.

Perley turned his innocent face to him. "Just like God, only different."

Great, Griffin thought, plastering a tight smile on his face as he scooped the papers from his bed, moving them out of sight just as Zebulon King walked in the room.

"You bothering Mr. Smith, boy?" he demanded, eyeing them both suspiciously. "I told you you were here to work, not to flap your jaw."

"I wasn't, Pa," Perley said, hanging his head. "I was just telling him about some things."

"What things?"

Shit, Griffin thought, steeling himself for disaster. "I told him about the fishing. He wanted to know where the best place was to catch a rainbow trout, and I told him." Perley looked as guileless as a puppy. He might be simple-minded, but he could lie with the ease of an expert.

"Takes more than the right spot to catch a rainbow," Zeb muttered, making it more than apparent that he thought Griffin didn't have the right stuff for such a task. "A man shouldn't hunt for something he's not ready to eat, and I reckon you don't know much about dressing a rainbow, now do you?" His contempt was almost genial.

As a matter of fact Griffin had caught many a rainbow trout during the last summer of his youth, and he was more than adept at cleaning and cooking them. "Just a thought," he said. "I probably won't get around to it, anyway."

"Too busy being on vacation," Zebulon said with a barely disguised sneer. "We'll be out of your way as soon as we can. In the meantime, I'd appreciate it if you didn't talk to my boy. He's a mite slow, and he can't concentrate with someone yammering at him."

There was no mistaking the warning in Zebulon King's flinty eyes, and Griffin gave him a slight nod. "No more yammering," he said. "Maybe I'll just get out of your way for now. Go for a drive, maybe find a place to eat."

"The Village Diner is open in Waybury," Zeb said, suggesting the next town over.

"Maybe I'll just take a picnic and go wander through the town. I'm particularly interested in old graveyards." It was deliberate, and he half expected Zeb to react.

He'd underestimated the man. If Perley looked distressed, Zeb just shrugged. "Suit yourself. Can't imagine what a grown man would find interesting about a bunch of tombstones, but there's many who find them of interest. Just be careful."

"Careful?"

"The one on the lake road gets a bit swampy at the edge. That old rattletrap of a car wouldn't have too good a time in the mud. Wouldn't want you to get stuck."

Like hell, Griffin thought. "Nice of you to warn me," he said.

"Doesn't hurt to be too careful," he said in his iron-hard voice. "You take your time, and we'll be finished for the day by three."

It wasn't even eight-thirty in the morning, which made for a long, empty day, but Griffin couldn't very well object. He couldn't go up to the inn— people were crawling all over the place at this hour, and he didn't expect Sophie to greet him with open arms. Besides, there were three or four cemeteries in the old town, some going back to the 1700s when the town was first founded. Finding the graves of the murdered girls might take some time. Particularly if it included looking for other, unidentified murder victims.

The two King men were looking at him, clearly

waiting for him to take his leave. "Can I shave first?" He didn't bother keeping the sarcasm out of his voice.

"If you make it snappy. I've got work to do in the bathroom."

Griffin managed to take almost a full hour showering and shaving, a petty revenge that nevertheless left him inordinately pleased with himself. By the time he got back to the kitchen Addy King was busy sweeping the back porch, and she didn't look up when he filled a travel mug with the last of the coffee. Maybe she was deaf.

He didn't think so.

He grabbed his keys, heading for the front door, then came to an abrupt halt.

Sophie Davis was standing on the porch, a plate of cookies in her hand, a wary, determinedly pleasant expression on her face.

Griffin leaned against the doorjamb, barring the entrance. "What's this?"

He frightened her. It was fascinating how easy it was to unnerve her, but it suited him just fine. Sophie Davis didn't strike him as someone who'd respond to charm or seduction, both of which he could turn off and on with sublime ease. She didn't trust him, wisely. And he couldn't rid himself of the notion that she had something to hide.

She was too young to have remembered the media coverage of the murders. She was maybe in her early thirties at the latest, more likely late twenties, and she'd been in Colby for only a few months. Not really time enough to develop secrets, unless she'd brought them with her.

He knew nothing about her, apart from the fact that she didn't particularly like him. Normally that wouldn't have bothered him, but he couldn't afford to ignore any anomaly while he was here. So he managed a faint, predatory smile, just to see her squirm.

"I brought you cookies," she said in a nervous, breathless voice.

"I can see that. Why?"

"To thank you for bringing my mother home."

"I could hardly let her wander around alone at that hour, could I?"

"You strike me as the kind of man who'd do just that," she said.

He didn't blink. She'd taken her white kid gloves off, ready to get down and dirty. He was more than willing to join her. "So this isn't really a social call," he said. "You want to tell me why you're really here?"

There was a muffled crash behind him as Addy dropped something in the living room. He didn't bother to turn and look, but Sophie turned pale. "Who's here?"

"Marge Averill sent the people you recommended out here to do some of the maintenance. You haven't answered my question. Why are you here?"

"I need to talk to you." She looked about as happy as a woman facing a firing squad.

"Fine. We can't talk here—too much going on. I was going for a drive—you can come with me."

"I've got things to do...."

"You want to talk to me or not?"

She hesitated. "All right. Where should I put the cookies?"

"Bring them with you. I haven't had breakfast yet." He moved past her, onto the porch, noticing with wry amusement that she backed well out of his way, just to make sure he didn't get too close to her. You'd think she suspected him, the way she was acting. He hadn't had people treat him like a leper since he'd gotten out of the Chittenden Correctional Center. It wasn't a pleasant feeling.

But she followed him, anyway, ten paces back like a dutiful Muslim wife, only to come up short at the sight of his car.

He was prepared for her caustic reaction. Few people understood or appreciated his attachment to his car—even Zebulon King had thought it was an old junker. Old it certainly was. Worth more than Zebulon King probably made in a year. The simple fact that it was a Jaguar was far outweighed by its advanced age and seeming state of decrepitude. The damned thing ran like a top, and he kept it in prime condition. The interior was perfect, from the refurbished leather seats to the burled-walnut dashboard. Only the outside looked disreputable—a mangy collection of bondo, rust and dark gray paint.

He went to the passenger door, opening it with an exaggerated flourish. "Not what you're used to, I know, but it will have to do. Your carriage awaits, madam.''

She approached it cautiously, as if she were expecting spiders to jump out at her. But when she spoke, her voice held a totally unexpected note of reverence.

''It's an XJ6,'' she said softly, her voice husky. ''What is it, a '74, '75?''

''It's a '74,'' he said, startled.

''It's beautiful,'' she breathed, totally entranced. She handed him the plate of cookies and slid into the soft leather of the front seat like an angel entering heaven. She closed her eyes and took a deep, appreciative breath. ''It even smells right.''

He didn't move, just stared at her. Annelise had always hated his car, insisting on taking her Mercedes or his more respectable Lincoln SUV. If he'd ever really needed the four-wheel-drive, it would have been in Vermont, but he'd decided to take the Jaguar on a last-minute whim. The Lincoln Navigator was huge and ominous; the Jaguar deceptively battered. And he'd wanted the excuse to take the Jag out on the highway, see what she could do after all the work he'd put into her.

He hadn't wanted a soft, flowery woman to practically have an orgasm the moment she climbed into it. Especially when he suspected that Sophie Davis had never had an orgasm in her life.

He opened his mouth to suggest they take her car, then closed it again. So she liked his car. Obviously she had hidden depths, something to recommend her. He took one of the ginger cookies and popped it into his mouth. More than one thing to recommend her, he corrected himself.

She had long legs beneath her flowered skirt, and he closed the door, feeling like a damned footman. She'd settled into the leather like a kitten on a blanket. He wondered if she was actually purring.

He gave himself a shake that was more mental than physical, then moved around the back of the car to climb into the driver's seat.

Her eyes were still closed, and he wondered if she'd fallen asleep. The leather was soft, but not that soft. He stared at her for so long that she finally turned her head and opened her eyes. She had a dreamy expression in them, like someone in the midst of sex, and he realized he was getting an erection just from watching her. He'd never had sex with anyone in the roomy back seat of the sedan, but clearly Sophie would be someone worthy of the privilege. The privilege of the car, not him, though he intended to make it very much worth her while.

He tried to break out of the erotic spell. "It's just a car," he said, not too sure of that.

"You know as well as I do this is more than just a car." A sudden frown creased her forehead. "Do you have other classics? I suppose you collect them, have someone fix them up for you...."

"No one touches this car but me. And this is my only one. I have a new car for transportation, but this is..." He wanted to tell her the truth. That it was his heart, his soul, the one thing he loved most on earth, more than any human being who'd ever crossed his path. "My hobby," he finished, deliberately downplaying it.

She ran her hand across the soft leather seat, and he could picture that hand running across his skin. She'd look quite glorious, sprawled naked on the golden leather of his wide back seat. And if he didn't stop thinking about that he was going to have to put the plate of cookies on his lap to hide his condition.

"It's quite..." She suddenly seemed to realize what she was doing. She stopped stroking the leather seat, sat bolt upright and blinked, trying to dispel that erotic haze. "It's quite nice," she said. She took the cookies from him.

He turned the key, hearing the throaty rumble of the motor with anxious pleasure. He put it into Reverse, backing out the narrow, weed-choked driveway with consummate care. "Don't even think it," he muttered.

"Think what?" She bit into one of the small, wonderful cookies, her white teeth severing it, her tongue pulling the rich flavor into her generous mouth. *Shit, he had to stop thinking about sex.*

"I'm not letting you drive this car, no matter how much you appreciate it. No one drives it but me. It's got too much power for most people, and besides, you probably don't even know how to drive a standard shift."

He'd managed to get her back up. Not much of an improvement over her dazed, erotic reaction to his car. Basically everything she said and did was turning him on.

"I like to drive stick," she said in an ominous voice.

"Oh, yeah? You don't look to me as if you've had much practice," he murmured. "You strike me as someone who's been cruising on automatic for years."

He had no idea whether she knew they were talking in sexual innuendoes. If she did, she was staunchly ignoring it. Making him even hotter.

"I don't think my driving experience is any of your business," she said.

Maybe not ignoring it, after all. "I could make it my business," he said in a low, seductive voice. "I could put you through your paces. See how you are on short hops, and how you stretch out on long, flat places. How smoothly you shift, and whether you throttle down with a rumble or a purr."

"Cut it out!" she said, her voice severe. "I didn't come with you to talk about cars."

"Is that what we're talking about?"

"What else?"

"I thought we were talking about sex."

"Not likely," she said. They were already on the road that wound around the lake, the Jaguar cruising perfectly.

"Then why are you here? Not for my charming company, I presume," he said.

She fidgeted with the seat belt. Her hand kept

creeping toward the leather for a surreptitious caress, then pulling back again.

"If I was looking for charming company it wouldn't be with you. I know who you are and I know why you're here, Mr. Smith." Her use of his phony name was filled with sarcasm. "And I want you to keep away from my family."

9

It wasn't the reaction that Sophie was expecting, but then, the supposed Mr. Smith wasn't anything like Sophie thought. He didn't protest, didn't get angry, didn't do more than blink.

"Okay, who am I?" he said in a reasonable voice.

The car was vibrating beneath her, a beautiful velvet hum, and more than anything she wanted to lean back and close her eyes and absorb the sound and the feel of it. Clearly he was a man with unsuspected depths, to own a car like this one, but even that didn't make him any less of a ruthless snake. A dangerous one.

"You know as well as I do that you're a reporter, trying to dredge up interest in the old murders." She concentrated on pleating the fabric of her flowered jumper. "People like you have no sense of compassion for the victims—it's over and done with. Why do you need to start ferreting around in someone else's pain?"

He didn't bother to deny it. "I would have thought the victims would be past harming."

"The three girls weren't the only victims. Their

families, the whole town suffered.'' She couldn't keep the anger out of her voice.

"You weren't even here at the time. Why would you care?"

"How did you know I wasn't here?" she asked suspiciously.

"If I were a reporter I would have done my homework, found out who still lived here so I could question them. As a matter of fact, though, you told me you'd just moved here a few months ago. Or had you forgotten?"

She couldn't remember telling him any such thing, but that wouldn't prove anything. "That doesn't mean I didn't used to summer here. I could have remembered it all."

"You were probably not much more than ten," he said. "And you weren't here when it happened. Don't waste your time trying to convince me you were."

"So what are you doing here?" she persisted.

"I thought you'd figured all that out. I'm a reporter on the trail of a very old crime. Though why a reporter should care about ancient history is beyond me."

Some of Sophie's conviction started to fade. "It's unsolved. People are always fascinated by unsolved mysteries. Besides, it had all the things people like to read about—sex, drugs and murder."

"People usually like money and fame involved in

their murders, as well, and I haven't heard about any missing treasure or famous politician mixed up in it. And who says it's unsolved? Just because the boy was eventually released on a technicality doesn't mean everyone doesn't believe he didn't do it. He was a bad one to begin with—anyone who was here could tell you that. And it makes it so much easier for the good people of Colby to think that an outsider would kill their young women, rather than one of their own.'' There was a grim undertone in his voice, one she couldn't quite define.

''Well, there must be some question, or otherwise you wouldn't be here,'' Sophie said, not about to be swayed.

''And what tipped you off that I was a reporter? Something I said? Something I did?''

''Common sense. I saw the books in your bedroom—normal people don't have books about serial killers for light reading.''

''Any number of people are interested in true crime. Just look at the bestseller lists.''

''So you're writing a book,'' she said, jumping at it. ''I should have guessed as much. You probably have a million-dollar advance and you don't care who you hurt.''

He turned off onto a back road, driving away from the lake, an unreadable expression on his face. Not that she dared take more than a passing glance at him. She didn't want to be caught staring at him, trying to figure out what it was that disturbed her so much about him.

"It sounds like you've got it all figured out," he said, concentrating on the narrow dirt road. "If you're so good at solving mysteries, then maybe you ought to be writing the book."

"I don't like true crime," she said coolly. "I don't enjoy other people's pain. If I'd known about the Colby murders I might have chosen another place to move to."

"You'd have a hard time finding a town without some kind of bloody skeleton in the closet." His voice was absolutely without emotion, but Sophie shuddered at the image his words summoned. "There's always trouble behind a bucolic atmosphere."

"That's a pretty cynical attitude. If you're not a reporter or a true-crime writer, who are you? And for that matter, where are we going?" The first hint of uneasiness tickled her stomach. What the hell was she doing, going off alone with a perfect stranger, one who filled her with illogical misgivings? The Kings would have seen her leave—they could testify if she disappeared and...

"I doubt you'd believe anything I told you," he said, interrupting her panicked thoughts. "I'm on vacation, and I wanted some peace and quiet. Not old ladies wandering around in my kitchen in the middle of the night, not uber-housewives delivering cookies.''

''Uber-housewives?'' she said, her panic replaced by outrage. ''I've never been married.''

''There's a surprise,'' he muttered under his breath.

She couldn't very well hit him while he was driving, not and risk the Jaguar. ''Where are you taking me?'' she demanded.

''I'm not taking you anywhere. You insisted on coming along with me, so you're stuck with it. And if you're so good at jumping to conclusions you should have figured out where we're going by now.''

Sophie looked out the window. ''There's nothing on this road but the old Mackin farmstead and the...'' she stopped.

''The graveyard.''

Sophie's throat felt suddenly tight. ''You haven't done your homework,'' she said after a moment. ''The girls aren't buried in the old McLaren graveyard. They're down in the village cemetery.''

''I'm not looking for those graves.'' He'd pulled to a stop along the side of the road and turned off the engine. The deserted McLaren graveyard was on their right, the white fence peeling and rotten, the grass growing high around the old, sagging headstones.

''Then why are we here? No one's been buried

here in over thirty years—they don't even bother to keep the grass properly mowed. Most people don't even remember there's a graveyard out here. Certainly no one ever comes here anymore.''

''You knew about it.'' He climbed out of the car, and for a moment Sophie didn't move. She still didn't trust him. She could lock the car, slide into the driver's seat and drive away. There were two advantages to that—one, he made her nervous. She couldn't believe he'd really hurt her, but a tiny sliver of doubt had settled in the back of her mind.

Two, it would give her probably her only chance at driving his glorious car. He'd left the keys in the ignition, and it would only take a second...

He reached in and took the keys. ''Don't even consider it,'' he said, his voice expressionless. ''You aren't driving this car. Are you coming?''

She didn't really have much choice. She set the plate of cookies down on the back seat and climbed out, following him past the sagging gate into the graveyard.

He seemed to be looking for something, though she didn't have the faintest idea what. He moved through the small graveyard at a leisurely pace, reading each headstone, until he stopped at one.

''I guess we're not the only ones who ever come here,'' he said. ''So tell me, who do you think brought those flowers?''

She looked down at the headstone. A handful of

bright yellow flowers sat in front of it, wilting from
the bright sun. It was the grave of Adeline Percey,
who died in 1973 at the age of nineteen. Sophie
racked her brain, trying to remember who the Perceys were, and a moment later came up with it.
Their daughter had been killed in a boat accident
during her first year in college.

"Presumably her parents. The Perceys still live
just outside of Colby."

"Maybe," he said. "What kind of flowers are
those?"

"I don't know."

"What do you mean, you don't know? Aren't you
some kind of Martha Stewart wannabe? They must
be fairly common around here."

"Mr. Smith..." She stopped, furious. "I'm not
calling you that phony name anymore."

"You can call me anything you want."

"I don't use that kind of language. I don't recognize the flowers because they're not common
around here. I've seen them before, but I can't remember where. And why does it matter?"

"It doesn't," he said.

"Then why are we here and why are you asking
me these questions, and what does it have to do with
the three girls who were killed?"

For a moment he was silent, glancing back at the
neglected grave with its spray of dying flowers.

"I'm thinking there were four," he said. "Maybe more."

"Don't you think someone would have figured that out before now?" she said caustically.

"Not when the authorities had a built-in scape-goat." He knelt down by the gravestone, staring at it as if it held the answers to a thousand unnamed questions.

And Sophie stared at him, finally given the chance to indulge herself.

He was wearing an old denim shirt and jeans, and his glasses had turned dark in the sunlight, obscuring his eyes. Not that his opaque brown eyes gave anything away in the first place. If the eyes were a window to the soul, then his were firmly shuttered.

After a moment he rose, and she could feel him looking at her. "Any more questions? Not that you had any—you've already figured out the answers."

"Look, I didn't want to come out with you in the first place. I just wanted to thank you for bringing my mother home."

"And warn me to keep my distance in the future. What did you think I did—lure her to my cave? I'm not here to be invaded by batty old ladies or nubile young ones."

"I'm not nubile!" she protested.

"I meant your sister."

"Oh." The idea was somehow deflating. "Well, I'm glad to hear that," she said briskly, recovering.

"I'll keep a closer eye on my mother so she won't bother you."

"What about the brat?" They were almost back at the car. The sun had disappeared behind a cloud, and there was a hint of chill in the air.

"I'll keep her as far away from you as humanly possible. She's young enough and foolish enough to think you're hot, and I don't want..."

They'd reached the car, and she was about to go around to the passenger side when his arm shot out, stopping her.

She turned to move in the other direction, but his other arm came up, trapping her against the side of the car. They were miles from nowhere, on a dirt road that might as well be a dead end, and no one would hear her scream. She swallowed, looking up at him with as fearless a look as she could muster.

It wasn't very effective. She couldn't see his eyes behind the dark lenses, but his mouth curved in a faint, cool smile. "Young and foolish enough to think I'm hot?" he repeated. "I guess you don't consider yourself young and foolish."

"Not really." There was a slight quaver in her voice, one she hoped he didn't notice. The only way she could escape from this situation was to show no fear. His long legs were brushing up against her skirt, and she could feel the warmth of his body in the cool air. Too close. Much too close.

"Then why are you so skittish around me? If I

didn't know better I'd say you were downright terrified.''

She didn't move. Not that she could, with his arms trapping her against the hard steel of the car. So much for showing no fear, she thought helplessly. It would be a waste of time to deny it. ''You just make me nervous,'' she said after a moment.

''Do I? Is it just me, or is it all men?''

She would have shoved him, but shoving him would have meant touching him, and if she did that he might not move, and then what would she do, with her hands on him? ''I don't like being pinned against a car out in the middle of nowhere,'' she said in her coldest voice.

''Yes, but it's a classic Jaguar XJ6,'' he mocked her. ''Surely that makes up for the indignity. And you've been skittish since I first saw you. Why are you afraid of me? What do you think I've done?''

His question startled her. ''Absolutely nothing. I just don't like—''

''Men in general? Or just me?''

Her fear was abating, just a little, replaced by justifiable anger. ''I sure as hell don't like you,'' she said. ''Now, let me go.''

''Convince me,'' he said in a low voice.

''What?''

''Convince me,'' he said again. And to her absolute horror he leaned down to kiss her.

It was just as well she had the car behind her and

his arms on either side of her. Otherwise she might have slid to the ground in complete astonishment. She tried to duck, but he caught her face in his hands, holding her still as he brought his mouth down on hers, a slow, deliberate kiss, open-mouthed, wet, thorough.

She closed her eyes. She told herself it was because there was nothing else she could do, no way to escape, and she didn't want to look at him. He pulled her arms around his waist and she held on, absorbing the feel of his body pressed up against hers. Hard, strong body, wet mouth, hands that held her and wouldn't let her go.

And she didn't want to escape. She wanted to be kissed in the sunlight by a gorgeous man. She just wanted some other man, not this complicated creature who had more secrets than she could even begin to imagine.

But it didn't matter what her brain wanted. Her body, her mouth, her soul wanted him, and she heard a quiet little sound of desire and knew that it had come from her.

He stopped kissing her, but he didn't move away, his hips pinning her against the car, his hands still cradling her face. She opened her eyes, dazed, to look up into his unreadable face, shielded by the dark glasses, and she wondered if he made love with his glasses on. And then she realized she was clinging to him, her arms tight around his lean waist, and she slid them up to push him away.

He didn't budge, just looked down at her. "So that's not it," he said obscurely.

"Let go of me."

"In a minute." His voice was lazy, provocative, and he kissed her again. And this time she kissed him back.

He slid his hands behind her, pulling her up against him, and she could feel his erection. It should have startled, even disgusted her. Instead she arched her hips against his, rubbing, needing. He reached behind her, fumbling for the car door. "Get in the back seat," he said in a husky voice, his other hand starting to pull her skirt up her leg.

Reality came crashing down. He wasn't expecting her to shove, and it took him off balance, so that he fell back from her. She sprinted around to the passenger side before he could grab her again, jumped in the car and quickly locked all the doors. Then she sat there, panting, staring out at him in grim triumph.

He wasn't even breathing heavily. She couldn't help it, her eyes went to his crotch, now at eye level, wondering if she'd imagined his erection. She hadn't.

She waited for him to demand that she open the door, and then she could tell him to go to hell. Instead he calmly reached in his pocket, stretching his jeans even tighter across the telltale bulge, and pulled out the keys.

She leaped over to slam down the lock again, but he was too fast for her. He opened the door and slid into the front seat, catching her wrists in one hand and forcing her back into her own seat. "All you had to do was say no," he said mildly enough.

"I did."

"I didn't hear you."

"No," she said, furious. "Keep your goddamned hands off me."

"Yes, ma'am. Hands off your mother, hands off your sister, hands off you. Any other orders while we're at it?" He started the car, and it was all Sophie could do to resist the hypnotic rumble beneath her.

"Leave town."

"I don't think so. I'm here for a vacation and I intend to take it."

"I'll make your life a living hell," she said furiously.

"Stronger men than you have tried," he muttered beneath his breath. He pulled out onto the narrow dirt road, making a U-turn that almost sent them careening over the hillside.

He drove like a bat out of hell down the narrow dirt road, but Sophie was beyond panic, still too profoundly shaken. She didn't say a word until he pulled up in front of the inn. Gracey was sitting in one of the rocking chairs, with Doc beside her, and they both stared at the ancient Jaguar with unabashed curiosity.

She started to get out of the car, then stopped, unable to help herself. "Why did you do that?"

"Do what? Drive too fast?"

"Kiss me."

No expression on his face at all. "Curiosity, I suppose."

She bit the inside of her cheek to keep from exploding. "And was your curiosity satisfied?" she asked in her iciest voice.

"For the time being."

She slammed the car door behind her, hoping the window would shatter. But Jaguar XJ6s were too well made for such indignities. Even with all her force, the door closed with an elegant little thump as she stalked up to the porch.

Griffin was humming softly beneath his breath as he drove back down the narrow drive to the Whitten cottage. In fact, it had been a very productive day. He'd learned three things of monumental importance.

One, that there might very well be a murder victim from 1973. He'd been eleven years old in 1973, and living with his father in California. And if he didn't kill one victim, he probably hadn't killed anyone.

Two, Sophie Davis was as innocent as he'd suspected, or else she knew damned little about kissing. He probably shouldn't have given in to temptation, but it had been irresistible, and he'd wanted to find out what her luscious mouth tasted like.

Her mouth had tasted like honeyed ginger, and longing, and fear. And he still couldn't be sure why she was so afraid of him.

And three—and what should have been the least important discovery, but for some reason it was making him uncharacteristically cheerful—the virginal Miss Sophie Davis wanted him. And she didn't know what to do about it.

In another time, another place he'd show her. She wasn't his type—innocence and ruffles and soft curves weren't his style. But in Sophie's case he would be more than willing to make an exception, if it weren't for the fact that he was here to find out what had happened twenty years ago, not to get laid.

He was a fool to let her distract him. He'd been here two days already, and he wasn't any closer to getting inside the abandoned hospital wing. Or to remembering what happened that night.

No, Sophie Davis was the very least of his problems, an annoying, irresistible attraction that he had every intention of resisting.

At least for now.

10

―――

"Was that your beau, darling?" Grace asked in a cheerful voice. "Who is he? I've never seen him before."

Sophie mounted the wide front steps to the porch, suppressing a sigh. "He's not my beau, Mama," she said. "Far from it. He's just a neighbor. He's renting the Whitten place. You remember."

"I don't remember anything," Grace said sweetly. "But if he's not your beau, why do you look like you've been necking?"

So much for Spacey Gracey, Sophie thought. She could feel the color rise in her face. Grace would see that as well, or at least Doc would. He was watching them both with benign fascination—she wouldn't get any help from that quarter.

"I haven't been necking with anyone," she said calmly. It was technically true. Two thorough kisses didn't quite constitute necking. "You're imagining things."

"It's my memory that's shot, not my powers of observation," Grace said with one of those lightning shifts of rationality that always threw Sophie for a loop. "Is he nice?"

"Who?"

"Don't try that with me, Sophie Marlborough Davis! I'm talking about your young man. Is he nice?"

Escape would be lovely, Sophie thought, eyeing the kitchen door longingly. In a few minutes Grace wouldn't even remember that Sophie had been gone for a while, much less think to ask questions about her companion. "I really need to go inside and wash up..." she began, but Doc, the traitor, forestalled her.

"Oh, sit down and tell us about it," he said with a mischievous look in his faded blue eyes. "It's not often your mother shows an interest in her daughter's romances."

Caught, Sophie thought. Hooked and landed, and if she didn't face the music she'd end up gutted. She plastered a phony smile on her face and dropped into one of the Maine rockers that overlooked the quiet lake.

"It's not a romance, he's not a young man, he's not my beau," she said patiently.

"Then why were you kissing him?" Grace asked.

"I wasn't!"

"You shouldn't lie to your mother, Sophie," Doc said with gentle reproof.

Sophie glanced at him. The old codger was enjoying this, she thought, annoyed. Maybe her own discomfort was a small sacrifice for her mother's temporary interest in the real world.

"I didn't kiss him," she said patiently. "He kissed me."

Her mother's hoot of triumph almost sounded like the old Grace. "I knew it! Was it love at first sight?"

"It's not love, and it certainly wasn't first sight. I have no idea why he kissed me, but I doubt he'll want to do it again."

"I wouldn't doubt it at all, Sophie," Doc said gallantly. "If the man has eyes in his head and half a brain he'd be smitten."

Sophie repressed a sigh. Smitten, eh? She could just imagine Mr. Smith's reaction when he heard the old folks were calling him a smitten beau, and *her* young man. It might almost be enough to drive him away.

"I wouldn't get your hopes up, Mama," she said wryly. "Mr. Smith isn't my type, and the last thing he's looking for is true love. I have no idea why he kissed me, but it had nothing to do with being attracted to me." Belatedly she remembered the unmistakable bulge of his erection, and she could feel the color rise in her face again. Well, maybe he was attracted to her, or maybe he just got hard every time he kissed a woman, whether he liked her or not. She'd managed to avoid that kind of information, and she'd just as soon never learn about such things.

No, that wasn't strictly true. She simply hadn't been sufficiently tempted before. And wasn't now, she reminded herself sharply, the moment the thought drifted into her unruly consciousness.

"My Sophie's still a virgin," Grace said with the air of someone announcing a terminal illness. "I don't know what I'm going to do about her."

It could have been worse, Sophie thought bleakly. She could have announced it in front of someone other than Doc. She could have announced it in front of Mr. Smith.

"Good for you," Doc said approvingly. "It's refreshing to find a girl who's saving herself for marriage."

Sophie shuddered at the thought. It sounded old-fashioned and priggish, when she was afraid it was simply a matter of her being cold-blooded. "It's not that," she said frankly. "I just haven't found anyone who interests me enough. God knows I don't plan to die a virgin, and I doubt I'll be waiting for my wedding night. I'm just a little...picky."

"It's a good way to be," Doc said fondly. "Don't listen to your mother, Sophie. Virtue is a highly underrated commodity nowadays. Treasure yours."

Sophie resisted the impulse to make a moue. She'd started to think of her relatively untouched state as more of a liability than a selling point, and there had been a number of times when she'd been determined to get rid of it with the next available man. Unfortunately the next available man had always proved unacceptable for one reason or another, and she was now the oldest living virgin in the Northeast Kingdom. Maybe in the entire United States.

"Speaking of random sex, where's Marty?" she asked, changing the subject. Grace laughed, but Doc's sweet face drooped in sorrow.

"Last we saw she was chasing around after the Laflamme boy," he said. "Whatever made you decide to hire him to do the yard work? There's no denying he's a hard worker, but I would have thought you'd try to avoid temptation as far as your wanton younger sister was concerned."

That was going a bit too far. Sophie was allowed to criticize Marty and her flagrant habits—Doc had no right to disapprove.

"She's not wanton," Sophie protested. "Just... young. As for Patrick Laflamme, he seems like a levelheaded young man, and Marge Averill assured me he wouldn't be interested in Marty."

"He's a man," Doc pronounced. "The worst kind—halfway between being a kid and being grown up. He may mean well, but his hormones will make him crazy, and practically unable to resist any kind of temptation. I know his family, and he's a good, smart boy, but your little sister could tempt a saint." His genial tone took the sting out of the words.

"I'll keep an eye on them. As a matter of fact, I'd better look for her right now. Make sure she hasn't dragged young Patrick into the toolshed," she said cheerfully.

"Oh, she wouldn't do that, Sophie," Grace said with all seriousness. "There are too many spiders in there. Ghosts, as well."

Doc's teacup dropped to the porch floor, smashing. "I'm so sorry!" he said, leaping up. "I've broken your pretty dish."

"Don't worry," Sophie said, already picking up the bigger pieces. "All the china is mismatched—I just bought anything that took my fancy." In fact that had been one of her favorites, but she wasn't about to tell Doc that when he was looking so mortified. She turned back to her mother. "What were you saying, Mama?"

Grace just gave her a vague smile. "I don't remember."

"I'm trying to talk your mother into coming to town to have dinner with us. Rima hasn't seen her for a week now, and she gets a little isolated."

"You should go, Mama. You know how you enjoy your little outings," Sophie said, heading for the door, the broken cup in her hand. "If Doc can't pick you up I can drive you."

"I'll come fetch her at five," Doc said. "If that's all right with you, Grace?"

Grace waved an airy hand of acceptance, looking

rather like a youthful Queen Elizabeth for a moment, and Sophie disappeared into the kitchen before another awkward question surfaced.

His face was as good as his body, Marty thought, breathing a sigh of relief. She'd put her contacts in, showered and was wearing a halter top and the shortest shorts she owned, the ones that showed off her long, tanned legs to perfection. She knew she looked gorgeous, but Sophie's new gardener was looking at her out of the most beautiful, liquid eyes she had ever seen in her life, and he actually didn't seem interested.

"Hey," Marty said. She'd wanted to wear her high-heeled sandals, the ones that made her legs look even better, but she figured that would have been a bit much. Subtlety had its uses.

"Hey," he said, unpromisingly. He had a gorgeous chest, but to her dismay he quickly pulled a T-shirt on. "Can I help you?"

"I'm Marty Davis. My sister's your boss."

"Yeah," he said, again not very enthusiastic. "I've cut up the three poplars that came down in the last storm, and I was going to start in weeding the flower bed on the east side of the house. Did she have something else she'd rather have me do?" He didn't have a Vermont accent, thank God. Not that she actually minded the Yankee twang of the Northeast Kingdom, but she preferred not hearing it in someone she was trying to seduce.

"I haven't the faintest idea," Marty said. "Isn't it time you took a break? You've been working non-stop for hours."

"I took a break at eleven. I'll stop for lunch at one."

"How do you know which side of the house is east?" she asked, suddenly curious.

"Any fool knows what's east and what's west," he said with barely disguised impatience. "Is there anything I can help you with? Otherwise I need to get back to work."

She'd been told she had a very sexy pout, so she tried it on him. "Don't you like me?" she asked plaintively.

He looked her up and down, slowly, from her toes with their blue polish and three toe rings, up her admirably long legs, over her bare stomach and all the way up to her fuchsia-tinted hair. And then he shrugged, clearly unimpressed. "I don't even know you. Should I?"

Marty's sexy pout turned into a frown. "You tell me."

"I've been trying to tell you I have work to do. So if you haven't got a message from your sister or something you need me to do, I'd appreciate it if you let me get on with it."

"Oh, I have something I want you to do," Marty said in a soft, cooing voice.

"What is it?"

"Go to hell."

She stalked away, majorly pissed. Trust Sophie to find the best-looking homosexual she could find in the area, just to make Marty's life miserable. Well, there were other boys around, men as well. Marty just hadn't made the effort. Maybe she'd hitch a ride with Doc when he went back into town. Of course, Doc gave her the creeps, but then, most old people did. Maybe she could...

"Hey."

She was just about to turn the corner by the inn when she heard his voice. She was half tempted to keep on stalking, but curiosity got the better of her. She turned to glare at him. He was as unmoved by her anger as he'd been by her sexy pout.

"What do you want?" she snapped.

"I'll be eating my lunch down by the lake," he said. "At one."

"And I care because...?"

He grinned then. Big mistake—he had the most delectable smile she'd ever seen in her entire almost eighteen years. "You tell me," he said. And then he turned his back on her, and she could hear him whistling under his breath.

She stomped around the front of the building, in

time to see Doc rise and pat Grace's hand. "I'll be back at five," he was saying.

Perfect opportunity. She could get a ride into Colby with Doc, and even get a ride back out if she ever felt like returning to this epitome of boredom. It should have been an easy decision. Doc and freedom, at least for a few hours. Or meeting that smartass down by the lake where anyone could see them.

It was a no-brainer. Sophie's new handyman was the best-looking thing she'd seen since she arrived in Colby—she doubted she'd find anyone nearly as interesting at Audley's. If fate had decided to deliver such a hunk to her own backyard, then he was probably worth the effort.

Besides, she didn't like Doc. It was one thing for her sister and Grace to worry about her, another to have a stranger doing it. She wasn't part of Doc's clientele, and what she did with her time, what she smoked, who she saw, was her business, not his. And if she rode into town with him he'd probably cross-examine her.

No, she was better off staying behind. Seeing if she could make the sourpuss smile again. And seeing if there was any way she could lure him out of sight of the big house.

The book was gone.

One of the odd twists that Grace's illness had brought was a sudden concern with neatness. Grace had always been someone who left her clothes scattered on the floor, who had papers and scarves and paraphernalia trailing after her, who believed making a bed was a waste of time when you were just going to sleep in it again that night. In fact, Sophie hadn't even learned to make a bed until she had gone to live with her father and Eloise in their neat home in Michigan while Grace traveled the world. There were times she thought her almost obsessive fascination with all things housewifely was simply a reaction against her globe-trotting mother, but that seemed too obvious an answer. All she knew was she found safety and comfort in making jars of apple butter and raspberry jam, and old china soothed her soul.

Sophie really had no intention of searching Grace's room. She was merely interested in snitching her resurfaced copy of *Murder in the Northeast Kingdom.* It should have been lying on top of Grace's neatly made bed, or in an orderly pile on the floor beside it.

It was nowhere.

There were books arranged neatly, by size, in the bookcase, but amid all the Ted Bundys and Boston Stranglers there wasn't a Vermont killer to be found. On a whim Sophie looked under the bed, but there wasn't even a stray dust bunny. When she opened the closet it was more like the old Grace—clothes piled on the floor, hung on hooks instead of hangers, her shoes caked with dried mud.

Sophie closed the door again, thoughtful. When had Grace wandered out on a muddy path? She tried to keep track of her—the only time she thought Grace wasn't accounted for was when she'd visited their surly neighbor in her bare feet. So when had she gone traipsing through the mud? And why?

She leaned against the closet door, staring at her mother's room as if looking for answers. Her windows were open, and she could hear Grace's soft voice from the porch as she said goodbye to Doc. She'd come inside then, only to find her daughter searching her room, Sophie thought, suddenly ashamed of herself. If she wanted to read the book all she had to do was ask her mother.

Except that the book had disappeared, and Grace wouldn't remember where she'd put it.

There was something deeply shameful about spying on one's mother, Sophie thought, opening the dresser drawers as quietly as possible. Even if it was for Grace's own protection, it felt strange, uncomfortable. After all, what did she expect to find? She'd stopped looking for the book—if she really wanted it she could probably get it online. It wasn't as if she had any interest in the old killings, apart from trying to figure out what John Smith's particular fascination with them was. So why was she rifling her mother's drawers?

They were like the closet, jumbled, messy, every-thing mixed together. The expensive lacy stuff that Grace had always preferred, mixed with the utilitar-ian cotton that Sophie had bought her on the premise that they were easier to launder. No missing paper-back to be found, and Sophie had no earthly reason to keep searching.

Until she found the knife.

He would pray for their souls, he thought, bowing his head. His true path was being pointed out to him, and there was no way he could shun his duty, much as it pained him. The righteous must triumph, the wicked must perish, or there would be no meaning to life, and he had to cling to the belief that it all meant something, otherwise why would God have taken his children from him?

The wicked would die, the righteous would be born again, and he would grieve his part in meting out justice.

Not the fact that he must kill them.

But his pleasure in the act.

Three of them in that old house. Three women, all sinful in their souls, from the old, crazy one to the randy young one. And even the Madonna in the middle was courting temptation. It would be a gift, to have her die in a state of grace. He would tell her he killed the others, so she wouldn't worry. She worried too much about her small family. She would be much happier knowing they were no longer her responsibility.

He could do it all, though it grieved him. He was young, strong, immovable with the Lord's wrath to guide him. He would take them all. And then maybe he could sleep at night.

11

Sophie woke up with a start, her heart pounding, covered in a film of cold sweat. The moon was shining in her window, almost daylight bright despite the late hour, and she sat up, letting her eyes focus on the dark shapes in the room. They seemed to shift and move, but it was only the shadow of the tab curtains moving in the breeze from the open window.

She didn't move, waiting for her heartbeat to still, waiting for reality to wash over her. It was a cool, silent night in the country, and the only sound was the rustle of leaves as that same soft breeze stirred them. That, and the faint lap of the lake against the sandy shore were all that broke the stillness.

They were noises she was used to, soft, lulling noises that soothed her to sleep. Why had she woken up in such a panic?

She scooted back against the headboard, tucking the plump feather pillows behind her. It must have been a nightmare, though she wasn't quite sure what had set it off. In fact, she hadn't had the world's calmest day. At least Marty had been halfway cheerful, and she'd even taken her dishes out after they finished dinner. Grace had gone off with Doc, and by the time she returned she'd gone straight to bed. Nothing to panic about with either of them, at least for now.

Of course, there was the big hunting knife she'd found hidden beneath Grace's underclothes. That in itself wasn't terribly worrisome—Grace had a habit of appropriating strange things and leaving them in her room. Over the past few months Sophie had retrieved three of her most flowery dresses, a frying pan, four half-eaten boxes of cookies, a trowel, an electric razor from God knows where and a red wool hunting cap. She had no possible use for any of those things, except perhaps the cookies. Grace had never had much of a sweet tooth, and she'd seldom eaten store-bought cookies, but then, she was changing so radically that it was no wonder that Sophie couldn't keep up with her.

Still, it was nothing out of the ordinary in terms of Grace's recent behavior. Though the knife was intrinsically more dangerous—she could have cut herself on the dull, rusty blade.

But at least it was out of her reach now, tucked in the back of Sophie's closet. She could clean the rust stains off it, maybe give it to Doc to dispose of. It was a good-looking knife if one liked that sort of thing, and men seemed uncommonly fascinated with weapons. She didn't think Doc would be, but he probably knew someone in town who'd like it.

As a matter of fact, it had a distinctive handle, a carved white bonelike substance. Not the sort of knife that was kept behind the glass case in Audley's extensive hunting section. Maybe Doc would know who'd lost a knife like that one, and could get it back to its rightful owner. And even come up with a reason why Grace would have found it and hidden it in her drawer.

It was really nothing to worry about. No more than Marty's interest in the new gardener. Patrick Laflamme was immune to her, Marge had assured her. He was much too focused on going back to college and accomplishing things to be distracted by a young girl who meant nothing but trouble. Besides, he had a stern French-Canadian mother who'd keep him on the straight and narrow.

So that situation was safe enough. The inn was almost ready, everything was running smoothly. What was her problem?

She knew perfectly well what her problem was— she just didn't want to think about it. It could be summed up in one word. Well, maybe two. John Smith.

Why in the world had he kissed her like that? And why couldn't she stop thinking about him? It wasn't as if she'd never been kissed. She'd kissed any number of men, looking for one, anyone, who would entice her enough to make her throw caution to the wind. She still hadn't found the right one, but that wasn't for want of trying. She'd kissed more than her share of toads, searching for a prince in disguise. So far they'd all been toads.

Including John Smith—or whatever his name was. Who did he think he was, to grab her like that? What in heaven's name made him think she'd want him to kiss her? Had she been sending out erotic messages? Highly unlikely. Maybe he was just egotistical enough to think any woman would want him to kiss her, including someone who'd gone out of her way to show her dislike...

Had she? Had she been cool and unfriendly? She'd meant to be. But the question was, why? Why did John Smith bring out the worst in her?

Maybe because he was a liar. If his name was John Smith then her name was Madonna. She hated liars.

He also had the totally annoying habit of acting as if he could see right through her. Past the flounces and the flowers, past the jams and pies and soothing rituals. He could see something small and frightened inside her, something she tried to wash away. And she didn't want anyone looking that closely, particularly someone as unnerving as John Smith.

She scooted back down in bed again, closing her eyes. The shadows in the room shifted in the moonlight, and for a moment she cursed her obsessive attention to detail. The room needed light-blocking shades of some sort, or heavy curtains. So far she'd been more than happy to let the sun wake her up at the crack of dawn, and she didn't even mind when the strong moonlight occasionally roused her from sleep.

Tonight she minded. She lay there in the moonlight, listening to every creak and groan the old house made. She'd grown used to those noises, even loved them. It made her think of a kitten purring. Her huge old house was talking to her, making approving noises, telling her she was welcome.

Tonight it felt restless, nagging at her. Silly, Sophie thought. She was the one who was restless. Anxious about the opening of the inn, anxious about her family, anxious about being kissed by an unwelcome stranger who certainly wasn't inspired by love at first sight or even a passing attraction. He made it clear he found her just as tiresome as she found him.

So why did he kiss her?

And when was she going to get back to sleep? Tomorrow would be a long day—she had to call the bedding shop in Burlington to deliver the new mattresses, and the building inspector was coming in the next day or two, and sooner or later she had to get her software up and running. All before strangers started invading her inn.

And maybe that was the crux of it. She'd moved

to Vermont, bought the huge old house of her dreams in order to turn it into a bed-and-breakfast. She'd worked tirelessly, and everything was coming to fruition. And suddenly she didn't want to share her haven with a bunch of paying guests tromping through her peaceful rooms.

"Get over it," she muttered, keeping her eyes closed. *You have to make choices in this life—nothing was ever handed to you on a silver platter.* The only way she could afford to live in this peaceful place at the back end of beyond, the only way she could support such a huge old house and her sister and mother besides, was to take in paying guests. Whether she wanted them there or not.

She heard the noise, and for a moment she couldn't place it. Just a quiet clicking sound, coming from below. She had one of the front rooms overlooking the lake, though she knew she would have to give that up when she opened for business. Customers would pay more for a lake view, and Sophie couldn't afford to indulge herself. The wide porch ran directly beneath her open window, and she suddenly realized what she'd heard. The sound of the front door latching.

She scrambled out of bed and opened the door as quietly as possible. For a moment she stood in the hall, wondering if she was being the world's greatest idiot. Like a heroine of an old Gothic romance, she was wandering around in the middle of the night in her nightgown with a murderer on the loose.

But there *was* no murderer on the loose. She was just getting spooked by the unnerving reminders of those long-ago deaths. The boy had been caught, and even if he'd eventually been freed, in most people's minds there was no doubt he'd done it.

Though her unwelcome neighbor probably had some other theory, or why would he bother snooping around?

No, it was much more likely to be Marty or Grace sneaking out of the house. Marty slipping out for cigarettes or a boy. Maybe Patrick Laflamme wasn't nearly as stalwart as Marge had promised.

She opened Marty's door just a crack, breathing a thankful sigh that she'd oiled the hinges, and peered in at the bed. Marty was sprawled on top of it, her fuchsia-streaked hair startling against the pillow, her face innocent in sleep. For a moment Sophie couldn't move, as a wave of nostalgia washed over her. For all her sullen, teenager defiance, Marty was still a kid. The little sister Sophie had always loved, and somehow felt responsible for. Her parents' deaths had hit her hard, but Sophie had done everything she could to make up for it, to give her a home and security. Seeing her like that, her defenses washed away by sleep, reminded Sophie just how much she loved her and always had. And reminded her to thank God Marty wasn't in the garden shed with Patrick. And the spiders. And the ghosts.

That had been an odd thing for Grace to say. God help them all if she started seeing ghosts and apparitions. Sophie wasn't about to put her in a nursing home—Grace was her responsibility, and Sophie had every intention of keeping her home as long as possible. But how would a delusional old lady mix with her well-heeled clientele?

Sophie closed the door just as silently and made her way down the stairs, carefully avoiding the seventh one that always squeaked no matter how she tried to fix it. Sure enough, Grace's door stood wide open, her rumpled bed empty in the moonlight.

Sophie didn't hesitate. She grabbed a flashlight and a shawl she'd draped across a chair and ran out into the damp night air.

The moon had vanished behind a cloud. There was a mist rising from the lake, spreading out over the sloping lawn like a velvet fog. She tried to beam the flashlight toward the woods, but the light simply bounced off the rolling mist, and there was no sign of anyone.

She couldn't afford to wait. Grace would be heading back to the Whitten place—she'd developed a fascination for it. Or maybe it was a fascination for Mr. Smith, though Sophie doubted it. That particular weakness seemed to be left to her usually hard-headed daughter.

She plunged into the woods, fighting her way through the overgrown ferns and saplings, as the fog swirled around her. The air was cool and damp, almost clammy, and Sophie pulled the shawl tighter around her. At least she wore decent cotton nightgowns, not the skimpy shorty pajamas Marty favored or the slinky silk that used to be Grace's style. She was still shivering, probably because her feet were bare and cold, but she was determined to catch up with her errant mother before she happened to wake her mysterious neighbor. The last thing she wanted was another midnight confrontation with the man. Especially after that kiss this afternoon. Right now all she wanted was to keep her distance.

She could always head back home and call Doc. He'd come out and find Grace, and provide a buffer if Smith decided to come calling. But what if Grace had headed in the opposite direction? Did Sophie dare waste time?

No, she'd be at the Whitten place. Sophie had found her there any number of times, sitting on the porch, humming softly. Her mother seemed to have a fascination for the old house, and an entirely unhealthy fascination for the man who'd rented it. She wouldn't go anywhere else on a midnight stroll.

The Whitten cottage was set in a little clearing among the towering white pines, and the moonlight filtered through the darkness, glancing off the rolling fog. The mist was almost like a living thing. Some giant, lumbering beast, some strange enchantment from an old fairy tale, wrapping itself around the cottage. The house was dark, but the front door was open, and Sophie breathed a silent curse. She was too late.

Or maybe not. There were no lights on—clearly Grace hadn't woken the tenant yet. Maybe there was a chance she could get in there, retrieve Grace and get out before Smith even realized his privacy had been breached once more.

The porch creaked beneath her bare feet, and she tiptoed carefully across it, pushing open the screen door and peering into the house.

"Ma?" she whispered, not too loud. At least Grace still had all her faculties, even if her memory and reasoning power were shot all to hell. If she was there she'd hear Sophie calling her. "Grace, are you there?"

She couldn't see anyone, any movement, and she stepped inside, squinting in the darkness. Immediately the smell assailed her, the unmistakable scent of old wood and paint and years of lakeside living, mixed with the unexpected note of fresh lumber. She took a deep breath, inhaling it, fighting off the wave of pure longing. This should have been her house, Sophie thought for a blind, covetous moment.

And then she remembered what she was doing here. And who was upstairs asleep. "Ma?" she whispered loudly.

She didn't dare climb the narrow stairs to the second level. She was already playing with fire—besides, Grace wasn't the stealthy sort. If she was here, Sophie would have heard her. She tried one last time. "Grace?" she called in a stage whisper.

"She's not here."

Sophie shrieked. Smith had appeared out of nowhere, looming up in the darkness. Blocking the doorway. "What are you doing here?" she demanded in a panicked voice.

"I live here, remember?" he said with thinly disguised impatience. "And your mother hasn't wandered over here tonight. What made you think she had?"

"She's missing." It was bad enough that she was standing in his house in the middle of the night in her nightgown. Somehow the darkness made it worse. Not that she wanted bright lights to expose what she was wearing. Though in fact the nightgown had more fabric in it than some of her dresses. She was being stupid. "Why are you prowling around here in the dark?" she demanded.

"It's my house, I can prowl around all I want. In fact, the power's out. I was just calling the electric company."

"You told me your phone didn't work."

"It didn't work yesterday. They hooked it up today. Why don't you call your house and see if your mother's there?"

"She won't answer the phone."

"Your sister will. That way you'll know whether you really need to panic or not."

"All right," she said grudgingly. He sounded too damned practical for her, and she wanted to get away from him as fast as she could, but if Grace was missing she needed to get help quickly. "Where's the phone?"

"Over by the sofa. You'll have to feel your way there—I don't have a flashlight or candles."

"I do," she said, remembering it belatedly, and she switched it on, shining it on Smith.

Big mistake. He was wearing a pair of ragged cutoff jeans and nothing else. There seemed to be acres and acres of naked, tanned, warm male skin right in front of her, and she dropped the flashlight, which immediately went out, plunging them back into darkness again.

"Smart move," he drawled. "Did you see a ghost?"

There it was again. "I don't believe in ghosts," she said.

"Given the history of this place that's probably just as well," he muttered. "Give me your hand."

"Why?"

"I said your hand, not any other part," he said, annoyed. "I'm going to lead you over to the telephone, preferably without you breaking your neck in the process."

"I think I should just go back..."

He'd already grabbed her hand. He could see better than she could in the darkness, and she had no chance to pull away. His hand was big, strong, warm. Flesh. He moved past her into the pitch-black room. The doorway was empty. She could yank her hand free and run for it if she could just take him by surprise.

"Don't think you can run away," he said, tugging at her. "I won't be responsible for you getting lost in the woods any more than I would for your mother. I have at least a faint sense of decency. Come on."

She didn't bother struggling—it would have been undignified, and her tattered dignity was her only defense by that point. She let him lead her through the darkness, and she only banged her hip once against a wooden object before he placed her hand on the telephone. "There," he said, sounding impatient.

The impatience was both reassuring and annoying. He didn't want her there any more than she wanted to be there—he'd made that entirely clear. He just had a sense of responsibility beneath his remote exterior.

It was an old-fashioned dial phone, probably black and ancient. Touch-tone would have been hard enough in the dark. By the fifth attempt she could hear the phone ringing on the other end, and she only hoped to God that she'd dialed the right number and not some frosty Vermonter.

She let it ring. Her eyes were just beginning to get used to the darkness, and she could tell that Smith's body was once again blocking her escape route. Why did he have to be so damned big? So damned *there?* So damned naked? It was a cool night—he should be sleeping in pajamas like any sensible man, not in skimpy little cutoffs....

"Yeah? What is it?" Marty's sleepy voice finally answered the phone.

"Grace has disappeared. I've been looking everywhere for her—would you check her room and see if by any chance she's come back in? I'd hate to call the police for nothing."

"All right." She sounded martyred, as always, and Sophie clutched the phone tightly as she listened to Marty's footsteps shuffle away.

It seemed to take her forever. When she finally got back on the phone she'd gone beyond begrudging to outright annoyed. "She's sound asleep in her bed, Sophie."

"Are you sure? I heard the door close and..."

"I'm sure. You must have been dreaming. Where the hell are you, anyway?"

"I'm at the Whitten place. I thought she might have come back here...."

"The Whitten place? O-kay." There was no

doubt Marty knew exactly who she was with. "Don't wake me up when you get back home."

"It'll only take a couple of minutes. You'll still be awake."

Marty's laugh was far from comforting. "Maybe," she said. "Maybe not. Have fun, sis. Don't do anything I wouldn't do."

"Marty..." But Marty had already hung up the phone—leaving Sophie with no choice but to hang up the other end and somehow figure out a way to get by her unwilling host without him touching her again.

He wasn't there. He'd disappeared while she was talking to Marty, obviously having lost interest in her. Again one of those moments of regret-tinged relief. At least he wouldn't interfere with her leaving.

She headed straight for the door, bumping into two more objects and almost knocking down a table in her haste. "Thanks for letting me use the phone," she called out into the darkness as she pushed open the screen door.

"Anytime," he said from the porch. "Now, why don't you tell me why you really came here."

12

She should have known she couldn't escape that easily, Sophie thought. Not the way her luck had been running. He was standing on the porch, leaning against the railing, and the moon had come out again, sending a silvery light over the landscape, a shimmering trail on the mirror-still lake. He was even better-looking in the moonlight, she thought irritably. Why couldn't life ever be simple?

She pushed open the screen door, letting it slam behind her as she stepped out onto the porch. Into the night. "I told you why I came here," she said patiently. "I was looking for my mother."

"Who was sound asleep in bed."

"It was a logical assumption. She was here the other night," Sophie protested. "I thought I heard the outside door closing, and when I went down to check on her, her room was empty."

"Did you think to check the bathroom?"

"No," she muttered. "That was probably where she was. She gets up several times during the night."

"Too much information," he drawled. "So why

the panic tonight? It would have taken only a moment to see if your mother had wandered off, and presumably no one could have gotten in without jimmying the door. You do lock the doors, don't you?''

"Do you think I'm some kind of idiot?" she demanded huffily.

Wrong question. "Yes. What kind of lock do you have?''

"Whatever came with the house.''

"Jesus Christ, woman, don't you have any sense at all?" he exploded. "The first thing you should have done was have the locks upgraded on the place. Three women alone out here at the end of the lake, with no one around..."

"You're around," she pointed out.

"I just got here. And you trust me about as far as you'd trust Jack the Ripper. Don't you have any sense of self-preservation?" He sounded really annoyed with her.

"The crime rate around Colby is very low," she said in a haughty voice.

"This year, maybe," he muttered. "Get new locks for the doors. It won't keep anyone out who's really determined, but it could slow them down."

"Why would someone want to break in?"

"People do all sorts of strange things. Maybe someone's developed a mad passion for you."

"Thanks a lot," she said wryly. "The notion is not *that* strange."

She couldn't see his expression in the shadows. The moon was behind him, silvering him with an almost eerie light. He had bony shoulders. She liked bony shoulders. Oh, God, she liked him, she realized with sudden horror. Not his personality or his presence or anything about him. Except his body. And his mouth.

Why the hell was she reacting like this to the most disturbing man she'd ever met? At this time in her life?

She didn't show a glimmer of what was racing through her mind. "I better get home," she said after a moment.

He was watching her. He leaned against the porch, lazily, as if he hadn't a care in the world except to bait her. Maybe it was only her crazy emotions, roiling around beneath her determinedly calm exterior, or maybe he was just as tense as she was despite his negligent pose. She couldn't tell what was going on under his enigmatic exterior.

"Yeah," he said, not moving. For her to leave, he'd have to move out of the way. But he showed no signs of moving. "Tell me something. What the hell are you wearing?"

Presumably he couldn't see the blush that warmed her face. She pulled the shawl more tightly around her shoulders. It was a warm night for late August, she was wearing a voluminous Edwardian night-gown, and he was making her feel naked.

"It's a nightgown. Haven't you ever seen one before? I would have thought a man of your vast experience would have seen women in nightgowns before." Shit. In her effort to be arch and cool she'd inadvertently brought up the subject of sex. Obliquely, but it was there, between them, and she didn't want to talk about sex with John Smith or whoever the hell he was.

The slight curve of his mouth, his very sexy mouth, was his only reaction. It was enough. "I have to admit that most women I sleep with are naked. They certainly don't wear things like that. You look like a doomed bride. All you need is a bouquet of dead flowers and a tattered veil and you could haunt this place quite nicely."

Ghosts weren't any improvement over sex as subject matter. Not when she had to walk by what had once been a murder scene.

"It's a nightgown, and I'll have you know it came from Victoria's Secret!"

"Not the Victoria's Secret I know. Trust you to consider that sexy."

"I don't consider it sexy!" she protested.

"Then why are you wearing it?"

"Because I don't care about sex." *Shit.* He'd trapped her into it. And in fact, it was a lie. She hadn't cared about it before. All he'd had to do was kiss her, and she couldn't stop thinking about it. And why the hell didn't he put on more clothes—his chest, his stomach, everything about him was distracting her, making her think about things she didn't want to even consider.

He pushed away from the post, and she thought he was going to let her leave. She was wrong. He came right up to her, and there was no place for her to retreat. The screen door was pressed against her back, and he was blocking her way with his body. His moonstruck shoulders. His mouth.

"Oh, yeah?" he said mildly enough. He reached out and took the shawl in his hands, pulling it from her. She made a futile grab at it, but it was too late. He let it drop on the porch floor, at her bare feet beneath the ruffled nightgown. Then he began to unfasten the pearl button at her throat. She was having trouble breathing. "Prove it," he whispered, unfastening the second button.

She finally looked up at him, stricken. "What are you doing?" she demanded in a strained voice.

"Seducing you." He sounded remote, almost clinical, as his long fingers moved down the front of her nightgown, parting one button after another. It had too many buttons. "I would have thought a woman with your vast experience would have figured that out by now."

"But...why?"

His low laugh was even more unnerving. "Because I want to."

In another minute she was going to be naked in front of him, she realized dazedly. Why the hell hadn't he shown up ten years ago—twenty pounds ago? She was not going to get naked with a man who hadn't even told her his real name, who was nothing but hostile, who was looking at her out of hooded eyes that seemed filled with impossible desire, as the last button gave way beneath his deft fingers and the yards of white cotton fell to a heap at her feet.

At least it was dark. His eyes drifted down over her body, the ripe curves in the moonlight, and a dreamy expression crossed his face, just before he leaned forward and put his mouth against the side of her neck, tasting her hammering pulse.

She stood very still, like a doe caught in the headlights, hoping maybe he'd forget she was there and go away. But he held her wrists, and he was sliding his hands up her arms to hold her shoulders. He moved his mouth to the base of her throat, and she could feel his tongue.

That worried little moan of pleasure couldn't have come from her, could it? Maybe the loons were out on the lake, floating safely in the silver water. Maybe it was an owl....

He reached behind her and opened the screen door, pushing her back into the house with only the lightest touch. "I'm not doing this," she warned him.

"Sure you are. The only question is whether we're going to do it standing up, on the dining room table or make it all the way up to my bed."

Her eyes widened in shock. They were back in the dark again, the moonlight barely making it in one window, and she should have felt less vulnerable. But his hands were still on her, and she couldn't even make another token protest. Not when he'd slid his arms around her waist, pulling her up against his hot, strong body, and he was kissing her. Slowly. Lazily. Thoroughly.

Skin against skin. His hard chest against her soft breasts. Her chilled flesh against his heat. Now she was shivering. Silly, she thought absently. It wasn't that cold. Why was she shivering?

He broke the kiss, swearing softly. "The hell with this," he muttered, and she felt a sudden panic that he'd changed his mind, that he didn't want her. And then an even greater panic as he simply scooped her up and laid her down on the floor.

The carpet was scratchy beneath her back. And then it wasn't her back she was thinking about, as he leaned over her in the darkness and slid his hands down her shoulders to her breasts.

She opened her mouth to protest, but he filled it with his tongue, and for some reason she arched beneath him as his fingers touched her nipples with the lightest, most unexpectedly erotic touches. And she wanted more.

Maybe if she closed her eyes here in the dark it would be accomplished as if by magic. She could finally get rid of her virginity, and then she could go on to find someone more suitable....

He put his mouth on one breast, sucking at it, and a stripe of hot pleasure speared down between her legs. He must have known, because he put his hand between her legs as his mouth pulled at her breast, his fingers sliding inside her, rubbing against her with a slow, deliberate rhythm that matched the tug of his mouth at her breast, and she couldn't speak, couldn't argue, couldn't make much more than a choked gasp that caught in her throat as a spasm of pleasure hit her body.

She knew what an orgasm was like—she was a modern woman who knew her own body. It was nothing like this. It was...

She stopped thinking coherently as her body convulsed beneath his relentless touch. He stopped then, but she had no words to argue, when she heard the unmistakable rasp of his zipper, the quick fumble of clothes, of paper tearing.

She surfaced long enough to realize he was using a condom, to realize he was back, kneeling between her legs, and she knew this was going to happen unless she said something. She couldn't remember how it had gotten to this point, so fast. The man was certainly efficient. She only knew that if he stopped she'd die.

He stretched out over her body and kissed her, and for the first time she kissed him back. "Put your arms around me," he said in a harsh voice, "and hold on."

"I should tell you..." she began, obediently putting her arms around his neck.

"Just tell me whether you want to do this or not," he said impatiently. "Yes or no?"

She wanted to shove him off her, but for some reason her arms were tight around his neck and her mouth was saying, "Yes."

He slid his hands under her butt and she could feel him pressing against her, hot and hard and sleek. And then he thrust inside, deep, fast, burying himself inside her, breaking past whatever trace of innocence she still had remaining.

She let out a stifled yelp of pain. She'd forgotten that it would hurt. She'd even assumed her hymen was long gone. Apparently not.

He was frozen, buried deep within her body, and that nice, sensual haze that enveloped Sophie began to fade.

"Shit," he muttered in her ear. Not the romantic uttering she would have imagined, and she felt him begin to pull away.

"No!" she said, clinging tightly to his neck. "Don't stop."

"I wasn't going to." He kissed her, and she thought she could taste regret on his mouth. "Shit," he said again. And then he reached down and pulled her legs around him, so that he was deeper, further, harder.

He began to pull out of her, and she almost protested, but then he filled her again. "Don't worry," he muttered, his voice thick with strain. "I know how to do this. I have lots of experience."

Forget tender, romantic musings. It didn't matter. What mattered was the feel of him inside her, thick and heavy, the surge of his hips against hers, the feel of his beautiful bony shoulders beneath her hands. The heavy, glorious weight of him. The movement, deep and rocking. She wanted to wrap herself around him, dissolve into his skin, lose herself completely, if only for a short while.

Somewhere along the way her shivering had stopped, and she was covered with a film of sweat, slick, sliding against his hard body. The pain wasn't even a memory, and now she wanted this to last forever, soaring, sailing, faster, deeper, harder. She couldn't catch her breath, didn't want to, she just wanted him, more of him. Neverending. Relentless. Forever.

It started slow and hit her with the force of a sledgehammer, a cataclysm of such power she could only hold on to him and let it happen. He went rigid against her, rock hard in her arms, and he probably muttered ''oh, shit'' again, but she was beyond hearing, lost in some mind-scattered cloud of inexpressible pleasure. She fell back, limp, awash in shimmering sensation, and she knew an odd, faint trace of regret that he'd used a condom. She'd wanted all of him inside her, a total giving, and he'd withheld something.

He collapsed on top of her, heavy, damp with sweat, his heart slamming against hers, his breath rasping in his chest. As the powerful sensations began to ebb, regret took their place. She hadn't seen him in the dark, hadn't touched him. She'd lost her virginity in the darkness to an experienced predator, in exchange for a moment of fleeting pleasure.

Well, it was more than a moment, she thought fairly. And *pleasure* was a pretty tame word for what she'd just experienced. If he just said something sweet to her. Something gentle, something even mildly flattering.

''Shit,'' he said, and pushed away from her, rising from the floor.

She could feel the scratch of the rug beneath her back. She could feel the chill returning to her overheated skin. She could feel the worst shame she'd ever felt in her life. Not shame that she'd finally done this. But that he'd walked away from her, cursing.

She heard a door close in the darkness, heard the water running. She didn't hesitate. She practically sprang to her feet and had to steady herself on a nearby piece of furniture as her legs wobbled beneath her.

She had to get out of there, fast. She didn't know which of them would be more embarrassed, and she wasn't about to find out. All she knew was that she had to escape before he said "shit" one more time.

It was getting light outside. She didn't let the screen door slam. Her nightgown was on the floor of the porch, and she grabbed it and ran into the murky, predawn light, pulling it on as she went.

She half expected to hear him calling after her, but no sound emanated from the old cottage. She'd escaped, and he could only be grateful. No morning-after recriminations or difficult small talk. Hell, with luck he'd leave town after that debacle.

Maybe *debacle* was the wrong word for it. He certainly hadn't been happy to find out that she was still technically a virgin, but it hadn't seemed to slow him down any. Still, it must be embarrassing to face someone you unwittingly deflowered. He'd probably rather leave town. Or at least she could hope so.

She felt close to tears by the time she reached the open expanse of lawn in front of the inn. The day was getting brighter—it must be after five. Not that anyone in the house would be waking to ask her embarrassing questions. Both Grace and Marty liked their beauty sleep.

Sophie walked down to the water's edge, stepping out onto the dock. It was too early even for the most devoted of fishermen, and if they came by she didn't care. She dropped her unbuttoned nightgown onto the dock, looking down at her body.

There was blood between her thighs. Well and truly de-virginized, she thought, and she dove into the lake, a neat, clean surface dive that barely made a ripple in the still, cool water.

She was gone, of course. He should have known she'd run like a scared rabbit, Griffin thought, cursing. Hell and damnation, he couldn't even have two minutes in the bathroom without her taking off into the woods like a ravished virgin.

Which, in fact, was exactly what she was. How in the world did someone with a body like hers make it into her twenties without ever getting laid? Had she spent years in a convent or on some deserted island? What was wrong with the men she'd met, that no one had taken advantage of that sweet mouth and delectably lush body?

It wasn't as if she'd put up a hell of a fight. He liked women, liked sex, and he knew perfectly well when a woman was attracted to him, even if she didn't want to be. Sophie Davis couldn't keep her eyes off him, in between snapping at him, and all he'd had to do was taste her mouth this afternoon to know he could have her.

He hadn't been in any particular rush to do anything about it, but she'd shown up on his doorstep in the middle of the night, dressed in that ridiculous nightgown, and he was hardly a man to refuse such an unexpected gift. So he'd taken her, she'd been willing, and he had no reason to feel guilty. Though why in hell she was still a virgin was beyond his comprehension.

He couldn't figure out why she hadn't told him. Maybe she'd tried and he'd been too busy concentrating on getting inside her to listen. And if she had told him, what would he have done? Been noble, had second thoughts, put her away from him and forswear being a cad?

Like hell. He probably would have made it all the way up to the bed instead of taking her fast and hot on the rug like a horny teenager, but that was about the limit of his self-control. The moment she'd appeared out of the woods he'd known this was going to happen, and nothing was going to stop it.

It was a mistake, and her being a virgin had nothing to do with it. From now on she'd be so skittish around him he'd have an even harder time getting into the old inn. He'd screwed things up big time, and if he had any sense at all he'd keep his mind and his hands off his neighbor. He should be kicking himself. In fact, though, she'd almost been worth it.

Of course she'd run off, refusing to face him. She was probably crying, probably hating him. That, or even worse, she'd decided she was in love with him. He shuddered at the thought. That was the last thing he needed at a time like this. Women tended to be sentimental, particularly when it was their first lover, and she'd probably convince herself it was the romance of the century that made her give up what she'd been hoarding for too damned long.

She'd be hard put to fashion a romance out of this, he thought, pulling his abandoned cutoffs back on. He stared down at the rug, trying to imagine her lying there beneath him. The early morning light was creeping in the cottage window, creating strange shadows. With his luck the lugubrious Kings would show up on his doorstep. At least they hadn't walked in on him and Sophie.

He went to the kitchen and made himself a pot of coffee. He'd actually been looking forward to stretching out in the bed upstairs with Sophie and taking his time. A virgin deserved more than a quick tumble and a good orgasm, and he'd intended to take care of her properly once he got her upstairs. He should have realized she'd run, and he now had no interest in going back to bed alone. Maybe he'd take a nap later on. Maybe Sophie would find some excuse to come back and yell at him, and they could take a nap together.

He took his coffee out to the porch and sat with his legs propped on the railing, watching the lake. He reached for his glasses. Someone was out swimming at that hour, someone at the beach next door. It didn't take much to figure out who it was.

He rose and strolled down to the edge of the water where he could get a better glimpse of her. She swam well, slicing through the water with an elegant economy of motion. He shivered, remembering Lorelei, dead in his arms, weighted down by the water.

Lorelei hadn't been able to swim. She'd been childishly nervous about the lake. It had always bothered him that that was where the killer had dumped her body. He only hoped she was dead before she hit the water. She wouldn't have wanted to feel the cold wet darkness closing over her....

He spun around, heading back to the porch. He didn't want to think about Lorelei and how she died. Not right now. That was what he was here to find out, to see if he'd had anything to do with it. But for just a few hours he'd rather think about Sophie. And the deliciously erotic squeaking noises she made when she came.

He was watching her, and in the darkness he wept. Whore of Satan, with her virgin's blood staining her thighs. The waters of Still Lake wouldn't wash the sin from her. It would take his hand to do it.

He had never shunned his duty, and he wouldn't this time. Sophie Davis had given herself over to the wickedness of the flesh, and there was no hope for her. He would cleanse her body and her soul. And she would enter the kingdom of God, purified.

He just had to decide when.

He watched her move back up the lawn, her nightgown wrapped around her wet body. In the early morning light he could see her quite clearly, the calm determination on her pale face. If she'd shown remorse he might have hesitated. But there were no tears, no regret. She had sinned, and she must suffer the consequences.

Much as it pained his heart to do it. She would die, and be born again in rapture. He only had to decide when to act. And how much to make it hurt.

13

The buzz was insistent, ripping into Sophie's fog-shrouded sleep. It had all been a dream, she thought. An erotic, unsuitable, thoroughly enjoyable dream that she wouldn't have to give a second thought to. Her body felt lazy and luscious and utterly relaxed, and if erotic dreams did that to her every night, then she'd make a habit of fantasizing about men, even one as unsuitable as her unwelcome neighbor.

It was the phone, but she wasn't going to answer it. She was going to stay in the nice cozy afterglow of her sexy dream and enjoy herself, and someone else could either get the phone or the answering machine would take care of it.

It stopped, abruptly, and she figured the machine must have picked up. After all, she always got up hours before Grace and Marty did, and why should today be any different? Apart from the fact that she'd had a dream that had been so luscious it had been downright embarrassing....

She slid down in the bed, and then froze. She wasn't wearing a nightgown. She never slept nude—she just couldn't feel comfortable without some kind of clothing on. Gracey had always been a bit of an exhibitionist in her own nudity, and Sophie had reacted by being prudish. Fortunately in her currently foggy state Grace had decided to stay decently clothed, but the aversion had lingered with Sophie.

But there was no doubt she was naked in bed. And her hair was damp. She turned over and squinted at the alarm clock, then let out a squeak of horror. It was after ten o'clock. She never slept that late, even when she was sick.

There was a sudden rapping on her door, and she jumped nervously as her sister's sharp voice called out to her. "Phone's for you, sleepyhead. And you've got a visitor downstairs."

"Shit." The reaction was instinctive, and immediately more details began to flood her mind. It *was* a dream, wasn't it? She couldn't have been so stupid. And if it wasn't, then that was probably John Smith downstairs, and how was she going to face him...?

"Phone," Marty said irritably, then she stomped off down the corridor.

Sophie sat up, groaning. She was most definitely naked, and her hair smelled like the lake. Her hand was shaking when she picked up the phone, but she managed to keep her voice steady and businesslike.

"Yes?"

"I think you already said yes." He sounded cool and faintly ironic.

She almost slammed down the phone, but at the last minute pride stopped her. Okay, so it wasn't an erotic dream. He must have drugged her.

"I don't know what you're talking about," she said in a frosty voice. It was a weak defense, but the only one she could come up with at the last minute.

He laughed. If his reaction hadn't been so annoying it might have sounded sexy. Sophie wasn't in the mood to find anything sexy.

"If that's the way you want to play it," he said amiably enough. "I just have one question."

"And that is?" she said icily.

"If you were saving it for so long, why'd you give it to me?"

She slammed the phone down.

The day went from hideously awful to even worse. Marty was lying in wait for her when she dragged herself downstairs, probably wondering why John Smith was calling her, wondering why she'd slept in. Sophie ignored her, heading straight for coffee, only to come face-to-face with Doc in her kitchen, peering at her from beneath his bushy white eyebrows, his kindly eyes worried.

Grace was the worst of all, of course. "He's a very handsome young man, our neighbor," she said artlessly as she poured more and more sugar into her coffee. Grace always drank her coffee black, without sugar. Doc finally realized what she was doing and he took the sugar bowl away from her, putting it out of reach and patting her hand.

"He's not that young," Sophie said with just a trace of a snarl. Marty had made the coffee, and it was too weak, on a morning when she needed the strongest coffee known to man.

"Just right for you, darling," Grace said with a dreamy smile. "He'd look after you, keep you safe."

"Why would Sophie need anyone to keep her safe?" Doc asked. "She strikes me as someone who can look after herself."

"I certainly can," Sophie said, but the two of them didn't seem interested in her opinion.

"She needs a man, and our Mr. Smith is a perfect candidate. Sexy, ruthless, just a little bit dangerous," Grace said. "He's got a good heart, and he'd be very loyal. He wouldn't let anyone hurt you."

"And you can tell that on the basis of two meetings?" Sophie said.

"No one's going to hurt Sophie, Grace," Doc said patiently.

Grace took a sip of her coffee, then pushed it away. "What did you do with the coffee?" she demanded. "It tastes like poison."

"You put too much sugar in it, Grace," Doc said. "Have mine."

She cast him a suspicious glance. "You didn't poison it?"

Doc patted her hand. "No, Grace. I promise you, I didn't poison it."

"All right then," she said, taking a sip. "Much better, but it's too weak. Sophie, where were you last night?"

The question jarred Sophie out of her abstraction. Doc and Grace were so busy arguing that she'd hoped she'd have a chance to sneak out before she got their attention again. Obviously that was a vain hope.

"In bed, Grace," she said, rising from the table in an attempt to forestall any more conversation.

"I imagine so. The question is, whose bed?" Grace tried to look arch, but the effect was ruined by her flyaway hair and her broken reading glasses.

Sophie had just enough time to notice Doc's stricken expression and Marty's avid interest before she rose from the table. "No bed but my own, Ma," she said firmly. In fact, it was the truth. She'd had sex on the floor, on a scratchy rug, and she had carpet burns on her butt to prove it.

"Too bad," Grace murmured. "But I haven't given up hope. Why don't you go see what Mr. Smith is doing today? Maybe you could seduce him."

"That's enough, Grace," Doc said gently. "You leave Sophie alone now."

But he didn't follow his own advice. Sophie escaped onto the porch with a mug of weak coffee, desperate for a few moments of peace to try to regain her usual calm, when Doc followed her out.

"Your mother's getting worse," he said, and Sophie almost felt relief. At least he wasn't going to question her about her sex life. Now that, inexplicably, she seemed to have one.

"Yes," Sophie said, rocking back on the padded glider. "You told me she'd deteriorate. I didn't think it would be this fast."

"Paranoia and hostility are key aspects of this stage of Alzheimer's. She's going to start accusing people of stealing things from her. Of trying to kill her. It'll be a difficult time, and you'll need patience. I'll do all I can to help."

She wanted to cry. "You're so good to us, Doc," she murmured. "I don't know what we'd do without you."

Doc sat down beside her on the glider. For all his seeming fragility he was a heavy man, but the glider was built to take it. "I just want to do what I can. Rima will help, too. She doesn't leave the house much nowadays, but she loves it when Grace comes to visit. Maybe we could make it a regular thing. Bring her in for a few hours every day. Rima would enjoy the company and you wouldn't have to worry about Grace getting into trouble."

"I couldn't ask that..."

"You're not. I told you, Rima would love it." He paused, as if trying to figure out how to broach a difficult subject, and Sophie braced herself for more questions about John Smith. Part of her wanted to tell Doc what happened, take advantage of his age and wisdom and calm good sense.

Maybe if he'd been a woman. The thought of telling Doc she'd had wanton sex on the floor of the old Whitten cottage with a man she barely knew, and then seeing the disappointment in his face, was unbearable.

But Doc didn't want to talk about sex or John Smith. "Grace says someone's been going through her room," he said. "Stealing her clothes, stealing her books, stealing all sorts of things. I'm sure it's just a fantasy on her part, but I thought I should warn you to be extra careful about her stuff. Even if you ask to borrow it she may not remember. If you take her clothes to be laundered she'll probably feel threatened. The best bet is to make sure she sees what you're doing and understands it. And if you find anything that worries you, don't hesitate to come to me. I'm here to help you, Sophie. You know that."

"I do know that, Doc," she said. "Thank you."

She should tell him about the knife. The stained, rusty hunting knife she'd found in Grace's drawers, but she stopped at the last minute. She didn't want anyone jumping to the conclusion that Grace was dangerous. Her mother must have found the knife somewhere and taken it, part of her magpie tendencies. Sophie was always finding strange things in Grace's room—tiny rocks and dried flowers and chewing gum and odd bits of jewelry. The knife was just a piece of that fascination with garbage.

"Promise me you'll tell me if you find something that worries you," he said.

"I promise," Sophie said. The knife didn't worry her. Grace was harmless, and the knife meant nothing.

He rose, and the glider slid back violently. "What about your neighbor? Has he been any bother? I can go talk to him if you want. You don't need your life complicated by sex at this point."

Her eyes flew open in shock. "Doc!" she protested.

Doc chuckled. "Yes, I know, you think I'm an old fart, but I understand human nature, and the desire for sex is very normal and natural. I just don't want to see you getting into any trouble. You like him, don't you?"

"Like him?" Sophie protested. "I can't stand him! He's a sneaky, treacherous human being who lies about everything, including who he is."

"And who is he?" Doc asked, curious.

"Some kind of reporter or writer, I think. Something to do with the old murders. I don't know what his name is, but it sure the hell isn't John Smith."

"Fascinating," Doc murmured.

"So trust me, I'm not going anywhere near him if I can help it."

"That's good," he said. "Because Marty said you came from his place just after dawn this morning, and you looked like you had a rough night."

"Marty must have been dreaming," Sophie said flatly. Funny, she never lied. But she was lying now, and quite easily.

Doc smiled down at her, but there was no disguising the worry in his eyes. "I hope so," he said. "But call me, any time of the day or night, if you need me."

What did he expect, Sophie wondered irritably after he left. That Grace would climb onto the rooftop like Mr. Rochester's crazy wife in *Jane Eyre?* She could take care of Grace, she could take care of Marty, and she could take care of herself.

It was the element of surprise, she decided. If she'd had any inkling that John Smith was interested in sleeping with her she would have kept her distance. Of course, there was no denying he'd kissed her yesterday afternoon, which should have given her a hint, one that she had studiously ignored. And she'd had no choice but to go there last night, when she thought Grace was missing. She couldn't let her mother wander around in the night.

So instead Sophie had ended up on the floor beneath a stranger, and she couldn't stop thinking about it. Stop thinking about him. How could her life have changed so much in one night?

It was silly to think she was somehow different. People made too much of a fuss over sex—it was a perfectly natural bodily function, and just because she'd avoided it for longer than most didn't mean it was any big deal. And it wasn't as if she were frigid. God, no. Maybe even the opposite. She shouldn't have enjoyed herself. Women weren't supposed to have orgasms the first time, were they? Especially women with underdeveloped sex drives who didn't know or trust their partner.

Well, maybe she didn't have an underdeveloped sex drive, maybe she'd just been too busy to notice. Or too picky. Or maybe, just maybe, John Smith was really good at sex.

She didn't want to think that. It would be a major problem to have started out with an expert and then have to settle for someone less competent. It would be just her luck to have him spoil her for any worthwhile man who might come her way.

There was always the remote possibility that she'd inherited the curse of the Wilsons, Grace's family. According to Grace, Wilson women loved only once, and then it lasted forever. It was no good trying to find someone else, someone more acceptable. Once they fell in love they were doomed.

Which was hogwash. Sophie was a practical

woman. She simply needed to find someone more suitable. Someone who was equally talented at sex.

If she was going to keep having sex, and eventually get married and have children, then she was going to have to find someone from the area. Doc would know of any eligible bachelors around. She couldn't very well ask him if they were any good in bed, of course, but maybe she'd be able to pick up on that before she tried them out. After all, there was no denying John Smith was a very sexy man. The way he moved, the way he touched things, the way he looked at you out of his dark eyes, the shape of his mouth...

"Shit." Oh, God, now she was going to be using his favorite curse word all the time. She was always getting after Marty for her language—there was no way she could get away with it herself. And every time she said the word she could see him, feel him, buried deep inside her tightly clenching body, his heart pounding against hers, his breath rasping, his hips moving, her body damp, wet, clinging, shaking...

She practically tumbled off the glider in her haste to get away from her own lascivious thoughts. What the hell kind of mess had she gotten herself into this time?

14

Griffin laughed when Sophie slammed down the phone on him. His work here was done—she was so pissed off she wouldn't indulge in a weeping fit. She'd be so focused on her anger she wouldn't make the mistake of thinking she was in love with him. God knows, that was the last thing he wanted. He'd had women make that mistake in the past, and it only led to disillusionment and bad feelings. At least his former fiancée had been too hardheaded and practical to suffer from those kinds of delusions.

But Sophie wasn't hardheaded and practical, she was as soft and yielding as her luscious body, and she'd be just sentimental enough to read more into a good fuck than there was. And he didn't want that happening.

The Kings were already hard at work, tearing up the floorboards around the chimney where the dampness had set in. They'd started their morning with a group prayer, and the mutters about sinful ways seemed clearly directed at their employer. Griffin ignored them. He had a certain fondness for sin, particularly the sin he'd committed last night. The

Kings could pray over his soul all they wanted—as long as they didn't interfere in his life.

Mrs. King was scrubbing the same areas she'd scrubbed yesterday, probably with the vain hope that she could get them even cleaner, keeping her head bowed and her lips moving in silent prayer. She jumped every time he walked into the kitchen to get more coffee, and after a while he took pity on her and decided to take his supposedly satanic self off for a while. He needed a nap, and he wasn't going to get any peace in his own place.

He wasn't going to get it up at the inn, either, even though the thought was appealing. At the moment there was nothing he'd like better than to wrap himself around Sophie's lush frame and fall asleep, but she'd be more likely to stab him. Sophie's second lesson in the art of lovemaking would have to wait.

He got in his car and headed out, aimlessly. It was an overcast day, still warmish, with the threat of a storm in the air. He could remember those storms well—the pristine blue of the Vermont sky darkening with rage, the wind whipping through the trees, the hail that would destroy crops and even break windows. It usually took days to build up to a storm like that, but he'd long ago lost touch with nature and the weather, and for all he knew a hurricane might be approaching. And he didn't give a damn, unless it got in the way of what he was trying to do.

His time was running out. He'd rented the Whitten cottage for six months, but he had no intention of staying more than a couple of weeks, three at the most. Time was passing, and he wasn't any closer to the truth than he had been before, with the possibility of other, earlier murders clouding the issue.

He didn't feel like a killer. He never had, but that proved just about nothing. The fact of the matter was, he didn't remember a thing about that night, not until he woke up with Lorelei's blood staining his body. For all he knew he could have been the one who killed her. Or he might have been passed out, unable to help her as she struggled for her life.

She'd fought her killer. He remembered that much from the trial. He'd brought the transcripts with him to remind him of what had happened. Twenty years ago DNA testing was in its infancy, and no one had bothered to see whether or not the skin and blood under Lorelei's fingernails matched his. Particularly when he had scratches down his back, anyway. Lorelei was fond of leaving her mark on her lovers, and it gave her a perverse thrill to see her scratches down his back.

The blood and skin beneath her fingernails were more than the remnants of faintly sadistic passion. Her nails, always her pride and joy, were broken from the struggle. Surely he would have had more marks on his body if he'd done that in some kind of drug-hazed frenzy. But the important question was why? Lorelei had annoyed the hell out of him. She'd teased him and taunted him and cheated on him, and he'd been a horny kid, full of pride and testosterone. But he'd already made up his mind to leave. Why would he kill her?

Instinct and common sense weren't enough to put his mind at ease, though. Not when he couldn't remember, not when he'd been convicted of the crime. It didn't matter that the conviction had been overturned on a legal technicality—there was still enough doubt left in the back of his mind and he couldn't move on until he knew the answer.

What if it was the wrong answer? What if, when he got back into the deserted section of the inn, he remembered something he didn't want to remember? He'd been back in Colby for four days and all he'd accomplished so far was a quick midnight reconnoiter of the old grounds, looking for a way to break in. The windows were boarded up tight, and pulling off the planks would have made a hell of a racket. He was going to have to get in through the old kitchen door, which made things a little dicey since the queen of that particular kitchen hated his guts.

Hell, he had too many excuses. Maybe he didn't want to remember. Maybe he wasn't ready to live with the truth.

What if the truth about that night came back and

he didn't like it? What if he suddenly remembered killing Lorelei, and maybe even the others? How would he live with that knowledge?

He'd survive. There'd be no noble gesture of turning himself in and confessing. He'd done five years already, and he hadn't been in his right mind if he'd actually been the killer.

There were too many loose ends. What about the other women, if indeed there were any? He needed to find out more about the girl in the old McLaren graveyard, with the fresh yellow flowers. He needed to check the other graveyards, see if there were other young women with unusual yellow flowers on their graves. If he couldn't show his face at the inn right now he could at least do something to find the answers.

It wasn't the first time he'd visited Lorelei's grave. When he'd gotten out of prison he'd driven over here. He'd never been sure why—maybe he still couldn't really believe she was dead. It was raining that day, and he'd stood at her grave and wept. The last time he ever had. He couldn't remember if there were any flowers—the harsh words etched in granite wiped out everything else.

It was going to rain today. The clouds were scudding across the sky, ominous, depressing, and the first few drops were splashing down on the windscreen of his Jaguar when he pulled up to the tiny, picturesque graveyard by the edge of the lake.

Most of the year-round residents were buried in the village cemetery. This graveyard had mainly been populated by summer people for the last seventy years, but Lorelei's family had been burying their kin there since the early 1800s, and Lorelei had been buried there, as well.

He saw the yellow flowers first, a splash of color against the lichen-stained granite stone. He walked slowly, ignoring the rain, stopping in front of her grave to look down. Not that he was any expert on flowers, but he didn't recognize them among his spotty knowledge of various perennials. The one thing he knew was that they were identical to the ones at the McLaren graveyard, and they were fresh.

Lorelei's family was long gone. Her mother had died when she was young, and her father died of cancer a few years ago. She had no siblings, no one left to mourn her. So who would have brought fresh flowers to her grave, and why?

He looked out over the rows of gravestones toward the lake, blinking in the ever-increasing rain. At least half the graves had flowers, ranging from wild roses to freshly cut flowers to gaudy, artificial memorial sprays. He walked down the center row of the small cemetery, ignoring the rain, until he found what he was looking for. One small stone with the same yellow flowers.

Marsha Daniels, age sixteen, born in 1957, died

in 1973. No other information, just the telltale spray of flowers.

He scribbled the information on a scrap of paper, watching the ink run in the driving rain. And then he headed back to his car.

He'd felt uncharacteristically cheerful when he'd started out that morning. Sex tended to have that effect on him, even ill-advised sex, and he'd been celibate since he broke up with Annelise. Besides, he found Sophie oddly, irrationally appealing, with her frills and her cooking and her fierce determination to protect her family. By now his good mood had faded completely—graveyards had a habit of doing *that* to you, he thought. And he suspected he was going to have a hard time getting to Sophie for a while. She had to sulk, and fume, and be embarrassed first. Then she'd start to remember just how good it had felt, and her defenses would start to drop. Or he'd put a little effort into tearing them down.

For purely recreational reasons, he reminded himself. And because he damned well wanted to.

Of course, if she decided to trust him he would be able to gain easy access to the house. That was all he needed, just a few short hours to make his way through the ruins of the old wing and see if he could remember what had happened there so long ago. If it didn't work, he'd get the hell out of Colby, give up on trying to remember what he obviously wasn't supposed to remember. He'd let go of it, as he should have long ago.

The rain had let up by the time he drove through the tiny picturesque town of Colby. Audley's General Store was booming, as always, with cars cramming the street in front of it and the parking lot by the town green. People were crossing the street to get to the public beach, the country-club crowd in their tennis whites were mingling with the locals in their bathing suits. None of the summer people had to use the public beach—they all had cottages on the lake and their own private swimming area. It was only at Audley's that the two classes ever mixed.

He didn't stop. The old general store still unnerved him—he was happier using the supermarket in the next town over, where there was little chance he'd run into someone he'd known twenty years ago. Someone who'd testified against him.

The village cemetery was just past the center of town, on the way to the nursing home and the old dump, which he'd always found somehow fitting. This was a more sprawling affair, with no safe white picket fence to guard the departed. No view of the lake, either, but he imagined the residents didn't particularly care. This was where the locals were planted, where Valette King's and Alice Calderwood's remains were buried. He didn't know exactly where on the terraced levels of rolling green grass. He figured he'd start by looking for the yellow flowers.

The village graveyard went in more for plastic crosses than fresh flowers. He found Valette's grave immediately. The yellow flowers sat next to a weather-beaten teddy bear. A slug was crawling across its matted tummy.

Unlike the others, Valette's stone had an epitaph, courtesy, no doubt, of her rigid father. *Lost to Satan,* it read beneath her name. The stone itself was small, cheesy-looking. He wondered who left the teddy bear. Probably her slow-witted brother, who might not be as dim as everyone thought he was. Hell, he would have been fifteen when the girls died. Close to full grown, probably, and not too aware of right and wrong. Maybe he'd taken his father's religion to heart and decided to punish the ungodly.

There were a hell of a lot more ungodly people in Colby than three teenage girls who liked to have fun. And Perley King had the innocence of a child in his eyes. As convenient as it would be, there was no way Griffin could make him into an easy scapegoat.

The hilly grass was slippery beneath his feet, and he moved through the graveyard carefully, keeping his eye out for the telltale splash of yellow. He had no doubt whatsoever that when he found those flowers he'd find Alice Calderwood's grave. It might mean nothing—Zebulon King might have a fixation for girls who had died young, and he might be the one to bring the flowers. Or maybe he was driven by guilt.

Maybe.

Or maybe it was someone else. Whoever killed the three young women had killed others, as well, and maybe he still lived in town and visited the graves of his victims.

There were a hell of a lot of maybes.

Alice Calderwood's grave was at the very top row of the cemetery, tucked beneath an apple tree. The flowers were fresh, the headstone scrubbed free of moss and bird droppings. Someone still mourned Alice, just as they mourned the other young women.

He didn't know how long he stood there, looking at the stone, before he realized someone had joined him. He looked up into the kindly blue eyes of one of the people who had put him in jail. Doc Henley was the last person he wanted to run into—those eyes might be friendly but they were still bright with intelligence. Sooner or later he'd recognize Griffin.

Maybe sooner. "I thought I recognized you up here," he said, genial as ever. He nodded toward the tombstone. "Sad, isn't it? Did you know her?"

"I've never been to Vermont before," Griffin said automatically, and Doc didn't seem interested in arguing the point. Griffin had already planned his excuse if anyone asked him why he was visiting graveyards, and he presented it without Doc asking.

"I'm doing a little genealogical research. There were rumors that a branch of my family lived in the area, and I thought I'd check it out while I'm on vacation."

"Really?" Doc raised one of his bushy white eyebrows. He was as tall as Griffin, only slightly stooped with age, and their eyes were level. "What's the family name?"

"Smith."

"That's going to make research a little tough," Doc said wryly. "We've got a lot of Smiths in town."

Griffin shrugged. "It's not important. Just something I thought I'd look into while I'm here." He glanced back at the grave. "What happened to her? She was awfully young to have died. Car accident?"

"She was murdered," Doc said, not hiding the pain in his voice. "She and two of her friends. I'm surprised you haven't heard of the Colby murders since you've been here. People still talk about them."

"I haven't been socializing much."

"Just Sophie," Doc said.

Griffin hid his reaction with admirable control. He shrugged. "Can you blame me? She's available, she's pretty, and I'm bored. A little fling will do us both good. She's too straight-laced. She needs to loosen up a little."

"I don't think she needs a stranger coming into

her life, disrupting it, and then leaving,'' Doc said. ''I'm assuming your intentions aren't particularly honorable?''

Griffin laughed. ''Hardly. What are you, her guardian?''

''Just a friend,'' Doc said, his disapproval tempered with understanding. ''She's a wonderful young woman, hardworking, decent, responsible. I don't want her to throw it all away.''

''Sleeping with me doesn't constitute throwing a responsible life down the drain. Life hurts,'' Griffin said. ''At least she's doing better than that poor soul.'' He nodded at Alice's grave.

''Is that where Sophie was last night? With you?''

For a moment Griffin wondered whether Doc, with his stately, old-fashioned manners, was going to challenge him to a duel, or at the very least horsewhip him. ''What makes you think she spent the night with anyone?'' he hedged.

''Marty was worried about her. She said Sophie called her from your place, and then didn't come home for hours.'' Doc hesitated. ''I don't want to see her hurt.''

''I think if you want to know about who Sophie's having sex with, you better ask her yourself,'' Griffin said.

Doc looked at him. ''I don't need to do that, do I?''

Griffin shrugged. He never considered himself a

particularly decent man, but Doc was making him uncomfortable with his questions. He changed the subject. ''Those yellow flowers are pretty. Ever seen them before?''

Doc didn't bother trying to pursue the subject of Sophie. ''They're not very common around here,'' he said dismissively. ''You don't strike me as someone who's interested in gardening, Mr. Smith. Any more than you seem the type to care about genealogy. Why don't you tell me why you're really here.''

''Why does everyone think I have an ulterior motive?'' Griffin said. ''I'm here on vacation, nothing else.''

''Then leave Sophie alone,'' Doc said.

There was something in his voice that made Griffin jerk his head away from his contemplation of Alice's grave. ''Is that a warning?'' he asked in a calm voice.

For a moment Doc's eyes met his. And then he simply shook his head. ''Only a request. She's got a tough row to hoe, with her mother and sister and trying to make a go of the inn. She doesn't need complications. I'm sure you don't, either.''

''You're right about that,'' Griffin said easily. ''At heart I'm a simple man.''

''Oh, I don't think so, Mr. Smith. I don't think so at all.''

They walked down the hill to the road in a companionable-enough silence. Doc had issued his warning like a protective father, and Griffin had received the message. Whether or not he had any intention of listening was another matter entirely.

He'd have to come back. Doc was already getting too suspicious, and if he figured out who Griffin was it might very well put an end to any answers he might find. Hell, he might even end up at the wrong end of that lynch mob he'd avoided twenty years ago, if the good citizens of Colby were really convinced he'd gotten away with murder.

So he walked back to his car with Doc by his side. Keeping his secrets.

"I think my sister had sex last night."

Patrick looked up from the chain saw he was sharpening. "And I care because...?"

"I don't know if she's ever had sex before," Marty said, swinging her long legs. She had nice legs, she knew, and she wanted to make sure Patrick knew it, too.

So far he'd seemed remarkably unimpressed, but then, she was trying to get used to his laconic Vermont ways. She couldn't figure out whether he was interested or not. Her instincts told her yes, his behavior made it more murky.

Patrick said nothing, concentrating on the chain saw. "Even if she has," Marty went on, "I doubt she's as experienced as I am."

He didn't bother to look up. "That's something to brag about?"

"Sure," she said, nonplussed. "I've had lots of boyfriends. I don't even remember how many lovers I've had." Which wasn't strictly true. There had only been Jeff, who'd been fast and messy and rough, and Nate, who really didn't care who he stuck it into. Sooner or later she'd find the kind of lover she deserved. Looking at the care Patrick was giving to the stupid chain saw, she suspected he was a good candidate.

He was certainly gorgeous enough. All lean muscle, tanned skin, big, strong hands. So gorgeous, in fact, that he probably already had a girlfriend. Not necessarily a problem—she'd stolen Jeff from her best friend, Sally, only to find it wasn't worth it. This time she wouldn't be betraying anyone she knew.

Patrick grunted, unimpressed. "Don't you like sex?" she persisted, swinging her long legs. She was sitting on the stone fence beside the chain saw, but he seemed more interested in filing the damned thing than in talking to her.

He looked up. "I like sex well enough," he said evenly. "If I care about someone. If I don't, I can do without it."

"So how many lovers have you had?" she persisted. For a second she thought he wasn't going to answer, but eventually he spoke.

"Just my girlfriend, Abby," he said.

Damn. "What is she? A childhood sweetheart? You going to marry her when you graduate from college?"

"She died."

That shut her up, at least for a moment. It was hard to compete with a dead girl. On the other hand, she was here and the girlfriend was gone. Advantage, Marty.

First, though, she'd better figure out how strong her dead competition was. "How'd she die? Unless you'd rather not talk about it."

"I don't mind talking about it," he said evenly. "She died in a car accident three years ago."

"Were you driving?"

He shot her a sharp glance. "No. She was with someone else."

"Another boy?"

"Yes." He shrugged. "We were breaking up. She was going to California to college, I was going to UVM. She wanted to get away from here, I wanted to stay. She got away for good."

A stray shiver crossed Marty's exposed spine. There were too many dead girls in Colby, that was for sure. And she didn't want to talk about death anymore—sex was a lot more interesting.

"How old are you?" she asked lazily.

"Twenty."

"I'm nineteen."

"You're seventeen," he corrected her. "Too young to be having sex."

"Eighteen in three weeks," she shot back. "How old were you when you started having sex with your lost true love?"

He looked at her, and she was suddenly ashamed of her flippancy. "Sorry," she muttered. "I didn't mean it the way it sounded."

He nodded, accepting her apology. It might have been a full five minutes before he spoke. "We were in love. I'm not interested in sleeping with someone I don't care about."

"Then I guess I'm wasting my time here," she said, sliding off the fence.

He set the file down on the fence by the chain saw. "Is that what you're looking for?" he asked in his grave, calm voice.

"Isn't everyone? Oh, except you with your high standards," she mocked. "I just want someone to..." The words trailed away.

"Want someone to what? Treat you like a whore? Screw you silly and then dump you? I don't think so, Marthe."

"Then what do I want?"

"Someone to love you."

For some crazy reason she wanted to cry. "So?" she said, defiant. "I told you I was wasting my time here."

"Not necessarily." He said it so quietly she wasn't sure she heard right.

She stood there, feeling oddly vulnerable, not sure what to say. "I'd better go find Sophie. See if she needs anything," she said finally.

"Yeah, maybe you'd better," he said, picking up the chain saw with a practiced grace. It was heavy, and he handled it as if it weighed no more than a few pounds.

He couldn't touch her if he was holding the chain saw, and she wasn't sure anymore she was ready to have him touch her. Wasn't sure if she was ready to have anyone love her, particularly a somber, beautiful creature like Patrick.

"I'd better go," she said again, not moving.

A slow smile spread across his face. "If I'd known that would scare you away I would have tried it a lot sooner."

"I'm not scared."

"Yup, you are," he said confidently. "You think about it, Marthe Davis. I'm not someone you can come and play with when you're bored. I make commitments, and I stick to them. If you want casual sex you'll have to look somewhere else." And he walked off before she could come up with a suitable answer.

The best she could manage was to stick her tongue out at him, but since he was walking away he didn't get the benefit of the gesture. She had no choice but to head back to the house and her strangely unsettled sister. Maybe she could get rid of some of her restlessness by baiting Sophie. But for some reason she wasn't really in the mood.

Maybe she'd find something to do. There were three bedrooms left to be painted, and while she hated to seem compliant, activity was better than boredom. And then maybe she'd find out exactly what her straight-laced sister had been doing in the middle of the night with that mysterious stranger.

Sophie was not in a good mood. They were all watching her, and it was driving her absolutely crazy. By the time they'd finished dinner she was ready to bite everyone's head off. She resisted the impulse. Grace would dissolve into tears, Marty would jump into the fray with an energetic belligerence, and things would go from awful to god-awful in seconds.

She finally couldn't take it anymore, and once dinner was finished she walked out of the house into the warm night air. They'd either do the dishes or not—she wasn't going to worry about it. As a matter of fact, Marty had been surprisingly industrious today, putting a primer coat on the three back bedrooms. Her black-and-fuchsia hair now had a streak or two of white from the paint, but the effect was impish rather than bizarre. And for all Doc's worries, Grace seemed uncharacteristically peaceful, even calling out after Sophie as she stomped from the kitchen.

"Have fun, love. Make him use a condom."

It wasn't enough to make her turn back. She repressed the urge to snarl, continuing out into the gathering dusk. She wasn't going anywhere near the Whitten place, anywhere near John Smith. She was going to get in the car and drive, maybe even as far as Montpelier and find a movie. Hell, she could even go to a bar and see if she could pick up some sexy young bureaucrat. Maybe it would turn out that she just liked sex, and John Smith happened to be the first to demonstrate it. Maybe he was only adequate.

And maybe pigs could fly. It didn't matter—she was getting out of here, all by herself, for a few hours. She'd play the stereo in her car very loud, something upbeat and cheerful like the Beach Boys, and she wouldn't think about Grace, or Marty, or murdered women, or sex, or how strangers were going to come and take over her house. She wouldn't think about going upstairs to that big rumpled bed in the Whitten house and just hiding there. With him.

And most of all, she wouldn't think about the damned tingle in her body that had haunted her the whole goddamned day.

Shit.

15

He followed her. The rain had begun again, no more than a fine misting that coated his windshield. The roads were wet, even a bit slick. It would be simple enough. She was an out-of-stater, not used to the peculiarities of Vermont roads. It wouldn't surprise anyone if she had an accident. After all, she'd been working too hard, worrying about her mother and sister. She'd been distracted. Could happen to anyone.

He hated to do it. He was starting to repeat himself, and he knew that was dangerous. As long as he used a different method each time the police were helpless. Most of the time they didn't even realize there was anything suspicious about it. Just another tragic accident.

But he'd already done a car accident, just three years ago, in the same area. The victim had been a teenage wanton, and she'd died with her lover. This time it would be a presumably virtuous newcomer, old enough to know better. There'd be nothing to connect the two. Only the fact that he knew them both. But then, everyone in Colby knew everyone else—there was nothing suspicious about that. God spoke to him, told him what he must do. And if he was directed toward a stranger, he had no choice but to listen to the Word and act accordingly. Faith was a lost virtue. He took the Word on faith, and dispensed justice and God's wrath without compunction.

As he would tonight, with Sophie Davis.

He kept his distance in the rain, a set of anonymous headlights in the murky darkness. She was driving a little faster than usual—he couldn't blame her. She was running from her wickedness, from her lost soul. She was a good girl—he'd known that when he'd first seen her from a distance. But even virtuous women could fall.

She was heading out toward Route 16, and he nodded to himself. It was a sign. Route 16 between Colby and Hampstead was usually deserted, and there were sharp curves, a steep drop-off, and a deep pond near the road. There was even Dutchman's Falls. He could choose any of those places.

He reached over and pushed the tape into the player mounted in the dashboard of the old truck. He'd put different labels on the tapes, and no one would ever search through his belongings, play one of his tapes. None of them would ever know that he listened to whores, singing their siren songs in his ear as he sought to do justice.

It was Madonna tonight, particularly fitting since

he'd thought Sophie Davis was a good woman. The bitch was singing about prayer, and his hands clenched the steering wheel tightly.

He didn't want to run her off the road. His distress and disillusionment was so deep he wanted to use his hands, so that she'd know why she was dying. He didn't want it fast and anonymous. She needed to know why, so she could repent.

The curve by Dutchman's Falls would be the spot. The road fell away sharply there, and her Subaru would tumble end over end, crushing her. It was steep enough that nothing would slow the car's descent, and he could drive back to Colby, secure that he had done his duty.

He passed her on the flat stretch, driving fast so she wouldn't recognize the truck. Not that she knew his truck, of course. But he hadn't survived for so long doing God's work without paying attention to details. He'd considered borrowing a vehicle, even stealing one to keep attention away from his old Ford, but decided that was even more dangerous. No, he was safer using his own truck, taking only a slight chance someone had seen him.

He pulled into the picnic spot that overlooked Dutchman's Falls and flicked off the lights. When she approached the turn he'd pull out, fast, bright lights on full, and she'd jerk the wheel out of the way and go over that cliff with a crash of shrieking metal. And he'd pray for her immortal soul.

It was possible she was a good enough driver to miss him, to keep control of the car, to drive around him. He hoped it wouldn't come to that. He didn't want to chase her through the darkness. Didn't want to terrify her—she'd been a good woman most of her life. Surely God wouldn't want him to frighten her too badly.

But her sin was all the greater, because she knew right from wrong. She'd kept herself pure, and then given herself away to a stranger. A stranger who wanted to hurt him.

Over the years many men had sought him, trying to stop the Lord's work, but none of them had ever guessed the truth until it was too late.

She'd surrendered her purity to such a creature. He knew it without anyone telling him. He watched, he observed, he knew things. He knew how to add two and two. And he knew how to subtract. Take one Davis woman out of the picture. Then the others would follow.

The lights of the Subaru appeared on the horizon. She was still driving fast, though not as fast as he would have liked. The teenagers had been easy—they were speeding, enmeshed in each other, barely paying attention to the road. The autopsy showed they'd both been drinking.

But even upset, Sophie drove with relative care. Making his job all the harder.

He hadn't asked for the easy way. He'd been chosen for this holy work, and he wouldn't flinch from his responsibility.

The car rounded the sharp corner by the falls, and he flicked his lights on high beam and stomped on the gas pedal, heading straight at her.

He was coming down the road in her lane. The only way for her to avoid him was to move to the left lane, and then he'd simply move farther over, so that she found herself flying over the edge of the cliff. The engine of the old Ford roared, like a charging beast, and she swerved to the left, exactly as he'd planned.

He moved closer to her, blocking her escape. She had no choice but try to ditch it on the side of the road that overlooked Dutchman's Falls, and he knew how soft the shoulder was. It wouldn't take much to crumble beneath the weight of the car. It would take a miracle to save her, and there were no miracles for sinners like her.

The bright lights illuminated the interior of the Subaru, blinding her. He watched her, fascinated, as he bore down on her. The confusion and terror in her eyes. The tears that stained her face.

Tears? Remorse? Was it possible that this time he'd been wrong? That she'd repented of her sin? It was too late, though. The front fender of his truck clipped the side of her Subaru, and she went spinning toward the cliff, the lighter car completely out of control on the rain-slick highway.

He didn't hesitate, didn't slow down. He simply sped off into the darkness, Madonna singing about getting down on her knees in prayer, and he knew he'd done what he had to do.

It happened so fast Sophie didn't have time to think. Blinded by the headlights, she could only sense the huge vehicle coming straight at her. The crunch of metal, and she was spinning crazily, desperately trying to control the steering wheel as the car bounced off the road.

She slammed on the brakes, and the car kept skidding in the darkness, over rough ground, until it came to an abrupt stop.

She didn't know how long she sat there, numb with shock. She'd had her seat belt on, of course, but she'd still managed to hit her head on something, and she thought she was bleeding. With numb fingers she unfastened the seat belt. The car had stalled out, but the lights were spearing out into the darkness, into nothingness, and the rain was coming down in a steady mist.

Whoever had nearly run her off the road was long gone. It had to have been a drunk driver—the Northeast Kingdom seemed to have more than its share of DUIs. He probably didn't know he'd almost killed her.

She fumbled with the door and pushed it open. She swung her foot out, and felt nothing.

She scrambled back into the car in a panic, and it rocked beneath her. She was an organized woman—she kept a flashlight in the glove box. She found it and shone it out the door. And then dropped it into the cavern below.

It was a long time before she heard it hit. She could now identify that rushing sound. She had had the sheer, incredible bad luck to have come across the drunk driver right near Dutchman's Falls. Another inch or so and she would have gone over the precipice.

She leaned back in the seat, clutching the seat belt, taking deep, steadying breaths. She wasn't safe yet. At least one tire was hanging over the edge, and the car rocked beneath her movements, but it still felt basically secure. She climbed over the gear shift, careful to keep her moves smooth and minimal, and pushed at the passenger door. It wouldn't open more than a crack—the right side of the car was pushed up against a tree.

She got back into the driver's seat, cursing. The rain was still coming down, heavier now. Clearly she wasn't getting out of the car where it was. The only option was to move the car.

She turned it on again, and it started so smoothly she almost cried with relief. She put the gear into Reverse and stepped on the gas.

Nothing of course. Just the hopeless spin of wheels, as the car rocked with dangerous enthusiasm. She let off on the gas, nervously running a hand through her hair. She didn't bother carrying a cell phone—coverage was too sporadic up in the hills of northern Vermont to make it useful. One of the concessions she'd had to make when she moved up here, that and buy a four-wheel-drive vehicle...

She stared down at the gear shift. She'd never tried the four-wheel-drive except when she'd bought the used car, but it was fairly simple to shift. She pushed the button on the gear shift, watching the letters light up—4 WD. Lovely letters.

She put the car in Reverse again, putting just the slightest pressure on the gas pedal. For a moment it edged backward, then the tires began to spin and the car slid forward again.

Sophie squeezed her eyes closed, prepared to go over the cliff, but the car shuddered to a stop, and she opened them, letting her breath out. Then she shoved the gear shift into Low and stomped her foot on the gas pedal.

To her astonishment it moved backward, in a spray of mud and dirt and gravel, so fast that she barely had time to slam on the brakes before ending up against another tree.

The car stalled out again, but at that point Sophie didn't care. She was sitting in the middle of Route 16, just outside of Hampstead, and she'd managed to do a 180, facing back home. It was the right direction—she wanted to go straight back to Colby as fast as she dared to drive.

She turned the key and for a moment the engine spluttered and died. "No!" Sophie whimpered. Route 16 was habitually deserted at this hour, but that didn't mean someone couldn't come out of nowhere and slam into her stalled car. The drunk driver had done just that.

"Please," she whispered. "Please, please, please!" The engine caught, and she shoved the gear into First, skidding as she raced down the empty road.

Her face was wet, and she couldn't figure out why when she hadn't been able to get out of the car into the rain. She put her hand to her head, then glanced at it. She was dripping blood, down her face, into her lap.

As a matter of fact, her head hurt like hell, she realized belatedly. She wasn't quite sure how she'd managed to hit it while wearing her seat belt, but the fact was, blood was trickling down the side of her face.

She couldn't show up back at the house looking like something out of a horror movie, but she wasn't about to drive to St. Johnsbury or Newport to go to an emergency room. Maybe Doc would still be awake when she drove through town—he could be counted on to patch her up so that Grace wouldn't have a heart attack if she happened to be up and wandering.

She should probably go to the police to report the incident, but what good would it do? She hadn't been able to see the other car—her main impression was that it was huge. It might have been a van or a truck.

And it wasn't the kind of publicity she was looking for. Stonegate Farm was a brand-new business— the wrong kind of newspaper coverage and people would start canceling their reservations.

She drove with particular care, back down the long, empty stretch of highway that led to Colby. She was usually organized enough to keep tissues in the car, but Marty had been having allergy problems recently and she'd snitched them. Sophie tried to dab at the flowing blood with the hem of her skirt, but it didn't seem to be making much of a difference. At least it wasn't going into her eyes.

It was after ten when she drove back through the tiny town of Colby, past the quiet town green and up the street to the lake road. Doc's house was dark and closed up, only a faint light coming from one of the upstairs windows. He'd get up and help her, she knew, but at that moment it seemed too much to ask. She kept the Subaru pointed straight, her hands gripped tightly to the steering wheel.

She almost made it home. The aftermath of her near miss began to take effect just as she was turning toward the north-end road, and she realized she was trembling all over. Too much in twenty-four hours, she thought with a trace of hysteria. It was bad enough having sex with a stranger. Almost getting killed was carrying things a little too far.

The rain was coming down at a steady pace, and the road around the lake was more mud than dirt, slick and deceptive. She was driving too fast in her need to get home. She misjudged the turn, missed the corner, and ended up sliding off the road, tilted sideways in a ditch that no four-wheel-drive would get her out of.

Sophie considered herself a tough, unsentimental person. But she burst into tears, loud, noisy sobs, and put her bloody head down on the steering wheel, indulging herself.

She hadn't cried that loudly, that long, for years. She couldn't even remember when. Crying was supposed to relieve stress, but all it seemed to do was wind her up tighter than ever. She was gulping for air in between sobs, having a full-blown anxiety attack.

"Smarten up, Sophie," she muttered through her tears. "This isn't doing anyone any good." She tried wiping her tears away with her full skirt, but it was already wet with blood, and she hated to think what kind of mess she was making.

She knew she couldn't stay there all night feeling sorry for herself, as tempting as the notion was. For one thing, she'd run off the road before the fork, and she was, in fact, closer to the Whitten cottage than the inn. Too close for comfort. She needed to get home, soak for a long time in one of the claw-footed bathtubs, maybe have a nice cup of herbal tea, and crawl into bed. She'd gone through enough for one day.

She slid out of the car, into the rain, sending a mental note of thanks skyward that at least there was ground beneath her feet. She slid as she climbed up the embankment, going down in the mud, but she was beyond caring. If she'd had one ounce of energy left she would have run home. As it was, she could barely drag herself down the narrow drive.

She saw the beam of the flashlight through the rain, and she let out a low, miserable moan. She didn't want to see anybody. Not her family, not John Smith, not the Northeast Kingdom killer. She just wanted to get home. She halted, considering whether she could dive into a ditch again, hide from whoever was out on such a miserable night. It couldn't really be anyone dangerous, though in fact she'd rather run into a legendary murderer than the man she'd spent the night with.

The bright beam of the flashlight caught her, and it was too late to hide. She couldn't see who was behind the light, only a large, shadowed figure, dressed in a raincoat. Shades of teenage horror movies, she thought, standing her ground. If she tried to run he'd probably catch her with some kind of grappling hook.

The ominous figure came closer in the rain-soaked darkness, till he was only a couple of feet away from her. He let the flashlight run over her bedraggled body with impartial interest. "I should have known it was you," John Smith said in a resigned voice. "What the hell happened?"

She considered a Victorian swoon, a graceful faint, to avoid answering his question. Even a flat-out run would be preferable, but none of those options would work. She'd hurt herself if she flopped down into the mud; he'd probably either leave her there or throw her over his shoulder in an undignified fireman's carry, or he'd catch her if she tried to run. Assuming she didn't fall flat on her face.

Rancor might help make him keep his distance. "What do you think happened?" she shot back. "Someone tried to run me off the road."

"They did a good job of it."

"Not here. On Route 16. Down by Dutchman's Falls."

She was vaguely aware of the utter stillness in his body. "How'd you manage to get away?"

"I'm kidding. It was just an accident. Some drunk driver nearly hit me, then drove off without realizing he'd run me into a ditch. Fortunately I was able to use the four-wheel-drive to get back on the road, but then I lost it when I pulled into the driveway. I'm fine, I'm sure the car's fine, I just want to get home and get in a hot tub and get to bed.''

She could have cursed herself for saying the word *bed*, but he didn't seem to notice. The beam of the flashlight swung up the road to her bedraggled car tilted sideways in the ditch. The front fender was crumpled, and she wondered whether that had happened just now or if it was the result of her earlier encounter.

He turned the flashlight back on her, and she squinted through the rain and darkness. ''You're bleeding,'' he said, more an observation of fact than an expression of concern.

''I'm fine.''

''Sure you are,'' he said, flicking off the flashlight, plunging them into darkness. Now was the time to make a run for it, she thought. Not moving.

He took her unresisting hand. ''Your place or mine?''

''What?''

''I'm not going to let you wander around in the darkness like some gory lost soul. You're covered with mud and blood, you look like you just managed to escape from an ax murderer, and I doubt you're any more capable of finding your way home in this condition than your batty mother is. Therefore, I'm making sure you get cleaned up and get home safely. Your place or mine?''

''I can take care of myself....''

"I guess it's up to me," he said, more to himself, and began pulling her along after him. She was too dazed to resist, though she knew she ought to run. "And don't think I'm going to carry you," he added. "It's a treacherous night, and you're more of a handful than a sylph. You'll have to make it on your own two feet."

It was enough to galvanize her. "Asshole," she muttered, picking up her feet. "A gentleman would at least give me his coat."

"Yeah? You're wet and bloody and covered with mud. The damage has been done, and if I give you my coat that just makes two of us wet. Besides, what in God's name ever gave you the impression I was a gentleman?"

She had to concede that point. Except where her mother had been concerned, John Smith was a mannerless pig. She was going to tell him that, as well as several other things, and she composed them in her brain, full, flowery insults of really impressive inventiveness like "sour-assed satyr" or "foul-hearted liar." Then she realized they had somehow made it all the way to his front porch in seemingly no time at all.

He opened the door and pushed her through with his usual lack of courtesy, but she was past fighting. The room looked different in the lamplight, and he had a fire going, and for the first time she realized how very cold she was.

She had two choices. One, try to take him by surprise, knock him out of the way and run out into the cold rain again before he could stop her. Or she could move to the fire and let the blessed heat sink into her bones.

He was a lot bigger than she was, and even though he was occupied in taking off the enveloping raincoat he was still blocking the doorway, and he wasn't the type to be taken off guard. And she was so damned cold.

In the end it didn't matter. He took her icy-cold hand and pulled her over to the fireplace. "Stay there," he ordered, and she didn't waste more than a moment considering escape.

There was nowhere else she wanted to be.

Oh, God, not the Curse of the Wilsons, she thought somewhat crazily. Life was complicated enough. She should run away, back home, and lock the doors. Lock him out, lock her ridiculous fantasies inside, and maybe they'd go away.

But they wouldn't. She knew it with a depressing certainty. And she knew that all he'd have to do was come knocking on the door and she'd let him in.

She was doomed.

16

He'd never seen anyone look more pathetic in his
entire life. Sophie had just stood there in the rain,
staring at him out of whipped-puppy-dog eyes, and
he'd had the absurd longing to put his arms around
her and tell her everything would be all right.

He hadn't, of course. Not his style. And it would
have been a lie. He'd made a crack about her weight,
enough to jar her out of her pitiful daze and make
her move. He had to be careful, though. He hadn't
seen her in the light yet, but he'd come to the uncomfortable conclusion that her soft, luscious body
was almost perfect. It would be a damned shame if
he goaded her into starving away her curves.

He grabbed an armful of the threadbare white
towels that came with the cottage and headed back
into the living room. She hadn't moved from the
spot where he'd left her, and the firelight flickered
against her blood-streaked face. Her hair was clinging damply to her head, her dress was streaked with
blood and mud, and if anyone had ever looked like
a drowned rat, she did.

He knew what he wanted to do. He wanted to

wipe the blood and mud from her, strip off her ruined clothes and warm her from the inside out. Last night had only been a start, and he'd had a hard time concentrating on anything but Sophie all day long.

And here she was, vulnerable, full of possibilities, and he wanted to explore each and every one of them, slowly, thoroughly. He didn't want to think about murder, about the past, even about the future. He wanted to think about now, and Sophie, and the way she smelled like flowers and fresh-baked cookies.

He dumped the towels on a wicker chair. "Did you see what you look like?" he asked, trying to keep his hands off her.

She looked at him instead, numbly. "What?"

"Over the window seat. There's a mirror."

She turned to look, obedient for a rare moment, and stared at her reflection. He'd half expected her to burst into tears.

Instead, to his surprise, she managed a rusty-sounding laugh. "Damn," she said. "No wonder you're being nice for a change."

"I'm always nice," he protested, starting to dry her head with one of the towels.

"Yeah, right. Ouch!" She grabbed the towel out of his hand. "I hurt my head, remember? I'll take care of it."

"Fine," he said, reaching for another towel. "I'll take care of your body."

She took a step back from him, shooting him a warning glance. "I'll break your hands."

"You and what army?" She was cold—he could see the goose bumps on her arms, the faint shiver in her body. Damn, he really wanted to see her. The darkness had been a sensual treat last night. Now he was ready to get a good look at her.

But she was too miserable for him to push, at least for the moment. "Sit in the chair and I'll get you a blanket," he said after a moment. "Then I'll see what I can do about that cut on your head."

"I don't need your help."

"You've got it, whether you want it or not. And you've made your head bleed again."

"I didn't—you did," she snapped.

At least she was still capable of fighting back. As long as he kept her pissed off she wouldn't start crying again. He was really hopeless with crying women.

By the time he returned to the living room, a quilt in one hand and a poorly equipped first aid kit in the other, she'd done as he'd told her, sitting closer to the fire as she tried to dry her hair while avoiding the cut.

"Wrap this around you," he said gruffly, handing her the old quilt.

"I will not!" she said, horrified. "That's a double wedding ring."

"It's a what?"

"Double wedding ring quilt," she clarified, as if to an idiot. "It's probably from the 1930s. I'm not going to cover it with blood and dirt."

"Wrap the fucking quilt around you or I'll do it for you," he said between clenched teeth.

She pulled the quilt around her shoulders, gingerly, jumping when he touched her head. "Quilts can be washed," he added prosaically. She had a nice little cut on her temple, one that had bled profusely, but the bleeding seemed to have slowed. He dumped some peroxide on a swab and began cleaning it, more gently than he would have liked. He didn't want to touch her gently. It would lead to other things, and he was coming to the belated conclusion that that was a very bad idea.

"It's an antique," she said. "The fabrics start to break down. You have to use special care in cleaning a quilt like this. You'd better bring it up to the inn and I'll take care of it."

"What the hell are you, Martha Stewart?" he grumbled. The wound was shallow enough, and it finally seemed to have stopped bleeding, but he put a butterfly bandage on it, anyway, just to be sure.

"You might say so. In a way. I write a column on housekeeping for a women's magazine." There was just a touch of defensiveness in her voice.

"So how come you're not married?" Jesus, why did he ask a question like that? Was he asking for trouble?

Fortunately she was willing to avoid it. "None of your business."

"True enough," he agreed. He finished with the bandage. "That's the best I can do for now." The towel was streaked with blood, and he tossed it in one of the empty chairs.

"Why were you out there in the rain?" she asked, suddenly suspicious. "It's hardly the night for a moonlight stroll."

"Considering there's no moonlight." He pulled one of the chairs closer and sat. Close enough to reach her if he wanted to. He wanted to.

She turned her head to look at him. "Maybe you'd just come in from a drive up Route 16. Maybe you're the one who tried to run me off the road."

"Now, why would I do that?" he inquired in a lazy voice. "Killing you wasn't exactly what I've been thinking about all day."

She actually blushed. It wasn't just heat from the fire—her cheeks turned pink and she looked away from him, flustered. "Then why were you out on a night like this?"

"Your car's only a few hundred yards away from this place. I heard you take the corner too fast, heard the car end up in a ditch. For that matter, I heard you bawling your head off inside the car. At least you'd stopped by the time I found you. Trust me, going off the road is not enough reason for crying.''

"I wasn't crying about going off the road,'' she said, shutting him up for a minute.

Only for a minute. "Okay,'' he conceded. "So what makes you think someone was trying to kill you?''

"I didn't say that.''

"Yes, you did. You said you thought I was trying to run you off the road deliberately. It wasn't me, so it must have been someone else. You been making enemies around here?''

"Only you.''

He laughed at that. "Honey, you are so naive.''

Her cheeks turned pinker, and he knew he wasn't going to be able to let her go tonight. Even if he knew it was the best thing for both of them, he just wasn't going to be able to let it happen.

"It wasn't deliberate,'' she said. "It was a drunk driver, and he probably didn't even realize he almost killed me.''

"Maybe. What kind of car was he driving?''

"I don't know. He had his brights on, and it happened so fast I couldn't get a look at him. Or her, I suppose. I figured it would be a waste of time to go to the police. But maybe I should, after all.'' She started getting out of her chair, but he put his hand on her shoulder and pushed her back down, gently.

"You can tell them tomorrow,'' he said. "No

one's on duty this time of night—it would just be the state police in St. Johnsbury covering the area, and they're probably busy enough.''

She stared at him. ''How do you know that?''

He shrugged. ''St. Johnsbury's a small city with a lot of poor people....''

''No, I mean how did you know about the police coverage? For that matter, how do you know so much about St. Johnsbury?''

Shit. ''I thought you'd already figured out I was a reporter. I would have done research.''

''You're not a writer,'' she said flatly. ''I was wrong.''

''Glad you figured that out,'' he said affably.

''You're a cop.''

He blew out a disgusted breath. ''Are you sure *you* don't write fiction?'' he said. ''Why don't you just accept the fact that I am who I say I am?''

''John Smith? Yeah, right. You have something to do with those old murders, I know you do, and it's a waste of time trying to deny it. Maybe you were a young cop here at the time, and you've always been bothered that the killer got off on a technicality. Maybe you're looking for proof that he really did it.''

''And exactly what good would that do? God knows where the poor kid is now. If he really did it, then I'd think he'd be suffering enough for what he did.''

"Well, that proves you're not a lawyer," she said. "You'd be more interested in justice."

"It proves nothing but that you're as innocent as a lamb about the way the world works," he drawled. "Lawyers don't care about justice, they care about money."

He knew he was annoying her by harping on her innocence. Too damned bad. He was still reeling from the fact that she was a gorgeous, thirty-year-old virgin. Or had been, until he got his hands on her. Hell, it had been almost as traumatic for him. He'd made an effort to keep his distance from vulnerable young women, preferring experience and emotional detachment. Somehow Sophie had managed to get beneath his skin.

"I need to get home," she said.

"It's still raining."

"That's all right. I'm already soaking wet."

"I could dry you off."

She moved then, fast enough so that she was at the door before he reached her. She opened it, but he pushed it closed, and she turned.

"I want to go home," she said in a shaking voice.

"Then I'll take you home. If that's what you want. What did you think I was going to do?"

"It's what I want." She didn't answer his other question; she didn't need to. They both knew exactly what he wanted to do. What she wanted him to do.

But she'd said no. And as far as he could remember, there was never a time when he hadn't taken no for an answer. Unless maybe on a dark night twenty years ago. "Let me get my keys."

"I can walk..."

"It's pouring rain, and I don't let women wander around in the woods alone at night, remember? Not unless they walk out on me when my back is turned, and I'm not turning my back on you again. I'll drive you. The more you argue, the longer it will take. And I might try to make you change your mind."

She shut her mouth at that, no more objections. He would have been amused if he wasn't so frustrated.

No reason for him to be so edgy, he reminded himself, pulling his wet raincoat back on. It wasn't as if he hadn't gotten laid the night before, and very nicely, too, despite her inexperience. It wasn't as if he was insatiable.

Except when he looked at Sophie, and he felt damned near voracious.

There was a hooded sweatshirt hanging on a peg, and he handed it to her. "Put this on. It might keep away some of the chill."

She opened her mouth to argue, then closed it again. Smart of her. He would have stopped her mouth with his, just to see if she wanted to change her mind.

He half expected her to take off and try to make

it through the woods on her own, but she dutifully ran from the porch to his car, ducking inside.

It started on the first try, damn it, and he put it into gear, backing out into the rain-swept night. She sat beside him on the seat, muddy feet pressed demurely together, hands tucked in her lap, her bedraggled skirt around her ankles, and all he could think of was how much he wanted to see her in something skimpy and slinky and sexy. She shouldn't cover up all that lovely flesh with goddamned ruffles.

He turned the heat on, and they drove up the driveway in silence, passing her car as they went. "Do you want me to call the garage tomorrow?"

"I'll take care of it," Sophie said stiffly.

"Suit yourself." He headed toward the inn, and the Jaguar slid briefly in the mud. He could see Sophie's hands fisted in her lap, and he was half tempted to gun the motor, just to see what would happen if they went into a spin.

He was too mature for that. He drove up the winding drive to the inn sedately enough, pulled up to the kitchen door and parked. He expected her to leap out of the car while it was still moving, but as usual she managed to surprise him.

She turned around to face him and held out her hand like a perfect little lady. Her grubby, blood-stained hand. "Thank you very much for taking me home," she said, her voice stilted.

He could feel a smile tugging at the corner of his mouth, but he solemnly took her hand and shook it. "I live to serve." He didn't release her hand.

She noticed, but she didn't pull away. "Are you a cop?" she asked.

"No."

"Are you a writer? Reporter?"

"No." Her hand was growing warm in his grip, and she bit her lip. He was going to have to kiss her.

"Then what are you?"

"Extremely turned on." And he pulled her across the seat, onto his lap.

She struggled only for a minute, long enough to feel his erection beneath her, long enough to make him hornier than ever. And then she stilled, looking at him out of those huge, wary eyes.

"Sorry," he said, absolutely unrepentant. "I can't resist." He slid his hand behind her neck, beneath her wet, tangled hair, and brought her mouth to his.

He half expected another argument. A struggle of some sort. Again, a surprise. She made that soft, hungry sound that had already emblazoned itself in his senses, she put her hands on his shoulders, and she kissed him back, her tongue sliding against his.

His reaction was immediate. He pulled her tighter against him, sliding his other hand up under the baggy sweatshirt to cover her breast. Why the hell had he suggested she wear an extra layer of clothing, when all he wanted to do was pull it off?

He could feel her heart thudding beneath his hand, and he knew it wasn't fear—it was plain, simple desire. He turned her in his arms, his mouth never leaving hers, until she was sitting astride him on the bench seat, pressing against him, and he wondered whether he could talk her into doing it this way for her second try at sex.

He broke the kiss, moving his mouth down the side of her neck as he reached underneath her full skirt to touch her.

She let out a quiet little squeak, and pushed against him for a breathless, agonizingly wonderful moment, and he wanted to make her come that way, first, before he unfastened his jeans and pushed inside her. If he could hold out that long. He couldn't ever remember wanting a woman so damn much— he was practically out of control, and his hands were shaking as his fingers slid beneath her panties.

She was wet. The feel of her against his hand, her soft neck beneath his mouth, the movement of her hips against him, the soft whimpering noises she made just before she exploded in a little shimmer of climax that made him almost desperate to join her.

He reached down for his zipper, fumbling, but Sophie came back to her senses with a thud, and she scrambled off him with a choked sound of horror. A moment later she'd practically fallen out the door, and the last he saw of her she was running up the hill to the kitchen door. It slammed shut behind her.

He swore. Slowly, carefully, with as much vibrant obscenity as he could possibly come up with. He really needed to punch something, but there was nothing but the burled walnut dashboard, and he had his priorities straight.

He sat back and looked at the building through the driving rain. The dark, deserted wing stretched out behind the cozy inn—bleak, deserted, keeping its secrets. Now was as good a time as any—Sophie would be too upset to even notice where he'd gone.

But he'd left his flashlight back at the house. And he didn't feel like scrambling through the debris and mud to stand in a place that might have seen violent death. Not tonight.

Tonight he was going home to jerk off, thinking of Sophie's soft, sweet thighs.

That, or he'd punch something. Either one seemed a good release. The best he was going to hope for, on a long, frustrating night like this.

17

Sophie sat on the glider the next morning, legs curled underneath her, nursing a mug of coffee, as she watched the mist rise from the lake. Grace was up already—she was moving around her room, humming an off-key little tune. That was something new—Grace had always had perfect pitch. But as her illness had progressed, her tone had deteriorated, and it was hard to even guess what she was humming. It sounded a bit like Cole Porter crossed with Marty's Limp Bizkit, but if there was a hidden meaning to her tuneless little song there was no way Sophie could figure it out.

She didn't particularly want to. She had enough on her mind, not the least of which was wondering what the hell she was going to do about her car, her sister, her mother, her neighbor, her new business, her overdue column, the cut on her head and the miserable headache that even the strongest painkillers couldn't dispel. How had things gotten so out of control in a matter of days? With no warning? Four days ago she had never heard of John Smith. Now suddenly she'd been having wild sex with a total stranger, and she would have done it again last night in the front seat of his car if she hadn't come to her senses. Damn it.

She looked down at the Whitten cottage, its roof barely visible through the tall trees. She was tempted to walk down to the water's edge where she could get a clear look at it, but she stayed where she was, showing a rare bit of sense for a change. A plume of smoke was rising on the cool morning air, and she could smell the cozy scent of wood fire. She really did belong in the country, she thought, taking another sip of her strong coffee. Her two favorite smells in the world were wood smoke and fresh-cut grass. Coffee came in at third place, followed by fresh-baked bread. Both of those could be replicated in the city, but nothing smelled like the cool lake water on a morning in late August.

She thought of going for a swim. The water would be cold and refreshing, and it would wipe out the shadows that haunted her, at least for a short while.

It would also freeze her ass off, which in theory was a good idea but in practice sounded extremely unpleasant. Still Lake was a particularly pristine lake, but there were all sorts of organisms in it, and she was better off keeping her lacerated head out of water.

She probably should have had a couple of stitches. If she'd had the nerve to wake up Doc then she wouldn't have driven off the road, wouldn't have had another run-in with John Smith, wouldn't be feeling restless and anxious. Wouldn't be tempted to walk down the driveway to check out her car and maybe run into her neighbor, and this time maybe she wouldn't run away, and then...

She heard the sound of a car coming up her driveway, and she felt a momentary clenching in her stomach. One that dissipated when she realized it wasn't the throaty, sexy purr of the Jaguar.

It was Doc. He looked a bit more somber than usual when he got out of his car, but he managed a warm smile as he mounted the steps to the porch. "Got any more of that coffee?" he asked, looking at her a little too closely for comfort.

She started to uncurl her legs. "I'll get it for you..."

"Heavens, no! I can help myself. You haven't changed the layout of the kitchen that much since the old days. I'll feel right at home. Can I get you a refill?"

"Why do I have the feeling this isn't a strict social call?" Sophie asked, handing him her mug.

"It's a social call," Doc said. "But let's just say it's a concerned one. I'll be back in a minute."

Sophie let out a pent-up breath. Whatever Doc wanted to talk about, she didn't think she was going to enjoy it. Right now she had enough problems without facing any new ones. Though knowing Doc, he was probably there to help her, not make her life more complicated.

"Here you go," he said, coming back onto the porch with two mugs of coffee. He sat in one of the rocking chairs, then took a sip. "Wonderful," he said.

"What did you mean, like the old days?" she asked. "Were you friends with Peggy Niles?"

Doc laughed. "Everyone around here is related. Peggy was my older sister. I thought you knew that. This was our family place. My father was the town doctor, my mother the nurse, and they used the whole back end of the building as the hospital. I grew up in this house."

"I knew the closed-up wing had been a hospital at one time. For some reason I just didn't connect you with it. Why didn't you keep the place? How did your sister end up with it?"

"Times changed. Back when I was a kid every small town had its own hospital, but by the time I was growing up the local ones had closed and everybody started going down to Morrisville or St. Johnsbury. Or to Burlington for the big stuff. It made more sense for me to have an office in town, and Rima never liked being too far out in the country. Peggy married Burt Niles, and they stayed on here to farm for a while. Not that it worked," he said, leaning back in the rocker. "Burt was never good for much, and he took off eventually. Peggy tried to keep the place going, first as a nursing home, then as a bed-and-breakfast, but obviously it didn't work. She was about ready to give up when the murders happened.''

"She died, didn't she?"

"Peggy? She got cancer a few years later. There was nothing anyone could do," Doc said, grief and dignity etched in his seamed face. "All the training I had, and I couldn't save her."

"I'm so sorry, Doc," Sophie said.

He shrugged. "I'm a doctor—I should get used to death. But you know, you never do, no matter how many times you have to deal with it."

"No, I imagine you don't," she said.

Doc gave himself a little shake. "Heavens, I didn't come out on this beautiful morning to talk about gloomy things like death. I wanted to find out what happened last night and make sure you're okay."

"Last night?" she echoed, feeling guilty, immediately thinking of sex. She'd run at the last minute, she hadn't given in to temptation and gone back to bed with John Smith—no matter how much she'd wanted to. Besides, what did Doc care about such things...?

"I heard you had car trouble," he said. "Zebulon King was out early this morning, and he dragged your car out of a ditch down the road and hauled it to town. Said it looked as if you'd had a fender bender. He said there was blood all over the seat.''

''I hit my head,'' she said, feeling almost embarrassed.

''So I can see. You should have come to see me right away, Sophie. Or given me a call—I would have come out here. Head wounds are nothing to mess around with—you might have a concussion, or worse.''

''I'm fine, Doc. It just bled like crazy.''

''Was it your neighbor? Did he run you off the road?''

''Why would you think such a thing?'' she demanded. ''No one ran me off the road.'' And then she realized that wasn't strictly true. The drunk driver up near Dutchman's Falls had been the cause of it all, but whoever it was, he was long gone. ''I was driving home late, it was raining, and I wasn't paying enough attention to the roads. I missed my turn and ended up in a ditch. Embarrassing, but really quite simple.''

There was a long pause. ''Zebulon King says there's blue paint on one of the fenders. He's a bit of a religious kook but he doesn't tend to get these things wrong. Did you hit someone, Sophie? You can tell me the truth. Were you drinking last night? If you hit something, or someone, the best thing you can do is admit to it. I can help you...''

''Doc, I wasn't drinking last night!'' Sophie said

with a little laugh. "I don't drink much, anyway, and I certainly don't drink and drive. I was just distracted. Thinking about things, and the roads were slick in the rain."

She didn't tell him about her near miss. It seemed like a waste of time, and he'd worry needlessly, but it felt strange to be lying to him. Maybe it was simply because he was so ready to jump to the wrong conclusion. Why in the world would he distrust Smith? The fact that she did was inconsequential— she had every reason to suspect him of at least lying to her. Doc should have taken him at face value.

"That was very kind of Mr. King," she added. "I've seen him at Audley's a few times. He's the one who looks like Abraham Lincoln without his Prozac. I wouldn't have thought he'd be bothered. He doesn't seem to have much use for people in general and newcomers in particular. I pity his poor wife."

"He's a good man," Doc said. "He's just got old-fashioned values."

"Old-fashioned as in Old Testament? He makes me uncomfortable. He always looks like he's wanting to paste a scarlet *A* to my chest."

"Do you deserve one?" Doc asked gently.

"No."

Doc nodded, though he still looked doubtful. "I'm glad to hear it. I worry sometimes. And I'm glad to know that no one was involved last night. That no one tried to hurt you.''

"Why would anyone? I don't have any enemies.''

"Some people don't need to have enemies to be hurt. I'm being an old fussbudget, I know. Ever since that awful time I keep worrying, thinking it's going to happen again. That it's not over, that the man who killed those girls will come back again.''

"Why would he?'' Sophie asked, the coffee suddenly turning to lead in the pit of her stomach.

"Don't they say the murderer always returns to the scene of his crime? Maybe he can't help it. Maybe the killer wants to atone for his sins. Or maybe he wants to kill some more. Psychiatry was never my specialty—I don't understand homicidal maniacs, and I really don't want to. I just want to make sure that no one else gets hurt.''

Sophie leaned forward and put her hand on his rough, gnarled one. "Doc, it was twenty years ago.''

"It's not over,'' Doc said, his eyes haunted. "Something tells me it's not over yet. I want you to be extra careful, Sophie. Don't go trusting any strangers, no matter how nice they seem to be. And don't let Marty go wandering off alone. That girl is ripe for trouble, and it would break my heart to see history repeat itself.''

Sophie squashed down her immediate panic. "Nothing's going to happen to Marty!'' she said firmly. "She's surprisingly good at taking care of herself. It's Grace who worries me."

"She's the least of your worries. He kills young girls, remember? Not older women. All three victims were slightly wayward young women, not much older than your sister. I don't want to see it happen again."

Sophie set her empty coffee mug down on the porch. "Doc, the killer's probably dead himself. He's not going to come back twenty years later and kill again."

Doc just looked at her. "Can you be certain?" he asked in a quiet voice. "Maybe he never left. Be careful, Sophie. Both you and Marty."

"What are you talking about?" Marty appeared in the doorway, looking suspicious.

"You're up early," Sophie said, trying to change the subject.

"I told Patrick I'd help him stack wood," she said, trying to sound offhand. "I need a little exercise."

Sophie resisted the temptation to point out that there was plenty of exercise to be had clearing out the rooms in the old hospital annex, but she resisted. Ever since Patrick had appeared on the scene Marty's mood had improved dramatically, and Sophie wasn't about to jeopardize it.

"I think he's around back. You can take him

some coffee and muffins if you want,'' she said instead.

Marty was staring at her through the screen door. ''Okay,'' she said absently, squinting at her. ''What the hell happened to you last night?''

Sophie touched her forehead nervously. ''Just a bump on the head,'' she said dismissively.

''I don't mean that. I mean the monster hickey on your neck. What have you been doing, big sis? You've gone from straight-laced to wanton in sixty seconds flat.''

''Marty...'' Sophie glanced at Doc, but he was merely shaking his head, a twinkle in his eyes.

''Don't worry about me, Sophie,'' he said. ''I understand human nature better than most, and I know what temptation's like for healthy young people. But that doesn't mean I'm not still worried. You shouldn't be so trusting.''

''I'm not!''

''Keep away from your neighbor. I imagine it's the last thing you want to do, but I don't trust him. Give me a chance to check up on him before you spend any more time alone with him. Promise me that, Sophie.''

''Doc, there's nothing to worry about,'' she protested. ''I barely know the man, but I'm sure there's nothing wrong with him.''

''If you barely know the man, why do you have a love bite on your neck?'' he said, sounding almost doleful. "Will you at least promise you'll be careful?"

"Of course."

Doc nodded, though clearly he wasn't satisfied. "King towed your car to Ferber's, but they don't know when they can get to it. One tire's ruined, and he's not sure if you bent the frame."

"Great," Sophie muttered.

"Don't worry. If you need a ride anywhere just give me a call."

"We'll be fine, Doc," she said—wishing she felt as certain as she sounded.

"Old Doc Henley gives me the creeps," Marty announced when Patrick finally decided they could take a break. She was dirty, sweaty, aching, scratched from the bark of the trees, but in an oddly good mood. Maybe there really was something to the benefits of physical exercise. She would have preferred more body contact, but this was a surprisingly enjoyable alternative.

She should have known Patrick really wanted her to help. With anyone else it would have simply been a veiled invitation to a make-out session, but with Patrick Laflamme, what you saw was what you got.

He'd taken off his shirt in the bright, cool sunshine, but he pulled it back on while they took a break. She couldn't understand why—he had truly the most beautiful chest she'd ever seen. And back, and shoulders. Hard work obviously did wonders for the muscles. He was absolutely gorgeous, with no reason to be modest. If any of the boys she'd known had been even half as well-built as Patrick they would never have worn shirts, even in the dead of winter.

"What have you got against Doc?" he asked mildly enough, reaching for his thermos of coffee.

Marty shrugged. "I don't know. Maybe I just don't like old men. He's nice enough, I guess, but I don't like the way he's always looking at me. Like he thinks I'm a terrible burden to my poor sainted sister."

"You are," Patrick said, his generous mouth curving in a faint smile.

She was getting used to him by now, and his cool teasing only stung a little. "She's no saint. You should see the hickey on her neck. Speaking of which, do you want to go someplace and park?"

"Park?"

"You know. Go off in your truck and make out? We could even do more than that if you want." For all his seeming standoffishness she knew he wasn't as disinterested as he pretended. He liked her, whether he wanted to or not. And she wasn't about to let the first decent prospect in all of the Northeast Kingdom escape so easily, even if he was a little too serious for her tastes.

"No, I don't want to go off and park," he said patiently. "I'll pick you up at six."

"Huh?"

"We'll go out to dinner in Stowe, so wear something nice. I'll bring you flowers, and you won't smoke, and when I bring you home I'll walk you to your door and I won't kiss you. Not until the third date."

"You think there are going to be three of them?" she asked, caustic.

Again that slow, devastating smile. "I'm betting on it. But you're going to have to stop smoking. I don't kiss girls who smoke."

"You're a judgmental pain in the butt, Patrick Laflamme," she said, pouting.

"I know," he said. "But I'm worth it. Let's get back to work."

She would have loved to tell him to fuck off. That would make his beautiful brown eyes open wide, wouldn't it? He wouldn't like potty-mouthed girls any more than he liked ones who smoked.

But despite that, he seemed to like her, anyway. And maybe he was right. Maybe he was worth it.

She just might be willing to find out.

Griffin closed the door behind the Kings, stepping out onto the front porch, leaving his dour, judgmental help behind. He'd been here for five days and accomplished squat.

That wasn't entirely true. He'd come up with enough circumstantial evidence to know he wasn't a murderer. There were too many victims, too many graves with yellow flowers. Whoever killed Lorelei, Alice and Valette had killed countless others, as well. And he still lived in Colby.

How long had it been since a young girl had died a mysterious death? He'd seen nothing recent, but that didn't prove anything. Maybe the killer was dead, and whoever brought the flowers knew the truth and tried to atone.

Hell, he didn't even know for certain that he didn't kill Lorelei. Logic dictated that the same person killed all three, but he knew from years of practice that logic had little to do with reality. And he wasn't going to be at ease until he remembered the truth about that night.

Distracting as she was, Sophie wasn't a complete waste of time, either. She was a pure, sinfully rich indulgence on his part. An indulgence he'd enjoy a lot more if he knew what the hell was going on. The sound of the chain saw in the distance sent a tense reminder through his gut. Whoever was working at the inn would be down by the lake. Out of sight of the old wing. And it was as good a time as any to go snooping.

He'd always found an excuse not to go up there, and right now he was tired of playing it safe. Hell, he was bigger and stronger than any of the women who lived there. If someone tried to stop him he'd just walk right over them. If he couldn't have Sophie, at least he wanted answers.

There was no sign of Sophie's car as he approached the inn from the woods, but that meant nothing. Her slightly battered Subaru had been towed into town. She was probably sitting in the kitchen like a spider, just waiting to catch him.

He moved past the ramshackle toolshed, pausing for a moment as a cold shiver went down his spine. The roof had fallen in, the door was off its hinges, and no one had used the place in what looked like twenty years. Not since he used to duck into the dark, cobwebby interior for a quickie with a willing and eager Lorelei.

He peered in the broken window, but everything was a shambles. He thought he heard a faint rustling sound, and he remembered the mice. Lorelei had been terrified of them. Valette liked to kill them by hand.

Any mice left there deserved amnesty, he thought, moving past to skirt the perimeter of the inn. No sign of any possible way to break in—he'd have to figure out a way past Sophie's watchful presence.

Maybe he should just walk into the house, pick her up and carry her upstairs to her bed. He could fuck her senseless, then go down and check out the old hospital while she slept.

As a plan it had a great many flaws, and only one thing to recommend it. It was what he wanted to do.

Unfortunately he wanted to do it so badly he might very well not leave her to go wandering through the ruins. And the longer he waited, the more entangled he was becoming.

He'd forgotten how much he liked Colby, and the cool, pristine beauty of Still Lake. It felt like the only home he'd ever known, which was flat-out crazy. He'd been living in his house in Sudbury, Massachusetts, for six years. Long enough to put down roots.

Except he wasn't the kind of man who put down roots. Not here, not anywhere.

He was about to turn away when he saw a movement near the boarded-up wing. Someone was in the overgrown bushes, watching him. Possibly someone dangerous—maybe even the killer himself. Or someone who knew the answers to what had happened so long ago.

He didn't move, trying to peer through the undergrowth to see if he could make out anything about the person hiding there. And then to his surprise the bushes parted and Sophie's crazy old mother stepped out.

She looked just as peculiar as always, with her mismatched clothes and flyaway gray hair. She was looking right at him out of her beady eyes, and to his amazement she motioned him forward.

He had nothing to lose. He strolled across the open space to the edge of the overgrown shrubbery, only to have her grab his arm in her surprisingly firm grip and drag him deeper into the bushes. He had long enough to wonder if she'd flipped out entirely, when he saw the open window.

Someone had pried the boards off. The glass had been smashed long ago, and it was obvious that Grace had climbed through there. She was dustier than usual.

"Go ahead," she said. "You've been trying to get in there since you came back."

She sounded caustic, almost reasonable, but he reminded himself he was dealing with a woman who'd lost her mind. Funny, but she seemed saner than most of the people he'd been around lately.

"I've never been here before, Grace," he said patiently.

"Sure you haven't. And your interest in the murders is purely academic. You're bigger than I am, but you can fit through the window. Mind the broken glass." She turned away.

"Wait a minute!" he called after her. "Why were you wandering around in there?"

She looked back over her thin shoulder. "Same reason as you. I want to prove who killed all those girls."

"All those girls? There were only three." How

could she possibly know about the others? How could she possibly know anything?

Grace's mouth curved in a wry smile, and he could see a trace of the vibrant woman she'd once been. More than a trace.

"Don't take everything at face value, Mr. Smith," she said. And then she walked away before he could say anything else.

The window was a tight squeeze, but he made it through, dropping down on the littered floor lightly. It was dark—the one broken window let in only a little bit of light, but this time he'd brought his flashlight, and he turned it on, shining it down the hallway.

Twenty years ago the place had been a wreck. By now it was beyond repair. Interior walls had crumbled, exposing the Spartan rooms, and beneath the fallen plaster and debris the occasional hospital bed could be seen. He and Lorelei had used each and every one of those beds during the long summer. It seemed like another lifetime.

He moved through the dust and rubble, shining his flashlight into every corner, trying to open his mind to any lingering memory. They remained stubbornly elusive. He could recognize rooms, remember events prior to his last night in Colby. But the night of the killings remained a mystery.

Even the basement kitchen came up blank. He didn't remember ever going down there, though he imagined he'd checked out every square inch of the place long ago. He'd been here that night, he knew it. But nothing, not even returning to old haunts, was going to bring back the past.

He wanted to slam his fist into one of the crumbling walls in frustration, but it probably would have brought the whole place tumbling down on him, and he wasn't pissed enough to die. He'd wasted his time in coming here. The answers he needed just weren't ready to be found, and the sooner he let go of it all, the better. Maybe when he was as old and dotty as Gracey he'd suddenly remember what happened that night. Or maybe he never would. He could live with it. He had for twenty years.

He headed back to the broken window, throwing one leg over the sill. His shirt caught on something, and he heard a ripping sound. He looked down, and his sleeve was torn open, caught on a protruding nail. A long line of beaded blood followed the scratch.

Lucky he'd had a tetanus shot recently, he thought. And then froze, as the drops of blood swelled on his arm and began to soak into the torn shirt.

There'd been blood everywhere. On the ground, in her hair, in her torn clothes. Blood on her hands and even in her wide, staring eyes. He'd tried to stop the bleeding, but she was already gone, and he'd knelt on the ground, holding her body, howling in grief.

Not in the hospital. In the inky dark interior of the toolshed. It was no wonder there was no sign of blood anywhere here. He'd found her in the tool-shed.

Someone else was there, watching them. He'd known it, but he'd been too drunk and stoned to remember it. He'd held Lorelei's limp body until he'd passed out, and when he awoke he was alone, lying on the grass in the dark.

He'd stumbled back to his bed, convinced he'd imagined it. Even the blood smearing his body the next morning hadn't jarred his memory. Nothing had. Until now, as he watched the blood soak into the thin chambray of his shirt.

He hadn't killed her. He knew it now, with a deep, certain sureness. Someone else had, someone who'd been watching them. Someone who was still watching him.

It wasn't over.

He'd shown weakness, when he could ill afford to. He'd remained firm and true to his calling for so many years, and now, in the very twilight of his mission, his will had failed him. He'd seen her tears and felt her sorrow and foolishly thought she should have a chance to repent on her own.

He was older and wiser than that. It was a momentary failing on his part, but he wouldn't make that mistake again. And there was no harm done. She was only enmeshed further still in her sinfulness, and it would be easier to get away with it once more. If that's what he chose to do.

Two sisters would be likely to raise suspicions in even the most trusting of the local police. But he counted on God to shield him from their eyes. He would do what he had to do, no more shirking, no more questioning the mantle God had placed upon him.

He would kill Sophie Davis and her sister. And release their souls to paradise.

At least Marty was in a good mood tonight, Sophie thought, trying to count her blessings. The bad moods had been fewer and fewer, and tonight her sister had actually been pleasant. And very pretty. She'd come down to the kitchen, wearing a skimpy dress and subdued makeup, and even her fuchsia-tinted hair looked relatively normal.

"I won't be here for dinner. I'm going on a date," she announced.

Sophie merely raised an eyebrow. "It's a little late to be telling me, isn't it? Who are you going out with?"

"Patrick." There was just a trace of defiance in her voice, which surprised Sophie. But then, everything about the situation was a surprise. Patrick

Laflamme was supposed to be immune to Marty's jungle charms. And he was hardly the type Marty usually went for—he was steady, responsible and very polite.

But Sophie knew when to keep her mouth shut. "Sounds nice. Any idea when you'll be back?" She half expected a rude response, but Marty merely shrugged.

"Probably early," she said. "He's a hard-working little Boy Scout."

Sophie turned her face to hide her smile. "How depressing," she said.

"Not really." Marty was being almost chatty. "Have you taken a good look at him? He's worth the trouble."

"I hadn't noticed. Are you intending to corrupt him?" she asked lightly.

"I'm doing my best." Again that mournful tone. "And he's trying to reform me."

Sophie turned at that, no longer able to hide her curiosity. "Who do you think is going to win the battle?"

"I don't think I have a snowball's chance in hell," she said. "He'll probably have me going to church and singing in the choir before long."

"You're not usually that persuadable."

"Patrick's different."

Thank you, God, Sophie said inwardly.

The front doorbell rang. "That'll be him. I'll be back early," Marty said, running out of the kitchen.

Sophie dried her hands on her apron and followed her sister into the hallway. Patrick was standing in the doorway, freshly shaved, wearing a coat and tie. He had a bouquet of bright yellow flowers in his hand. "We won't be back late, Miss Davis," he said politely.

It always depressed her when the meticulously polite Patrick called her miss. At least it was marginally better than ma'am. "I have complete faith in you, Patrick," she replied.

Marty turned and stuck her tongue out at her sister with surreptitious malice.

"I won't let you down, ma'am."

Oh, God, there it was. The dreaded ma'am. "Call me Sophie," she said cheerfully.

"Yes, ma'am."

Maybe there was something to be said for bad boys and losers, she thought morosely, watching them as they drove up the driveway in Patrick's meticulously well-kept pickup truck. At least they never made her feel like an aging spinster.

Another car was coming down the driveway, passing Patrick's on a wider stretch. That was something else she needed to find the money for, she thought, depressed. The driveway needed work.

Doc pulled up by the kitchen door and got out. He wasn't alone, and Sophie could see Rima sitting in the front seat. She waved at her, and Rima nodded back, looking lost in her own world.

As sad as it was for Doc, Rima's illness had been a blessing for Sophie. While she didn't know the details of what kept Rima housebound and mostly silent, she did know that she hadn't ''been right'' in years, according to Marge Averill. Doc had had plenty of time to hone his skills, his patience and his caring on his own wife, and he'd helped Sophie deal with Grace's sudden, unexpected deterioration.

Sophie left the porch, heading for Doc's car, but he forestalled her. ''Rima doesn't feel much like talking today,'' he said, his gentle smile accepting. ''It was all I could do to talk her into taking a little drive, but I wanted to check on that cut of yours and bring you these.''

He handed her a bouquet of bright yellow flowers, and she looked down at them, smiling. So Marty wasn't the only Davis woman with a gentleman caller who brought her flowers. ''How sweet!'' she said. ''I don't know if I've ever seen these before. What are they called?''

''Judas tears. Rima grows them in her garden— they're pretty rare around here. Rima's flowers are her pride and joy—just about the only thing that interests her. I was thinking it might help her if we moved to a warmer climate, where the growing season was longer, but she won't have it. Born here in Colby and she'll die here.'' He glanced back at the car with tender care. "But not for a good long time, I hope. I guess we're just a couple of hardcore Vermonters."

"Shouldn't I thank her for the flowers?"

"No need," Doc said. "I'll tell her you appreciate them. She'll just wait in the car while I check on your mother. She was pretty restless this morning, and I'm a little worried that she might start getting delusional."

"Delusional?"

"Don't you worry, Sophie. You aren't alone in this. I'm here for you. If Grace starts imagining things we can control it with drugs. How's the head?"

"Just fine. Not even a headache."

"Why don't you put the flowers in water while I check on Grace? You wouldn't want them to die, would you?"

She looked down at the pretty bouquet. She'd been wrong, she thought. The flowers were unusual, but she'd seen them somewhere before, and recently. She just couldn't remember where.

They looked like the same flowers that Patrick had brought Marty. That had to be it, she thought. But for some reason that wasn't the connection she was looking for.

She was arranging the flowers in a small blue vase, trying to remember where else she'd seen them, when she heard Doc and Grace's voices coming from her room. The tone was a little strained, which surprised her. Doc was devoted to Grace, as he was to all his patients, and even as Grace deteriorated she'd shown a surprising interest in Doc's comings and goings. There'd been a time when she'd almost seemed jealous of the time Sophie spent with him—she certainly did her childish best to keep them apart. Keeping Doc for herself, it seemed. She had no choice but to share him with Rima, but she wasn't about to let Sophie and Marty spend much time with him.

She heard her mother's door close quietly, and she turned with the vase in her hand as Doc walked into the kitchen, his expression gloomy. "She's not good, my dear," he said gently. "I'm afraid she's going to need to be on some kind of tranquilizer. She's very agitated tonight. I think I'll take Rima home and come back out and sit with her. If need be, I'll give her something so that she'll sleep through the night."

Sophie didn't bother to hide her stricken expression. "But what happened? She didn't seem any different this morning. I know my accident upset her, but I made it clear that it was just a drunk driver...."

"What are you talking about?" Doc said sharply. "You told me you misjudged the curve and slid off the road. You didn't say a word about another driver."

Shit. "I didn't want to worry you, Doc," she said,

embarrassed. ''I was nearly run off the road up by Dutchman's Falls. It was an accident, and the driver was probably too drunk to realize he almost killed me.''

''Maybe,'' Doc said in a grim voice. ''And maybe it was no accident.''

''Don't be ridiculous. Who would want to hurt me?''

Doc just shook his head. ''I'll be back as soon as I can. Just keep an eye on Grace, will you? I don't want to risk her wandering back down to the Whitten place. I don't think she'd be safe.''

Sophie set the vase down on the kitchen table, her hands shaking slightly. ''What are you saying? You think John Smith is trying to hurt us?''

''I don't know,'' he said. ''All I know is that things have felt wrong, strange, ever since he moved in here. I don't know what it is, but I've always had good instincts. And it just doesn't feel right. Keep your mother safe, Sophie. I'd never forgive myself if something happened to her. Or you.''

Great, Sophie thought as he drove up the driveway. As if she weren't paranoid enough, now Doc was imagining murderers lurking in the woodwork. Leaving her alone to worry about it.

She put dinner on the table, then went to her mother's door and knocked softly. Not that Grace had shown much interest in food recently, but she couldn't afford to miss meals.

"Dinnertime, Mama," she called.

"Not hungry" came the voice from the other side of the door. She sounded like a cantankerous seven-year-old, and Sophie sighed. Just when it looked as if Marty might be improving, Grace was getting worse.

"You need to eat," she said. "At least come out and keep me company."

A long silence. "Are you alone?"

"Yes," she said, startled. For a moment she'd sounded like the old Grace, rational and on top of things. "Even Marty's gone out, and Doc took Rima home. Come on out and keep me company."

The door opened a crack, revealing her mother standing there, her gray hair tangled, her clothes mismatched, an oddly lucid expression in her faded eyes. "Poor Rima," she muttered obscurely. "What's for supper?"

"Shepherd's pie from the leftover roast lamb," she said, following her mother back into the kitchen, only to come up short as Grace blocked the doorway.

"Where did those come from?" her mother asked in a trembling voice.

"I bought the lamb at Audley's, Ma," she said patiently. "You had some last night, and you liked it—"

"I mean the flowers," she said sharply.

"They're from Rima. Doc brought them out for

me. They're pretty, aren't they? I thought that was so sweet of her, to think of us even while she's having such a difficult time...''

''They're not from Rima,'' Grace said. ''They're from him!''

God give me patience, Sophie thought wearily. ''Yes, Doc brought them in, but Rima sent them. Come and sit down, Ma. I'm sure the flowers were meant for all of us, not just me.''

''Oh, my God, maybe they were,'' Grace said obscurely, distressed. ''Sophie, I have to talk to you.'' She took Sophie's hands in her gnarled ones, and she looked deeply troubled.

''Of course, Mama. What's worrying you?'' Sophie kept her voice low and reassuring.

''Don't talk to me like I'm an idiot!'' Grace snapped. It was the first time she'd shown anger in months. ''You have to trust me. I know I'm a dizzy old broad, but I'm not nearly as wafty as you think.''

''I don't think you're wafty.''

''Of course you do. That's what I wanted you to think. I was hoping to keep you safe, but it's too late. It's gone too far. He's going to kill you. He's probably going to kill us all.''

''What are you talking about, Mama?'' Shit, Doc was right about the delusions. Grace was having a dilly of a one.

''Doc. He's a murderer. He kills women, Sophie. It wasn't that boy they convicted, it was Doc who killed them. Killed them all. And he's killed more than those three people.''

"Why would Doc kill people, Grace?'' Sophie asked gently. "He's a healer, and the kindest man alive.''

"I don't know,'' Grace said stubbornly. "I only know that he'll try to kill you, and soon.''

"And how do you know that?''

"The flowers.''

Sophie wanted to burst into tears. How could her mother have gotten so deluded so quickly? "I'll get rid of the flowers,'' she said patiently. "Then we'll have some supper and some hot tea, and then Doc will come back and you can ask him whether he really wants to kill me…''

"No!'' Grace shrieked. "You can't let him in the house, Sophie. You can't trust him. Where's Marty? He'll kill her too, I know he will. And me. He'll have to silence me before I tell everyone the truth. Of course, no one will believe me. Even my own daughter thinks I'm a crazy old loon.''

"I don't think you're crazy, Mama,'' Sophie said. "I just think you're a little upset, and you need to calm down. No one wants to kill me, no one wants to kill anyone.''

"I can prove it to you,'' Grace said, her voice high-pitched and desperate. "I have notes, pages and pages of notes, that will prove it beyond a shadow of a doubt. I've got them hidden in my room. Let me just get them for you...."

"Prove what?" Doc asked, his voice calm and soothing as he stood behind the screen door on the porch. Sophie hadn't even heard the car return, she'd been so caught up in worrying about Grace's delusional state. He would have barely had time to drop Rima off before coming back here. Thank God, Sophie thought.

"Grace is worried that—" she began, but Grace interrupted her before she could finish the sentence.

"I was afraid that the shepherd's pie had poison in it," Grace said. "I think there are spirits in this place, wanting to do us harm. Make the spirits go away, Doc. They frighten me." Grace's brief spell of paranoid lucidity had vanished, and she looked like a terrified, pathetic child.

"I'll take care of it, Grace," he said gently. "I brought something to help you sleep, and I'll stay with you so that no one can hurt you. Would you like that?"

Apparently Grace had forgotten all about her previous fantasies. "Would you, Doc? Would you promise to sit with me all night, never leave my side? That's the only way I'll feel safe."

"Grace, you can't—" Sophie protested, but Doc silenced her.

"Of course, Grace. Rima has already gone to bed, and she knows that sometimes I'm called out all night long. She won't worry. I'll stay right here with you, I promise.''

Grace smiled happily, back to the sunny childhood that had become her habitual home. She wandered toward her bedroom, humming beneath her breath.

"You shouldn't have to do this, Doc," Sophie protested in a low voice. "I can sit with her...."

"Nonsense. I brought a sedative with me, and once I give her a shot she'll be out like a light. I have a good book, and I can sleep anywhere, even standing up if I have to. The remnants of my training as an intern."

"It's not fair—"

"Enough of this, young lady. It isn't fair that you've been saddled with a disturbed mother. What happened to set her off this time? She seemed peaceful enough when I left."

Sophie shook her head. "I don't know. She just started babbling about murder. She said you were going to kill us all."

"Did she?" Doc sounded more amused than alarmed. "And how did she know this?"

"Apparently the flowers were talking to her," Sophie said. She felt close to tears.

"That's one of the sad things about senile dementia. They never seem to be happy delusions. If flowers started talking, wouldn't you think they'd have happy things to say instead of talking about death and murder?''

''I wouldn't know.'' She took a deep, shuddering breath.

''I think you need a nice cup of tea and a good night's sleep.''

Sophie shook her head. ''I can't. But I'll be happy to make you some.''

''You don't need to take care of me, Sophie. I'm here to help you out. Let me go sit with my patient, and you do whatever it is you need to do to unwind. Take a hot bath, read a book. And don't worry about us—we'll be fine. If Marty comes home and you're not up, I'll tell her you were tired and went to bed early.''

''All right,'' she said, not willing to argue anymore. She could no more sleep than she could swim across Still Lake. She was restless, anxious, deeply troubled. She needed to get out of this house, away from everyone for a little while. She needed space to think and just to breathe.

She knew what Doc's reaction to that would be. Just as hysterically paranoid as her mother's, though he seemed convinced that John Smith was the danger. If anyone scared her, it was the disapproving Zebulon King. He seemed just the sort of Old Testament patriarch who would decide to punish the unrighteous. Mind you, until a couple of days ago she'd been depressingly righteous herself, but who knew how the mind of a religious fanatic worked?

As long as she kept away from everyone she'd be fine. Doc might not agree, though. He didn't have to know she'd left the house. As far as he was concerned she could be sound asleep upstairs.

"Call me if you need me," she said.

"I won't need you. Grace trusts me, deep in her heart, despite her current delusions. I promise you, we'll be just fine."

Sophie leaned forward and kissed Doc's soft, shaven cheek. "Thank you for everything, Doc. I can't imagine where we'd be without you."

18

Sophie really did try her best to avoid temptation. She took a hot bath, and afterward, for some reason, decided to wear some of the ridiculous underwear Grace used to buy her. It had been an ongoing family joke—every Christmas and birthday Grace would swoop back into their lives and present her staid daughter with lacy, impractical underwear, which Sophie would leave in her drawer. Looking at them tonight, she remembered her mother as she was before, slightly naughty, sharp-tongued and clever. Now she was a poor lost ghost of that vibrant woman, and Sophie wanted to cry.

Tears were a waste of time, she reminded herself. On a whim she pulled the scandalous underwear from her top drawer, took off the tags and put them on. The bra made her look even more voluptuous than she already, unfortunately, was, and the panties were just this side of a thong. She slid them on, anyway, staring at her reflection in the wavering mirror above her dresser.

Not bad if you liked well-built women, she decided impartially. She was never going to be fashion-model thin, but all those muffins and slices of peach pie hadn't done any noticeable damage to her curves. She just needed to find someone she was willing to take her clothes off for and she'd be fine. Unfortunately, the only person she wanted to strip in front of was John Smith.

She was pretty enough, in a bland way, she decided. Blue eyes were boring, though at least hers were reasonably big. On the other hand, her mouth was definitely too large, and she didn't care much for her full lips, either. Nose and skin were good, except for that mark on the side of her neck. He'd probably done it on purpose, she thought darkly. Branding her, just so everyone would know what she'd been doing in her spare time. Son of a bitch.

She should have gone to thank Mr. King for towing her car earlier in the day, but the man made her uneasy. She should offer to pay him, though chances were she'd get it wrong. She either offered to pay for things that were simply considered neighborly, or she didn't offer to pay for acts that were considered services rendered. Maybe eventually she'd get it right, but for now it would have been better to offend Mr. King than cheat him.

She could walk down to the Whitten cottage, leave an envelope on the porch for Zebulon King, and then take off before she ran into anyone. Anyone at all.

Anyone like John Smith. Who the hell was she

kidding? The only reason she wanted to go down there was in hopes that she might run into him, that he'd put his hands on her and override any common sense that might get in her way.

She'd be crazy to go, as crazy as her mother. She was courting danger, and she was much too wise to do that. And she was going, anyway.

She pulled on the rest of her clothes, covering up the naughty underwear, and tried to read a book to get her mind off him. Why in the world did women actually choose to wear this kind of stuff on their bodies, she thought restlessly? She preferred her underclothing in plain white cotton so she didn't have to think about it. She kept trying to concentrate on the book, and all she could think about was the way the bra cupped her breasts. Hell and damnation.

She should take her clothes off and put on her nightclothes. And then lie in the bed, unable to sleep, for hours and hours and hours.

No, that was out of the question. So was sitting in her bedroom trying to read. Maybe she should just go down to the Whitten cottage and face John. She needed to make it clear she had no interest in him, in his hands and mouth and any other wicked part of his body. She wanted her old life back.

She slipped out the front door into the warm night air, as silent as she could be. Through her mother's window, she could see Doc sitting by Grace's bed, reading something out loud. It looked like the Bible, and Sophie had to bite back an inappropriate urge to giggle. Grace had never cared much for organized religion, but right now she had no choice but to put up with it from Doc's gentle company.

Sophie moved across the grass, her thin shoes making no sound. She had to be out of her mind, coming out on a night like this, going to face her nemesis. But she couldn't sit around and wait anymore. She had to find out exactly who and what he was, and why he was living in Colby, Vermont. There was no innocent excuse, she knew, and the only reason had to be something to do with the old murders.

He wouldn't have run her off the road—Doc was crazy to have thought so. If he'd wanted to hurt her, he'd had any number of chances to do so. Besides, what possible reason would he have to do her harm?

She'd walk down to the Whitten house, find the answers to her questions, then come back to relieve Doc. There was nothing to be afraid of. John Smith, or whoever he was, didn't want to hurt her. No one did.

At least she had the dubious protection of Doc back at the inn. If she needed help all she had to do was scream—Doc might have slowed down a bit, but his hearing was almost supernaturally acute. If she got in trouble he'd come running.

So why was she walking into danger when she really needed to keep her distance? She knew perfectly well she was taking the first excuse she could find to see him. Maybe she just wanted to finish things up—once she got it over with she'd have no more excuses to go down there, and she'd be safe, whether she wanted to be or not.

The battered old Jaguar stood in the clearing. There were no lights coming from the house, and for a moment she wondered if he'd gone for a walk. She should just go home, come back in the light of day when it was safer. Except that she wasn't quite sure she wanted to be safe anymore.

She should have turned and run. But the place looked still and quiet, and if he was anywhere around he would have seen her by now. She may as well walk right up to the front porch. If she was that stupid.

Still no sign, no sound from the dark house. She turned to go, both relieved and disappointed, when the Jaguar distracted her. She didn't believe a word John Smith had told her, not even the anonymous name he'd given her. Didn't she deserve to know whom she'd inadvertently slept with?

That wasn't fair of her—there was nothing inadvertent about it. No one forced her, and she couldn't really call sex an accident. Even if it felt like the most impulsive thing she'd ever done in her short, safe life.

She opened the passenger door of the car and slid inside. The glove compartment was right there, and she had no reason to feel guilty. She opened it and pulled out the leather case that held his registration.

Or someone's registration. The car belonged to someone named Thomas Ingram Griffin of Sudbury, Massachusetts.

So why did that name sound familiar? She'd never been in Sudbury in her life—there was no reason she would know him. Who the hell was he, and what was he doing there?

She put the registration away, memorizing the name and address, and turned to open the door again.

Only to let out a shrill scream.

He was standing by the car looking at her, an unreadable expression on his face as he reached for the door handle. She acted instinctively, slamming down the lock, then reached across and locked the driver's side, as well.

He took a step back, and if there was any humor in his dark eyes she didn't see it. Instead he simply walked back to the porch, sat in one of the rockers and propped his feet up on the railing. Preparing to wait her out.

Stupid, stupid, stupid, she berated herself. Why the hell hadn't she just bluffed it? So she'd been snooping. So he'd be pissed off. She wasn't really afraid of him, was she? He might be angry, but he wouldn't hurt her.

She leaned back in the leather seat, reviewing her

options. Her talents ran more toward stripping wall-paper and turning buckets into planters, not hot-wiring classic cars, and he hadn't left the keys in the ignition, damn it. Actually, if he hadn't left the keys in the ignition he must have them on him, and her locking the doors did her absolutely no good at all. She'd learned that the last time she tried this little stunt.

She looked up at him as he lounged on the porch, watching her. As if he could read her mind, he held up the keys in one hand, dangling them with a taunt-ing gesture.

All right, so he'd won this round. She still wasn't about to climb out of the car. Instead she rolled down the passenger window, letting in the cool lake air.

"We've already done this dance before," he drawled. "Aren't you getting tired of it, Sophie?"

"Who's Thomas Griffin?" she demanded.

"Ever hear the phrase, curiosity killed the cat?" he said.

"Are you going to kill me?"

"I'm not in the mood. Not right now, at least. Though I could always be persuaded to change my mind." He might have been talking about afternoon tea in that pleasant, unemotional voice.

"Who are you?"

"Who the fuck do you think I am?" he said. "Use your brain."

He was really beginning to piss her off. Not enough to make her get out of the dubious haven of the car, however. "I don't know! I've already figured out that you aren't a reporter, you aren't a cop, and you aren't a lawyer. That leaves a lot to go through."

"As a matter of fact, I *am* a lawyer," he said, as cool as the lake breeze. "But that's not all. According to popular belief I murdered three women here some twenty years ago. I was known as the Northeast Kingdom murderer."

He said it in such a calm, matter-of-fact tone that for a moment she believed him, and her stomach knotted in instant panic. And then common sense surfaced.

"Sure you are," she shot back. "That's why the place has been littered with bodies since you got back."

His smile wasn't the slightest bit reassuring. "You don't believe me? Think about it, Sophie. Where have you heard the name Thomas Griffin before? You're a smart woman underneath those stupid ruffles—it'll come to you."

Her momentary confidence faltered. She remembered the photo of the killer in the newspaper, the grainy features that looked nothing like the man lounging on the porch. He'd worn sunglasses and had a beard, and the tattoo of a snake coiling over one hip, and his name was...

Thomas Griffin.

"I don't believe you," she said, but her voice quavered.

"Oh, yes, you do. You've been so busy worrying about your mother and sister that you haven't been jumping to the logical conclusions. I think Doc must have figured it out a while ago, though I can't figure out why he hasn't said anything yet. He's always been so protective of his little town and its young women that he should have figured it out long ago."

"He said something to me. He warned me away from you. I thought he was just being a fussbudget."

"Did the warnings work? No, I guess they didn't." He answered his own question. "You're here, aren't you?"

"If you hurt me they'll know you did it."

"I'm not going to hurt you."

"Then why have you got me trapped in this car?"

"I don't. You showed up and decided to go snooping, and you're the one who locked yourself in there. I can unlock the doors any time I want."

"I'll lock them again."

"Honey, I hate to break it to you, but I'm stronger than you are. I've already proved that I can unlock the door even if you put your whole weight on it."

"Enough with the cracks about the weight," she snapped, her fear momentarily fading.

He laughed. "It's the only way I can get to you.

Besides, you know perfectly well how sumptuous you are.''

''Sumptuous?''

''Delicious,'' he said, his voice low and beguiling. ''Utterly succulent.''

''I hadn't heard the Northeast Kingdom murderer was a cannibal,'' she said.

''Not in the traditional sense of the word. What can I say? You make me hungry.''

She shivered, and she wasn't sure why. It was an unseasonably warm night, and she felt hot and breathless in the car. And chilled. She needed to get home, make sure Grace and Marty were all right. She needed to cool down, strip off her layers of clothes. She looked at him sitting on the porch in the moonlight, obviously amused by her. Oh, my God, she'd had sex with a murderer! And even worse, she wanted to again.

''If you're the Northeast Kingdom murderer, how many people did you kill?'' she demanded. He still hadn't moved, he just sat there watching her. Like a chef, trying to decide exactly what he was going to do with a plump young hen.

''I was convicted of killing one woman, and I spent five years in prison,'' he said in his cool, emotionless voice. ''They overturned it on a technicality, set me free and didn't bother to give me a new trial. I'd been working toward my law degree while I was in jail and they knew they'd be screwed if they tried anything.''

''A felon can't have a license to practice law.''

''Very informed, aren't you? But I wasn't a convicted felon—it was overturned, remember.''

''So you only killed that one girl?''

''I don't know what I did. I had a blackout that night, and I've never remembered what happened. That's why I came back here—to see if I could find out what really happened. To find out whether or not I really murdered anyone.''

''And what have you found out?''

''Not much. How much do you trust me, Sophie? Not very much, I expect. For all you know you could be my next victim.''

''How reassuring.'' She felt slightly faint.

His smile was oddly self-deprecating. ''I can give you a ten-minute head start. I'll promise to stay on the porch long enough for you to get home safely.''

''And I'm supposed to trust you?''

''You don't have much choice. There are problems with that scenario, though. What if I'm not the killer? What if someone else is lurking in the woods around Still Lake? Waiting to catch you alone?''

''I think I'll take my chances.''

Why did he have to have such a sexy mouth, particularly when he smiled that rueful smile? ''There's another thing, too.''

''And that is?''

"You don't want to go home. You want to trust me."

She laughed at that. "I'm not that much of an idiot."

"You're not an idiot at all. Your instincts tell you to trust me. Your brain tells you to run."

"So it looks like a draw."

He shook his head. "Throw in your hormones, and the answer is clear. Get out of the damned car and come upstairs."

"Upstairs? You're out of your mind," she said flatly. "You tell me you've been lying to me ever since you met me, you tell me you may be a mass murderer, and you expect me to sleep with you?"

"You already knew I was lying. You already slept with me. I haven't quite figured out why, but you want me almost as much as I want you. Which, trust me, is a hell of a lot. I'm here for a reason, and I don't need distractions, and yet all I can think about is you. So get out of the fucking car and come upstairs with me."

"I thought you said I could go home if I want."

"You can. I just don't think you want to."

"Watch me." She unlocked the door, half expecting him to jump her.

He didn't move from his spot on the porch, his long legs still propped on the railing. He just watched her out of dark, hooded eyes.

She opened the door, stepping out on the weed-choked driveway. He wasn't coming after her, she knew. He wasn't going to touch her, coerce her, force her.

"You know, if you're a serial rapist and killer, then you're doing a piss-poor job of it," she said, closing the door behind her. "You're not supposed to give your victims a chance."

"Maybe I like the idea of a chase. I only said I'd give you ten minutes."

She blinked. He sounded so calm, so matter of fact. She was standing in the middle of a deserted clearing with a man who'd been convicted of killing at least one woman, and he'd been warning her, plainly and obliquely, waiting for her response.

"So what is it, Sophie? Run like hell through the woods, or go to bed with me? Who do you trust?"

"Whom."

"Fuck you," he said genially. "Get in the house."

"Make me," she shot back.

He shook his head. "Those kinds of games can be fun, but we need to save them for later. Right now you have to choose. And it better be soon. I'm getting tired of waiting for you."

"Ten minutes, you said?" She glanced down at her wristwatch. It was a delicate, old-fashioned, marcasite one that had cost too much and didn't keep time very well. It had stopped.

He glanced toward the sky. "Better run now, Sophie. Darkness is coming. So's the bogeyman."

"It sounds as if you'd rather I ran," she said in an even voice. "Why? Why are you trying to scare me?"

For once she'd managed to surprise him. "Maybe because that's the smartest thing you could do. I'm a dangerous man, Sophie. For some reason I think I want you safe."

"I thought you just wanted me, period. And maybe I'm tired of being safe." She didn't even know where those words came from. She only knew they were true.

He pushed up from the chair and took a step toward her, but her momentary bravado failed. She took off, disappearing down the lake path as fast as she could run.

It wasn't the first mistake she'd made that night, nor the last. Just one in a long line of idiotic moves that were dumb enough to die for. She got lost.

It wasn't really her fault. She hadn't spent much time wandering in the woods in daylight, much less after dark. She'd been too busy with the never-ending projects at the old house.

And she'd had a horrendously unsettling couple of days, capped by Gracey's meltdown and John Smith's outing himself as Thomas Ingram Griffin. She wasn't quite sure if she believed him or not. All she knew was that she was scared shitless, and the one thing she wanted to do was get back home safely and lock the doors behind her.

At least Doc was there. The lying, treacherous snake who'd rented the Whitten house wouldn't dare try to break in with him there. Not that Doc was that magnificent a specimen as a bodyguard, but he was enough. Griffin wouldn't come anywhere near her.

She stopped her useless wanderings, heat flushing her face and roiling in her stomach. She had slept with him. Made love with him. Had sex with him. Fucked him. It was crazy, stupid, self-destructive, unbelievable. And she couldn't stop thinking about it, couldn't stop remembering the way his hands felt on her skin, the way he felt inside her.

She let out a useless little whimper. She'd somehow gotten off the main path and was now smack-dab in a thicket that unfortunately seemed to consist of thorny berry bushes. They caught at her hair, her clothes, scratched her hands as she tried to shield her face, but the more she floundered around, the deeper she got in the tangle.

She knew he was there seconds before he spoke, though she wasn't quite sure where he was standing. "If you hold still I'll get you out of there," Griffin said.

"I'm fine." She couldn't tell if he was behind her or ahead of her—but she knew it was no use trying to escape from him.

"I thought you were a bear caught in the bushes," he drawled. "You make enough noise for one."

"Go away or I'll scream."

"And what's that supposed to accomplish? No one will hear you out here—the trees muffle any noise, and the wind's heading toward the lake. They might hear something down at the village beach, but by the time it reaches there any kind of cry will be too faint. Someone will probably just think it's a loon."

She could hear him moving closer, though she still couldn't see him. She tried to free herself, but her skirt was caught in the tangle of thorns, and the branches were pulling at her hair when she reached down to try to release herself.

"Hold still," he said, closer. "You'll hurt yourself."

She could see him now in the moonlight, hear a snicking kind of sound as he approached her, and the tangled thicket fell away as if by magic as he loomed up in the dark. And then he was there, surrounded by the thorns, and she saw how he'd gotten there so easily.

He'd cut his way in with the hunting knife he held in his hand. It glinted silver in the moonlight, not stained with blood and rust like the one she'd found in Grace's drawer. It was a new one. Maybe this was the first time he'd get to use it.

She tried to back away from him, but the bushes

were all around her, trapping her. The moon was bright overhead, and she could see him quite clearly, the calm efficiency, the determination as he sliced his way toward her with that huge, sharp blade.

And he'd be able to see the total panic in her eyes as he finally reached her, and the glittering knife slashed through the night. She opened her mouth to scream, but the only sound that came out was a breathless, terrified squeak.

19

"That sounds like the noise you make when you come," he said in a conversational voice, slashing away at the branches trapping her. She heard the ripping sound of fabric as he sliced through the long hem of her skirt, but she couldn't even utter a protest, just stood there frozen as he cut around her.

And then she was free of the branches. With Griffin blocking her avenue of escape, his eyes glittering like the blade of the knife. "Come on," he said.

"That's not the way I got here," she said with a croak.

"No, you took the long way. I came in by the gazebo."

"What gazebo?"

He didn't answer, she didn't move. After a moment he lifted his arm, and she closed her eyes, expecting the knife to slash down. Instead he grabbed her hand and began hauling her through the rough path he'd cleared.

He was moving too quickly, and she had a hard time keeping up with him, but she knew she had no choice. Maybe once they were out in the open she'd be able to escape. Doc wasn't that far away—he could help her. She just needed the moonlight to guide her.

The damned moon went behind a cloud, plunging them into darkness. She stumbled after him, falling against him, as she stepped free of the thorny bushes.

He caught her, both hands on her arms, and she wondered where the knife had gone. He didn't release her, and his grip was strong, holding her, keeping her from escaping. She couldn't tell whether it was threatening or protecting.

Moonlight, she prayed silently. Just a tiny bit of moonlight, enough to guide her away from this frightening man, back to safety. That was all she needed. Please God, some moonlight.

As if on cue, the moon came out again, bright and clear, and there was no way she could get away from him. They were at the edge of a small clearing, a spot she'd never seen even in her exploratory walks. A long picnic table sat in the middle of the space, though the chairs were gone, and the turrets of a fanciful gazebo loomed against the night sky.

"You're a mess," he said, pulling her into the open space. "This is getting to be a habit."

"What is?" She sounded just as normal as he did. Bizarre, she thought distantly.

"Rescuing you."

"Is that what this is? A rescue? I thought you were trying to kill me. Did you change your mind?"

"I was trying to scare some sense into you," he said. His grip on her arms tightened suddenly, almost painfully, as he lifted her and set her on the picnic table. And then he let go of her, and if he'd just move, just turn his back for a moment, she could run...

"I wouldn't try it if I were you," he said, reading her mind. "This place is hard enough to get out of in the daylight, even if you're used to it. You run off again and I'll end up cutting your entire dress off. Which isn't such a bad idea at that. Feel free to go for it," he said helpfully, stepping back.

She looked down at her dress. It was now officially a rag—the hem was ripped and tattered around her long legs. She'd lost her shoes in her mad dash for the bushes, but at least she'd spent a lot of time barefoot that summer. Her feet would survive.

That is, if the rest of her did. She tried to take a calming breath, but it was hard going. Her heart was still racing, her breath coming unevenly from her crazy dash through the brambles, and the man looming over her in the silvery moonlight didn't inspire her with serenity. Particularly when he had a knife tucked in his belt.

He saw her looking at it, and a faintly ironic smile lit his face. He held it out to her. "Would it make you feel safer if you held on to this?"

"I don't think it would be much of a defense against you if you decided to hurt me. You're a lot bigger than I am, and faster."

"Yes," he agreed, not terribly reassuring. "But you'd cause some damage, and when they investigated your murder I'd be a prime suspect. It would be difficult to explain away the physical evidence. That's what got me the first time."

His calm words made the situation even more macabre. She couldn't be sitting here in the moonlight, conversing with a killer. Could she? He seemed perfectly ready to convince her that she was.

"Did you?" she asked suddenly.

"Did I what?"

"Did you kill those women? Any of them?"

He hesitated. "And you actually think I'll tell you the truth? That all you have to do is ask me?"

She thought about it for a moment. He was threatening her, with body language if not with the knife, trapping her against the picnic table. There were no witnesses, no one to know where she was. If he was a crazed killer, then the only way she'd survive was to be very, very careful. Asking him leading questions wasn't the smartest thing in the world.

She looked up at him. The moon was behind his head, casting his face into a canvas of light and shadows. His brooding eyes were hidden in the dark, but she already knew the expression that would be in them. His mouth was twisted in a cool smile, but she knew that mouth. Knew the taste of it. Wanted to taste it again.

And then she knew, with an absolute certainty she seldom possessed. The man looming over her, trapping her, might very well be Thomas Griffin, convicted murderer. But he'd never killed anyone, even in a drug-dazed rage. She could feel it in her bones.

"Yes," she said.

"Yes what?"

"Yes, I think all I have to do is ask you," she said patiently.

His mocking grin faltered for a moment. And then he nodded. "All right," he said. "I'll tell you. I don't know for sure. I was drunk, stoned in a haze I can't even begin to penetrate. I found her body in the toolshed. But I don't have any proof."

His voice was flat, unemotional, and the words should have chilled her. But they didn't.

She was suddenly in a perfect oasis of calm and quiet. The soft breeze from the lake had stilled, the moon hung bright overhead, and the only sound was their breathing.

Back at the inn her mother had slipped over the edge into a completely delusional state. Her younger sister was off somewhere, probably corrupting the morals of the only decent teenage boy left in Colby, and she was alone with a convicted murderer who just happened to be the first and only man she'd ever made love with.

And was about to make love with again. She knew it, in her heart, her stomach, between her legs. And she wasn't going to do anything to stop it. She was going to start it, because it was inevitable, because she wanted it, because she was out of her mind. The reasons didn't matter.

"I don't believe you killed anyone," she said.

He was singularly unimpressed by her declaration. "Prove it."

How could she feel so calm and so nervous at the same time? So certain and so afraid of what she was about to do? "I can't prove you didn't do it," she said. "I can only prove that I don't believe it." And she put her hands on his shoulders, drawing him down to her mouth.

He didn't resist, he simply braced his hands on the picnic table and let her brush her lips across his. She'd been expecting a more enthusiastic response, and she pulled back, quizzical.

"Honey," he drawled, "that ain't trust and it ain't true love. That's about sex, pure and simple."

It took her only a moment to rally. "And do I strike you as the kind of woman who has sex with a man who murders women? I haven't been known for my high-risk behavior."

"Being around me is high-risk enough," he muttered.

She looked at him, cynical, angry, irresistible, and she smiled. She couldn't help it. "Honey," she said

in a perfect mimic of his drawl, "you're trying awfully hard to be a bad boy. I'm just having a hard
time believing it, despite all your romantic brooding.
So answer me just one question. Do you think you
killed them?"

He stared at her, probably astonished at her calm
cheer. "No," he said finally.

She nodded, satisfied. "And do you want to go
back to the house and make love with me?" Her
heart was pounding. She knew she'd said it, knew
she wanted it, but hearing the words out loud, in her
voice, was shocking.

Not as shocking as his answer. "No," he said.

She felt the color drain from her face. She'd never
been so horribly embarrassed in her life, and she had
no idea what to say. Something breezy, casual, dis-
missing him, as well. Instead she sat on the picnic
table looking at him like a wounded puppy.

"I want to fuck you right here," he said simply.

Marty tried to keep the pout from her face as Patrick drove down the winding drive to the lake. It
had been a perfect night, from the flowers to the
dinner in Stowe to the drive home. They talked. She
wasn't used to talking with boys, and she and Patrick Laflamme had nothing in common. He was
from the country, hard-working, ambitious, moral to
the point of being judgmental. She was a city girl,
looking for a good time, which he was clearly not

about to provide her. And yet she found herself telling him things she hadn't told anyone in years.

He pulled up in front of the house, and she gathered her slightly bedraggled flowers in her hand and reached for the door. He'd assured her there wasn't going to be a good-night kiss, but she still was reluctant to leave him.

"I had..." She was about to say "a wonderful time," but that sounded too coy or too gushing. "An okay time," she finished, trying to sound jaded. "Thank you for the flowers."

"I got them from Doc," he said with a faint grin. He really did have the most delicious-looking mouth. He was wearing a jacket and tie—never in her life had she gone out with someone in a tie. She liked the novelty of it. "I didn't want to tell you since you said Doc creeps you out, but he said he heard we were going out and wanted me to take the flowers to make a good impression. I didn't tell him I'd already planned to bring you flowers."

"And you didn't tell him I didn't need impressing, either, did you?" Marty said. "You probably told him you had to beat me away with a baseball bat."

"If I had beat you away, then I wouldn't have asked you out, would I?"

There was no answer she could make to that, so she simply sat there in silence. He said nothing, as well, as if he didn't want to break the moment, either.

But they couldn't sit there forever, and he wasn't going to kiss her. She fumbled for the door handle, only to have the spotless truck cab flood with light as he opened his own door and got out, then walked around to open her door for her. He even gave her a hand to help her down from the high seat of the truck. The outside lights were on, and she caught him looking at her legs. Admiring them. At this point it was the best she could hope for.

She slid out of the truck and he shut the door behind her, but to her surprise he started up the hill to the porch, holding her hand.

Someone was watching them from the windows. Grace couldn't be bothered—it was probably Sophie, making sure her sister didn't get into trouble.

She liked his hand in hers. His hands were big, strong, callused, and yet amazingly gentle. She liked everything about him.

They reached the porch, the orangeish glow of the light swarming with tiny bugs. "Uh...you can't come in," she said nervously. "Sophie would kill me. If you want to go to your place..."

He did have the loveliest smile. "I told you, Marthe," he said patiently. "I'm not interested in sex without commitment."

"Oh, yeah," she said, shifting nervously. "And no kissing until the third date." He was still holding her hand, and she felt strange, awkward, as she broke his grip, transferred the flowers and reached out to shake his hand. It felt stupid, but she didn't know what else to do, how else to end the evening that she didn't want to end. "You have too many rules, Patrick. Don't you ever make exceptions?"

"There's only one thing that would get me to kiss a girl on a first date," he said. "If I was falling in love with her."

"Well, then, I guess I'm flat out of luck...." Her words were silenced by his mouth on hers.

It was quite a kiss for such a well-behaved young man. No groping hands, but he didn't need to. He was a very good kisser. Maybe the best she'd ever kissed. And then she stopped thinking and kissed him back.

When he drew away she stared at him, confused, entranced, half crazy. "See you tomorrow, Marthe," he said cheerfully, and bounded off the porch.

She could see the grin on his face as he got into the truck and drove away. He was pretty pleased with himself, she thought. Well, she was pretty damned pleased with him, as well.

She stayed on the porch until his taillights disappeared into the night, then she opened the kitchen door, ready to face her disapproving, eavesdropping sister.

Doc was sitting at the kitchen table, alone, a cup of coffee beside him, a genial expression on his face.

"Hello, Marty," he greeted her warmly.

And then she saw the gun.

Griffin liked the expression of outrage on Sophie's pale face. Hell, he liked everything about her,
from her surprisingly long, gorgeous legs beneath
the tattered skirt to her lush breasts. He liked her
full, sweet mouth, he liked her soft, clever hands,
and he wanted them on his body.

He pulled off his T-shirt. There was no such thing
as a warm night in August in Vermont, but it was
close enough, and the slightly cool air touching his
skin merely made him hotter.

"What are you doing?"

"Guess," he said, reaching for his zipper.

She let out a protesting shriek. "I didn't say I
would."

He unfastened the button, letting the zipper ride
over his erection as he reached for her. "You didn't
need to," he said, unbuttoning the row of tiny buttons down the front of that stupid thing she was
wearing. The buttons went all the way to the ripped
hem, and it required great concentration to undo
them all, when he wanted nothing more than to rip
them off and pull her across the table and wrap her
legs around his hips. "Just once," he said under his
breath, "I would like to see you in something
skimpy. Something that clings to your body and
doesn't end at your goddamn ankles." He reached

the last button, and spread open the jumper, only to find a ruffled petticoat beneath it.

He cursed. "This is like trying to strip a nun. What am I going to find next, a chastity belt?"

"A little late for that," she said in a shaky voice.

She was still frightened of him. Not afraid that he was a killer, but afraid of sex. Of him making love to her, even though she wanted it almost as much as he did. Hell, she had to want it, since she was still here and hadn't run screaming into the woods again.

He slid his hands up her legs, slowly, beneath the ruffled petticoat, and her eyes widened. She made a soft, gasping noise when he reached her hips. He was half expecting bloomers, or at least some enveloping cotton panties. Instead his hands reached thin strips of silk.

He pushed the petticoat up to her waist, exposing what looked like white-lace thong panties. "Now, that's more like it," he said. "Come here." He pulled her off the table, into his arms, and began to strip the layers of clothes off her and toss them on the table.

He found her bra to be as stimulating as her almost-nonexistent panties. Her breasts were magnificent—there was no other word for them. Full, luscious globes of pearly satin, spilling out of the lacy cups of her bra. It would have been enough to finish a lesser man.

He left the underwear on her. After all, she'd worn it for a purpose, and he had every intention of putting it to good use. "Get up on the table," he said, his voice tense.

She did, dressed only in her skimpy lace underwear, and she gave him a worried look. He leaned forward and nipped her lace-covered breast with his mouth, careful not to use his teeth.

Her nipples were hard beneath the lace and he licked her, feeling the bud tighten beneath his tongue. She was trembling. He looked at her in the moonlight, all ripe, abundant, silvery flesh, her hair flowing to her shoulders, her eyes dark with worried desire.

"Lie down."

"Why?"

"You'll see."

She lay back on the blanket of discarded clothes, wearily, helped by his slight push, and she closed her eyes to the bright moon overhead.

And opened them again when he touched her. Her panties were slightly damp now. He wanted her wet with need.

The panties were going to have to go, much to his dismay. And the bra—the satin and lace were exciting, but not nearly as delicious as her skin.

The bra fastened in front, and he wondered if she'd worn it on purpose. He unfastened it, though he would have had no trouble with a back clasp, and her breasts spilled free in the moonlight, the rosy tips beaded with desire.

He was momentarily distracted from his eventual goal. He climbed onto the table, feeling it rock slightly beneath his weight, and caught her breast in his mouth, sucking at it, letting his tongue scrape against the distended nipple.

He could make her come that way, he thought. Hell, he could make her come in any number of ways, any number of times, and he had every intention of doing so. Right now he didn't want to think about death and murder, about the blood-soaked past or the doubtful future. He didn't want to think about any other woman. He just wanted to lose himself in the scent and sound of this woman, the taste and texture of her, the rare, impossible delight of disappearing into pure sensation and bringing her with him. He'd never needed sex, never needed a woman, *this* woman, so desperately.

He ran his tongue down her stomach as he slid his hands beneath the thin strips that held her underwear on. He knew exactly where he was headed, and she wouldn't like it, at least not at first. And then she'd like it very much indeed.

She let out a soft murmur of protest as he slid the panties off her long legs, but he ignored her. What the hell did she expect? He needed her naked, needed her now, and he wasn't about to wait any longer.

He unzipped his jeans, freeing himself in the moonlight, and the feel of the cool air on his cock was a sharp delight. Not as good as her hot, damp body would feel, though, taking him deep inside.

Her hips bucked when he kissed the soft curls that protected her. And then he slid his tongue down against her clitoris, and she practically exploded.

She grabbed his head, and he half expected her to pull his hair in an attempt to move him, but somewhere along the way she changed her mind, and her fingers slid through his hair and her hips softened beneath his grip.

She came immediately, almost a disappointment, since he wanted to make it last. It was just a small climax, and he knew he could do better, so he ignored her efforts to tug him away, returning to his task with renewed dedication.

The next one was better, and he could prolong it for her, with his tongue, his lips, even his teeth, until she was sobbing and gasping for breath.

He'd wanted to get her to use her mouth on him—he'd been obsessed with the fantasy since he first noticed her full, lush mouth, but by now it no longer mattered. All that mattered was being inside her.

He pulled away from her, wiping his mouth on his arm, and reached for the condom he had in the pocket of his jeans. He had three of them with him, and he wasn't sure they'd be enough. He couldn't imagine ever having enough of her.

He tore the packet open with his teeth, ready to sheath himself in latex, and then in the sweet folds of her body, when she reached up and took the open packet from him.

He let her, though her hands were trembling, and she was struggling to breathe evenly. He was on his knees beside her, on the table, his cock jutting out straight and hard, and he expected his Victorian virgin to cover her eyes and shriek in horror.

Instead she touched him, and he almost came in her cool, soft hands. He couldn't stifle his agonized groan, and she quickly pulled back.

"Did I hurt you?"

He took her hand and put it back on his cock, wrapping her fingers around its thick length. "No," he said, moving her hand, showing her what he wanted.

It was sheer torment, exquisite pain, but he had himself under control again, and he could stand it, savor it, the awkward tug of her hand on him.

She moved, and he opened his eyes to see her lean over and kiss the coiled snake on his hip. And then she closed her mouth over the head of his cock, her tongue quicksilver light, tasting him, sucking at him, until he knew he couldn't hold out a moment longer. He needed to be inside her, now, or he'd fill her hungry mouth with his seed.

He touched her, and she came again at his touch, her mouth pulling at him.

He was beyond gentleness. He shoved her back against the blanket of clothes and moved between her legs.

He went in hard, fast, deep, only barely able to control himself. She wrapped her legs around his, and he reached down and pulled them higher, up around his hips, so that he was deeper still, and she was tight, clasping, milking him with the power of her climax, which was almost sweetly painful.

He'd had a vain hope that he could hold out, but he was past any chance of self-control, and he followed her, filling her, spilling deep inside her before collapsing on top of her.

He wasn't sure when he realized what he'd done. The condom lay forgotten, unused. The feel of her mouth on him had wiped the last vestiges of rational thought from his brain, and he hadn't remembered.

"Shit," he muttered. It was the first time he'd forgotten in fifteen years. The woman beneath him made him as randy and stupid as a teenage boy. "Shit," he said again.

"Please, don't" came her weary voice. "It's really disheartening to have your reaction to making love to me always be the word 'shit.' Couldn't you go for something a bit more positive, like 'well, that was pleasant,' instead of cursing?"

He was still inside her, still partially erect. Or maybe he was getting hard all over again. Anything was possible with this witchy woman.

"Shucks, we may just have to do it again." And he bumped his hips against hers, so she could feel his cock still hard inside her.

Her eyes widened in the moonlight. "That's not supposed to happen."

"Says you from your vast experience. Trust me, with you and me all things are possible when it comes to making love."

"I thought it was fucking."

He had to kiss her. The word sounded absurd coming from her soft mouth, but then, she'd shown herself to be surprisingly adaptable with that mouth. He kissed her, and he felt an answering shimmer of response from deep inside her.

He almost said "shit" again, but decided to spare her. Besides, he had more important things on his mind right then.

He took his sweet time, and nothing would make him rush it, not her breathless requests, her choked begging. He got her to straddle him, and she arched over him like a magnificent warrior goddess, and this time when she came she couldn't stop crying, collapsing on top of him, her limp body racked by hoarse sobs.

His usual style with crying women was to beat a hasty retreat until they got over it. With Sophie he simply wrapped his arms around her, pulling her closer to his body, and stroked her hair until the sobs died away and she fell asleep.

It was a hell of a place to sleep, Griffin thought lazily. A hell of a place to have sex. Right now they could be in his comfortable bed back at the cottage, not lying on a hard surface in the middle of the woods, buck naked.

He ought to wake her, drag her back to the cottage to finish the night in comfort. But he couldn't move. Didn't want to move. The smell of the lake and the pine trees and the cool mountain air surrounded him, and for the first time in twenty years he was at peace.

With the hard wood of the table hurting his back, with Sophie's hair tickling his nose, with a mosquito biting his butt, he felt almost...happy.

He wasn't used to it, he didn't trust it. But for right now he had no interest in fighting it.

He simply closed his eyes and waited, listening to the sounds of the night, while sweet, soft Sophie slept safely in his arms.

20

Doc hadn't meant to hit her so hard. He had a long night ahead of him, and he didn't want to rush things. He hummed beneath his breath as he carried her through the rubble-strewn hallways of the old hospital annex. She barely weighed anything, and Doc was a strong man. It was easy enough to toss her over his shoulder and make his way through the candlelit passage.

The electricity had been turned off long ago. He wasn't surprised—the wiring dated from the early part of the century, with exposed black wires and white porcelain insulators up near the ceilings. It was one of the reasons the hospital had been closed in the first place—the danger and the cost of replacing the electricity. Sophie had told him she planned to open the place, fix up the rooms when she could afford it. In the meantime it was tightly sealed, so no one could get in.

She hadn't bothered to board up the main door, relying on the substantial locks that were still there. And of course he had the key.

Marty groaned, and Doc quickened his step, heading down the narrow wooden stairs to the old hospital kitchen. It wasn't the first time he'd used the place, but it would be the last. He was going to finish the night in a blaze of glory. Like the fireworks over the lake on the Fourth of July, he thought fondly. A final burst of multiple rockets and then all would be silent.

He'd killed three in one night, long, long ago. He preferred to take his time, choose his subjects carefully, but twenty years ago Lorelei, Valette and Alice had given him no choice.

Valette had come to him first, bleeding from a botched abortion. He'd used the knife on her, a fitting justice. And her father never had to know that his daughter was capable of such a great crime. Alice had shown up a few hours later, looking for her missing friend, her makeup smudged, her hair mussed, smelling of sex and sin.

And then he went hunting for Lorelei, the third of the town whores, determined to finish it all, finish God's work, and take his punishment.

It hadn't worked out that way. No one even guessed that he was the one who'd dispensed justice. No one had known Lorelei was coming to visit him except Valette. No one had seen any of the girls in hours. Except that hellion who worked up at his sister's place.

He'd never meant for anyone else to take the credit for his work. He'd acted wisely, sparingly before that dark night twenty years ago, and he'd always felt a certain pride in his deeds. But the Lord worked in mysterious ways, and the boy had appeared guilty as sin. He was, of course. Guilty, sin-ridden, a thousand crimes on his young, twisted soul. Murder would have followed soon enough—he was simply paying for his crimes ahead of time.

Since then he'd been careful, more selective, and no one had ever guessed there was any connection between Abby Ling's car accident, Sara Ann Whitten's disappearance and Doc's frequent trips out of town.

Tonight there would be four of them. Three were sinners, all in one tainted family. He should have known there was deep wickedness there. He'd chosen Marty at first glance, knowing she had come to Colby to be cleansed of her sin by sword and fire. He had no idea the wickedness ran clear through the family, striking the witless mother, even devouring sweet Sophie. She would be better off dead than living in whoredom. It was only his duty.

And Rima. She lay in her bed at home, her sightless eyes staring out into the night. She'd wept when he told her. He couldn't make her understand that this was his calling. He brought life into the world, and he took it from them when necessary. It was his love for humanity that made him do it. Wickedness must be sought out and destroyed. Surely she understood that?

But she didn't. He knew his saintly Rima hadn't been corrupted—after all, she'd suffered as he had, the loss of their unborn children, blameless infants destined never to walk this vale of tears. The last one had been the hardest. This was the pregnancy that lasted, though Rima had grown sicker and sicker. And when she'd gone into labor two months early, she'd given birth to a monstrosity that had damaged her internally, so severely that she was never well again. And he'd buried the loathsome thing in the cemetery by the village, weeping, as he heard the tramp shriek with laughter from the public beach, mocking him. And he'd known what he had to do.

He'd silenced her laughter. Not that night, when he longed to, but later, when she came to him complaining of headaches. June's headaches came from her vain refusal to wear glasses, but the town had taken Doc's diagnosis of a fatal brain aneurysm with sorrow and acceptance. And he'd followed God's work ever since.

He thought Rima knew. He'd never told her, not wanting to share the burden. And it *was* a burden—death was a grievous thing to hand out, when he'd been trained to save lives. But there was no turning his back on his destiny, whether he wanted it or not. This duty had been placed on his shoulders, and he had no choice but to carry it out.

He'd always thought Rima would understand.

Even knew, deep in her heart, what he did when he went off to the cities of New England and came home weary and grieving. He took no pleasure in killing, only righteous justification.

But he never thought he'd kill Rima. He'd sat by her bed, his head bowed, hands clasped, as he made his confession. This would be the final night—he was going up to the inn and finish his work. Destroy the last nest of vipers in their community, and then take society's punishment. He had no illusions that the courts would understand.

There was always the chance that once more Thomas Griffin would be suspected. Doc had recognized him the first moment he'd seen him in Audley's General Store, and he'd been half tempted to do something about it.

If he'd known the man would corrupt Sophie he wouldn't have hesitated. He'd grieved over that mistake, though in truth he knew that if Griffin was able to corrupt her, then someone else would have done the same. She was ripe for temptation, another fallen angel, doomed to the sins of the flesh. He knew she would have to join her younger sister, and the others.

It was the mother who'd fooled him. He knew she'd lived a sinful life, but madness had touched her, and he thought it was punishment enough. But her madness had brought her special knowledge, and she'd known who he was and what he did. And he'd known she would have to join the children.

He set the candle he was carrying on the rubble-strewn counter and shifted his burden. She moaned again, but she didn't wake. He opened the walk-in cooler, and the stale air rushed past him, making the candlelight sputter and waver. Grace was still where he'd left her, sitting in one of the abandoned cane wheelchairs, her thin hands tied to the armrests, her head sunk low on her chest. He set Marty's unconscious figure down on the floor and moved to Grace's side, suddenly worried. Things weren't going as he'd planned. He might accidentally have given Grace a lethal dose of the powerful sedative. He might have fractured Marty's skull when he brought the gun down on her black-and-pink-streaked hair. Whore's hair, streaked now with blood.

But Grace's breathing was even. She was just knocked out, as he'd wanted. Nothing more. And Marty moved restlessly, still alive. He needed them alive. And he needed Sophie with them. He needed them to feel the bite of the flame as it cleansed their souls and sent them to heaven.

He had no doubts that that was where they would go. He was cleansing them of their sin, sending them on so they would live in eternal blessedness and never know sorrow or pain or wickedness again. His mission weighed heavily on him, but he'd never shunned it. Even when he'd had to put the pillow down on Rima's face to keep her from calling out, keep the screams from echoing over the peaceful village streets of Colby.

He had felt the tears running down his face when he'd finally pulled the pillow away. She didn't look peaceful, and it troubled him. He'd been tempted to bring her body with him, up to the inn, to join in the conflagration, but that would have looked too strange, and he was still waiting to see whether or not the Lord would once more rescue him from discovery. If so, he would simply state that Rima had had a fatal heart attack, and no one would question him. They knew his devotion.

He set the candle on the floor of the cooler. The room wasn't quite airless, and he doubted they'd suffocate. He didn't want them frightened of the dark. After all, they were facing a long journey, and he wished them no ill. He was doing this for them.

He closed the door to the walk-in cooler and stepped back. If either of them regained consciousness they could scream for help and no one would ever hear them. He knew that already—no one had ever heard Valette's screams.

He couldn't leave them in there, of course. The heavy metal walls would preserve their bodies from the cleansing fire. He'd have to bring them back out, into the makeshift chapel, and say prayers over them.

He wrinkled his nose. He didn't like the smell of gasoline—never had. But it worked the best for fires, and he didn't require that much. He'd been siphoning it out of his old truck for weeks now, the truck he'd used to try to drive Sophie off the road, so that no one would know where the gasoline came from. It would burn hot and fast and bright; there was no way the volunteer fire department could get there in time.

He walked back up the narrow stairs, whistling. All he had to do was wait for Sophie to reappear, and the night could reach its inevitable conclusion.

It only took him a few minutes to walk back through the darkened hall of the hospital. He'd been born in that building, some seventy-six years ago. He'd brought five hundred and thirty-three babies into the world—he never lost count of that number. It was only fitting that he should end this way.

There was no sign of Sophie when he reached the kitchen, shutting the door to the abandoned wing closed again. He knew where she was, he knew what she was doing. The greater the sin, the greater the repentance. He picked up the sprig of Judas tears and turned it in his hand.

Soon, he promised himself. Soon.

Marty heard the voice buzzing in her head. She didn't want to listen, she just wanted to sleep. Why were people always trying to interfere with her sleep? Was it so much to ask...?

"Marty! Wake up, child!"

She considered her options. She recognized Grace's voice, but Grace was the last person she wanted to talk to. She was also lying on something hard and disagreeable, and her head hurt like hell, and she made the mistake of opening her eyes.

"Oh, shit!" she said.

"Indeed," Grace said in a grim voice. "Untie my wrists, will you? That crazy old bastard drugged me and I can't move."

Grace's voice was sharp and cool, unlike her usual dreamy tones, and Marty struggled to sit up, peering at her through the gloomy candlelight. They were in some sort of dark, windowless room, and Grace was looking at her with thinly veiled impatience.

"Are you crazy?" Marty demanded.

"As a matter of fact, I'm not," Grace said in the brisk tone no one had heard in months. "I had the good sense to recognize that Doc was the Northeast Kingdom murderer. Not that any of you would listen. I tried to warn you all."

Marty began untying the straps around Grace's thin wrists. "Why didn't you just tell us, you stupid old cow?"

"Because I had no proof. The only thing I had was a knife I was sure he'd used. I found it in one of the old hospital rooms, and I was trying to figure out how to have it tested when someone stole it from me. I had no choice but to pretend to be as spacey as I could to keep Doc busy and away from the two of you. I should have known it wouldn't last forever.''

''Doc's a killer?'' Marty said in slow disbelief.

''He didn't hit you that hard, Marty. He kills women—God knows how many he's murdered over the years. I don't know why—maybe some kind of Jack the Ripper complex. Why doesn't matter. What does is that he's dangerous.''

''And he's got us both locked up in here.''

''But he doesn't have Sophie. With any luck she's off with that young man, and he'll have figured out what's going on.''

''Why should Mr. Smith care?''

''Because he's not Mr. Smith, you little ninny. He's the boy who was convicted of the murders twenty years ago. The rest of you were too dumb to recognize him, but I could tell right away. I even left a copy of the old newspaper with his picture in it so Sophie would find it and figure it out. But she didn't.'' Grace's voice was sharp with disgust. ''I told her she should read the books I read. She would have picked up on it in a flash.''

Marty shivered, suddenly afraid. She didn't want to die. Not with Patrick Laflamme's kiss still sweet on her mouth. "What are we going to do, Gracey?" she asked in a meek voice.

Grace slid out of the chair, putting her arms around Marty's shivering body. "I'll tell you one thing, love. I'm not going to let him hurt you. I promise you that."

Grace's thin arms held her tightly, but Marty had no illusions. Grace's mind might be clear as a bell, but she was still only a slender, middle-aged woman. If it came to a showdown between her and Doc, there was no question who would win.

But she didn't say anything. She just hugged Grace back. "Sophie's gonna kill you when she finds out you were faking," she muttered.

"That's the least of my worries right now," Grace said with ghoulish complacency. "She'll forgive me."

"I just hope she gets the chance," Marty said gloomily.

"She will, love. She will."

Griffin didn't sleep. The moon scudded behind the clouds, spreading a shadow over the clearing, and he felt a sudden chill. The evening had grown cooler, and in a few minutes he'd be freezing his ass off. As would Sophie, since her delectable ass was still pointing upward as she sprawled across his body.

He wasn't about to move her, wake her up. Her

skin was cooling, but she seemed so peaceful that he didn't want anything to change that. And then she sneezed, twice, lifting her head to stare at him.

"Something bit my butt," she said.

"It wasn't me. Not that I wouldn't be more than happy to, but you've been lying on top of me...." Before he could finish his sentence she'd rolled off him, scampering off the picnic table too fast for him to stop her. He could have kicked himself.

"Where are my clothes?" she asked in a worried voice, not looking at him now, intent on searching the night-shrouded clearing.

Damned shame about the moon, he thought, sitting up. He could still see her fairly clearly in the night—her pale skin and lush curves moved through the shadows with hurried grace. He reached behind him for the scattered clothing, tossing the petticoat in her direction.

"Here you go," he said amiably.

She pulled it on, and she looked quite fetching bare-breasted, barefooted in a white lacy petticoat. He really hated giving up the bra, but she was holding out her hand, so he handed the rest of her clothes over to her, with the exception of the skimpy panties. He saw his jeans come flying at him, and he caught them before they hit him in the face. He'd had every intention of walking back to the house bare-assed, but Sophie clearly had other ideas, and he climbed off the table and pulled them on. As he moved, the unused condom fell on the ground, and he just barely stifled a groan.

"What's wrong?" she said sharply.

"Nothing. Where do you think you're going?" It was a simple-enough question.

"Back home, of course. I need to check on my mother."

"Your sister can look after your mother. We haven't finished."

"We haven't?" she said, momentarily distracted. "What else were we going to do?"

"Well, I thought we could try it standing up...."

"I didn't mean that," she said hastily. "Besides, we don't need to do it tonight."

"I do," he said. "Your mother's sound asleep, Sophie. Wouldn't you like to do it in a bed for a change? Mattresses have a number of advantages, not the least of which is it's easier on the knees. Yours and mine."

He didn't need the moonlight to know she was blushing. "Come on, Sophie," he said softly. "You know you want to."

She was wavering, he knew it. He'd managed to turn a prim-and-proper spinster into a healthy animal almost as hungry as he was. He wanted her in his bed, now.

"I can't," she said. "My mother had a bad spell tonight, and Doc's watching her. I have to make sure Marty's home and that Grace is sleeping. And Doc should be able to go home and take care of Rima, and…''

''Go check on them and come back to me. They'll be fine. And when you do, find something slinky to wear,'' he said wickedly. ''It's a crime to keep covering yourself up in those stupid ruffles.''

''I like ruffles.''

''You're crazy,'' he said flatly.

''Actually, it's my mother who really went crazy tonight, accusing people of murder, saying that the flowers were talking to her.''

A sudden chill settled over him that had nothing to do with the dropping temperature. ''Flowers?''

''Doc brought me some pretty yellow flowers, and Grace started insisting that the flowers were talking to her, telling her he was a murderer. Sweet old Doc, who wouldn't hurt a flea.''

''Sweet old Doc,'' Griffin echoed in a hollow voice.

''I really have to check on her,'' Sophie said. ''But I'll come back.''

''Sure,'' Griffin said absently, his brain working feverishly. Pretty yellow flowers, in Sophie's kitchen, on the graves of the women who'd died. Pretty yellow flowers talking to crazy old women, telling them who killed.

He didn't even notice when she left. He was trying to remember something, and it kept eluding him. He couldn't even begin to guess what it was, he only knew it was important. A matter of life and death. And if he didn't capture that long-lost memory then disaster would flow down over all of them. One more time.

He looked up and realized Sophie was gone. She was going to be pissed, he thought. She wouldn't like the fact that he'd gone off into some kind of trance, ignoring her. He wouldn't be surprised if she went home, locked the doors to keep him out and went straight to bed, furious with him.

He'd learned more than prelaw in prison. He'd learned how to hot-wire cars and jimmy most locks. As soon as he figured out what was preying on his mind he'd pay Miss Sophie Davis a little moonlight visit. Her bed was as good as his for what he had in mind, though she was going to have to be a little quieter when he made her come. Which he intended to do, any number of times.

He headed back to the cottage, making his way through the dark woods unerringly. He hoped Sophie hadn't gotten lost again, but he imagined he'd hear her if she did. She was about as delicate as a stampeding elephant.

He chuckled to himself. She wouldn't like that comparison. She didn't seem to have the faintest idea how completely gorgeous she was. It was a crime to hide a body as fine as hers in all those layers. Though he had to admit it kept other men away, making her nicely vulnerable when he showed up.

He'd give her half an hour, and then he was going after her. He took a fast shower, threw on a clean pair of jeans and an old flannel shirt, this time pocketing half a dozen condoms. Nothing like locking the barn door after the horse was stolen, but with any luck they were still safe.

And if they weren't? He wasn't going to go there, not now. He couldn't even begin to think about what his reaction might be, and besides, he had other things occupying his mind, like talking flowers and Doc, and...

It hit him so fast he almost fell over. A shock of memory so intense, so unexpected, that he felt dizzy. He stumbled into a chair by the empty fireplace, staring sightlessly into the ashes.

Lorelei had flowers in her hair. Yellow flowers, that he'd never seen before, and when he'd questioned her, full of adolescent jealousy, she'd laughed and told him she'd gotten them from a gentleman admirer.

Things had gone from bad to worse then. He'd been angry, shouted at her, and she'd shouted back. She'd always had a fondness for rough sex, and that night had been no different, tinged with the knowledge that he was leaving her, getting the hell out of Colby with the morning sun.

She'd scratched him, as she liked to do. They'd

found traces of his skin under her fingernails, even though she'd been in the lake for hours when he'd found her. The yellow flowers had still been tangled in her hair. Her blood-soaked body covered with flowers in the toolshed as he held her and cried. And Doc watched.

He dove for the telephone, panic rushing through him. She said Doc had brought the flowers. Doc, who'd been around from the beginning, who testified against him, who knew everyone and their secrets. Doc with the yellow flowers and the gentle smile. And the murderous hands.

He dialed the old-fashioned phone, thanking God that he'd remembered to scrawl the number of the inn on the old green blotter. The telephone rang on the other end, an odd, hollow ring, and a moment later it clicked.

"Sophie, you've got to…" He didn't get any further, as a recorded voice droned on.

"We're sorry, the number you dialed is out of order. Please try again later."

Griffin stared at the phone in horror. And then he dropped the receiver and ran.

21

Sophie stormed up the hill to the inn, ignoring the pain in her side, the stickiness between her legs, the fury in her heart. How dare that son of a bitch simply forget she was there? How dare he do…what he did and then ignore her? She was going to kill him, it was that simple. Find a gun and shoot him.

Or at least she really really wanted to. She hadn't smacked anyone since John McKinney annoyed her in the fourth grade, but there was murder in her heart, even if it was never going to move past the point of fond desire.

The house was dark, only a faint light on in the kitchen. She wasn't wearing her watch, and she had no idea of how long she'd been out there in the woods with Thomas Griffin. Griffin with the snake tattooed on his hip. Griffin the convicted killer, who hadn't killed anyone.

Doc's car was nowhere to be seen. Marty must have come home a while ago. Doc would have headed home to take care of Rima, and Gracey would be sleeping her drugged, peaceful sleep.

Everything was fine, she told herself as she

climbed the steps to the porch. She'd just check on Grace, make sure she was sleeping peacefully, and then she'd take a shower and go to bed. And plan revenge on that lying, insensitive prick that she'd fallen in love with.

The moment the thought danced in her mind she kicked it out, angrily. If that was love she didn't want anything to do with it. It was nothing more than healthy, normal sex, it meant absolutely nothing, and she was out of her mind if she was going to start making up romantic fantasies about living happily ever after with such a lying, cantankerous pig no matter how tied to him she felt. She was much better off fantasizing about killing him. What's another murder or two in Colby, she thought, reaching for the kitchen door. It wasn't as if they hadn't had them before. Maybe the talking flowers would do it for her.

She pushed open the door and flicked on the light, then stopped. Doc was standing there, covered in dust and cobwebs, looking distraught.

"It's Grace," he cried. "She's disappeared. I don't know how she managed it, but I think she got into the old hospital wing. I've been searching for her, but there's no light, and she might even be hiding. She seems to think I mean her harm."

Panic raced through her, putting her fond thought of revenge on a back burner. "Where's Marty? She could help us look..."

"She's not back from her date."

"Goddamn her!" Sophie exploded. Doc winced, and she knew she should apologize for her language, but somehow she didn't have it in her. "Have you called for help?"

He nodded. "The police are coming out to help us look. They're over in Hampstead, though, and it may take them a while to get here. I'm going back in there and see if I have any more luck."

"I'll come with you," she said.

"Like that?" Doc was glancing at her bare feet and bedraggled gypsy appearance.

"I don't think my mother will care what I look like," Sophie said sharply, then immediately regretted it. She had no business snapping at Doc.

"I mean your bare feet. There's a lot of broken glass, boards with nails littering the place. You'd better get some shoes on." He didn't sound the slightest bit offended, and she took a deep breath. That's what she needed in the midst of this crisis. Calm, sensible Doc.

"Okay," she said. "I'll be right with you."

She stuck her feet in the barn boots she kept by the kitchen door, then headed for the front parlor. "I'll be there in a minute," she called. "I'm just looking for a flashlight."

"Hurry," Doc called urgently, his soft voice deep with worry.

She shouldn't have done it. She was furious with

Griffin, she didn't need his help. But her poor, lost mother did. She picked up the extension and started to dial.

There was no dial tone. She looked down to the baseboard, wondering if it had somehow gotten unplugged. The cord dangled loose, the plastic end crushed.

"Hurry," Doc called again, beginning to sound impatient.

Her yellow flowers were sitting in a bowl on the table when she walked back into the kitchen, the huge, industrial-strength flashlight in her hand. It weighed a ton, and the light it shone was a beacon. The door to the abandoned wing stood open, the door she'd personally nailed closed. Grace wouldn't have been able to open it by herself—it had taken all Sophie's strength to seal it.

She glanced at Doc's sweet, concerned face. She knew where she'd seen those flowers before. And they had to have come from Doc, on the grave of each murdered woman. On her grave, as well, if she let it happen.

She wanted to run. She had a fighting chance—she was closer to the door than he was, and she was faster. She might even be stronger, though she doubted it. Doc was in excellent shape for a man of his age, and he could probably stop her before she could even scream.

She looked at Doc standing patiently in the open

doorway. If she ran, who would save Grace? And Marty? Doc had lied to her about the telephone, lied to her about Grace. He had probably lied to her about Marty, too. And she simply couldn't run off and save herself at the price of her mother and sister.

"Where do you think she is?" Sophie asked calmly, stepping toward him.

"I've checked everywhere but the old kitchen. She might be down there."

That made sense. The kitchen was deep in the belly of the old building. No one would find them if they came looking, no one would hear her scream. She stepped through into the darkness and smelled the sharp, acrid scent of gasoline. And she knew what Doc had in mind.

"Maybe we should go for help," she said, pulling back. "It's awfully dark in here."

He clamped a hand around her elbow, and it was like an iron manacle. He was definitely stronger than she was, Sophie thought. And she was in deep shit.

"We'll find them, Sophie," he said earnestly. "I promise you."

He didn't realize he'd said "them" instead of "her," Sophie thought, letting him pull her along through the rubble. The dust rose around them, eerie in the bright light of the flashlight. She could see a faint glow ahead of her, and the stench of gasoline had grown even stronger.

"What's that light down there?" she asked, stumbling a bit as she tried to keep up with him. Not that she had any choice.

"I left a few candles burning to help us look," he said easily. "I know it's a fire hazard, but I thought it was worth risking. We don't want anything to happen to dear Grace."

"No, we wouldn't want that." She tried to slow him down. "Shouldn't we check the second floor? There are lots of places to hide up there."

Doc gave her a tug. "I already searched. She's not there, I promise you. Come along, Sophie. We'd better hurry."

And she had no choice but to follow him, down the narrow stairs to the basement kitchen, trying to keep the heavy flashlight from shaking. Her mother was down there, probably her sister, as well, and if she didn't go, he'd simply kill them, anyway, either before or after he killed her. Her only chance was to go along with him and try to take him off guard. Running would only ensure that someone would die.

"Coming," she said, gripping the flashlight tightly in one hand.

The basement kitchen looked grim and eerie, like some kind of pagan altar. No, not pagan. There was a tarnished silver crucifix on the old cast-iron stove. Grace and Marty were nowhere in sight, but the door to the walk-in cooler was tightly shut, when Sophie had carefully left it propped open. They had to be in there. The question was, were they already dead? Could they even breathe in that closed interior? Was she too late?

And then she heard it. The sinister crackle of flames, licking through the dry timber overhead. The smoke was rising, sucking the air from the cellar with it. Doc must have started it as he followed her down the narrow stairs, and Sophie turned to look at him in sudden panic.

"It's all right," he said in his soothing voice. "It will all be over quickly. Sin must be punished, so that you may find eternal life. Any pain or torment will simply bring you closer to heaven."

"Where are Grace and Marty, Doc?" She didn't know how she managed to keep her voice so calm. Maybe she was just numb. She could already feel the heat from the fire, and it was just a matter of time before it traveled down the rickety stairs to engulf them.

"They'll be joining you, Sophie," Doc said. "On your knees, child."

"Why?"

"You need to repent of your sins so you can meet your Maker with a clean heart."

"But if I repent of my sins why do I have to die?"

Doc frowned, as if she'd posed a complicated theological question. "Because you have to," he said finally. "Pray with me, Sophie." He sank to his knees, dragging Sophie along with him, and began praying in a loud, eerie voice, his head bowed.

She thought she could hear the faint cry of voices beneath the increasing crackle of the fire, beneath Doc's loud exhortations. They must still be alive, she thought, clutching the heavy flashlight in her hand as Doc clutched her other one with clawlike fervor.

The flames danced down the rough wood banister, bright and cheerful, bringing death.

"Bow your head and pray with me, Sophie," Doc shouted above the noise of the flames.

And Sophie looked at Doc's bowed head, the vulnerable nape of his neck, and brought the flashlight down with all her force.

The sound would stay with her the rest of her life. The sickening crush of bone. The blood.

He collapsed in an ugly sprawl, as the flames moved toward him. She didn't stop to think, she simply stepped over his body and ran for the walk-in cooler. She struggled with the huge latch, but finally it opened, revealing Marty and Gracey huddled in one corner, hugging each other.

"It's about time!" Marty scrambled to her feet, struggling to help Grace. "What the hell is going on? Where's that old psycho?"

"I think I killed him," Sophie said.

"Good. Let's get the hell out of here. Grace needs

help. He drugged her, and her knees are still wob-
bly.''

Sophie moved into the cooler, coming up on
Grace's other side. Her mother gave her a woozy
smile, looking saner than she had in months. ''I tried
to warn you,'' she said. ''But you wouldn't listen.''

''But how did you...''

''Now isn't the time for talking, Sophie!'' Marty
said irritably. ''Come on!''

The smoke was beginning to fill the cellar, thick
plumes of it snaking down the stairway. ''Cover
your mouth and keep down,'' Sophie said. ''And
follow me.''

She half expected Marty to argue, but for once
she didn't. She simply helped drag Gracey through
the billowing smoke, out into the swirling darkness.

''If you get us trapped I'm going to be really
pissed off,'' Marty said between choking coughs.

''Me, too,'' Sophie said. She was running her
hands along the wall, looking for the bulkhead. It
was covered with tarpaper, and she hadn't bothered
to nail it shut. She could only hope that Doc hadn't,
either—it was their only way out with the stairs
awash in flames.

Her hands found the thick wood plank that ran
across the door, and she shoved it up, ignoring the
pain in her hands. She kicked things out of the way
as she dragged the other two up the short flight of
stairs, and began banging against the door overhead.

It didn't move. He must have put something over it, trapping them down there, and they were going to die in the smoke and flames.

The hell they were. She slammed against it, and she felt it begin to give.

"Hurry up!" Marty shrieked.

The door gave way, opening into the cool night air, and someone was standing there, silhouetted against the smoky sky. A hand reached down for her, Griffin's strong hand, and Sophie scrambled out, collapsing on the ground as he reached to drag the two other women to safety. Above her the deserted hospital wing was a sheet of flames, and it was spreading toward the main body of the house.

For a moment Sophie lay in the grass, coughing, unable to move, as she watched the hungry flames lick over the beautiful old house.

"Would you get a move on?" Griffin snapped, catching her arm and dragging her away from the searing heat. And then the four of them were running down the sloping lawn toward the lake, just as the fire sirens sounded from the village.

"This is far enough away," Griffin said, finally releasing her.

She collapsed in the grass, still coughing. "Where's Doc?" he asked grimly.

She couldn't answer at first. It was Marty who was able to speak. "He's toast," she said. "Literally. Down in the cellar. And don't even think of going back for him. He's a murderer.''

''I wasn't planning to,'' Griffin said, stretching out on the grass, trying to catch his breath.

''He killed them,'' Sophie said after a moment. ''He killed them all.''

There was a long silence. ''I know,'' he said.

Sophie lifted her head to peer at him through the orange glow of the fire. He was lying next to her, trying to catch his breath. ''And when were you going to share that information?'' she demanded.

''I only just figured it out,'' he said.

Grace's cackle of laughter wasn't the usual vague sound. It was more like the old Grace. ''Took you long enough,'' she said. ''I've known for months. Anyone who's ever read a true-crime thriller would have figured it out.''

Sophie raised her head to look at her mother in the bright light from the burning inn. ''You knew? Why didn't you tell me?''

''I tried. You thought I was out of my mind. So I figured as long as I was senile I could keep Doc occupied and away from you and Marty. Not that it worked for long, but there was no way I could get you away from here without telling you everything, and then you would have gone to your good friend Doc and told him everything I told you.''

Which was exactly what she had done, on a number of occasions. She opened her mouth to say something, to apologize, to yell at her mother, when the first of the Colby fire trucks careered down the narrow drive, their small complement of volunteer firemen jumping into well-orchestrated action. A moment later the rescue squad pulled in, the lights spearing out toward the lake, illuminating their bedraggled group, and then time passed in a blur as too damned many helpful hands insisted on checking her out.

They ended up taking the remarkably lucid Grace to the hospital for observation, but her mother had suddenly recovered from her so-called Alzheimer's. She'd been faking it all along, doing a hell of a good job in her misguided effort to protect her family, Sophie thought grimly.

Patrick Laflamme had arrived a moment after the fire department and Sophie couldn't even bring herself to argue when Marty left with him. He was solid, sensible, and if he tried anything, his mother would set him straight. Madelene Laflamme was a notoriously intimidating figure—if anyone could put the fear of God into Marty, she could.

She could see Griffin's body silhouetted against the flames of her burning home. It was too late—there was nothing the volunteer fire company could do to save the old tinderbox. The best they could hope was to keep it from spreading, but the summer had been a wet one, and there was no immediate danger of the tall stand of pines turning into a torch.

Sophie sat in one of the Adirondack chairs as she watched her future go up in smoke. She should have been devastated, weeping, up there manning the fire hose and begging them to try to save the building. She didn't move.

She'd killed a man tonight. A deluded old man, guilty of great evil, but a human being, nonetheless, and she'd bashed him on the head and left him to burn to death in the funeral pyre he'd created.

She'd fallen in love tonight, with the wrong man, at the wrong time, in very much the wrong place. She could only hope that she could talk herself out of it.

She'd watched her dreams go up in smoke. She had no home, no job, no future. She should have been devastated. Instead she felt almost lighthearted. Free.

Was she free enough to run from Thomas Griffin? Or had she traded one kind of bondage for another?

She leaned back against the wooden slats, closing her eyes. The heat from the fire spread down over her body like the midday sun. She had the absurd notion that as she sat there she took some of the house into her soul, even as the rest of it disappeared into smoke and rubble. It had been part of her life for such a short time. But now everything had changed.

She heard a crash, and she opened her eyes to see the hospital wing collapse in on itself. Burying

Doc's body inside. The firemen had moved back, out of harm's way, clearly deciding there was nothing they could do but keep it from spreading. It was just as well. She didn't have the heart to rebuild.

Hell, she wasn't sure she had a heart at all. If she had, she'd handed it to the man next door on a silver platter. She could pick Griffin out easily among the silhouetted figures of the men of Colby. Someone had given him protective gear, but there was no missing that rangy stride of his, the way he held himself as he stood talking to another of the firemen.

She could almost hear their voices. She sat wrapped in heat, mentally identifying each of the firemen. Will Audley and his son Perry, John Corbett off to the left, and Zebulon King in furious discussion with Griffin. She couldn't tell who anyone else was, and it didn't really matter. She was bone weary. She needed a bath, she needed a bed. Both had gone up in flames.

Everyone seemed to have forgotten she was there. Maybe they thought she'd gone to the hospital with Grace, but the EMTs had told her to stay put. Maybe they thought she'd gone back with Patrick and Marty. Maybe they didn't give a shit where she was.

She pushed back from the chair, no longer able to watch the fire. Turning her back on it, she walked down to the little spit of land that jutted out into the lake. The huge white pines were between her and the burning building, though the sky was as bright as day. She stepped out onto the dock, glad that no one could see her. She needed to be alone, at least for a short while.

She should have known that the moment she decided she needed privacy, Griffin would show up. He came up behind her on the dock, and she glanced back at him for a moment, then stared straight ahead, watching the reflection of the orange flames on the stillness of the water.

"Are you okay?" he said, his voice stilted.

"Just peachy. Go away."

"You're a mess."

She turned at that, looking up at him. "If you don't have anything constructive to say, go away." She turned again, keeping her back rigid.

He came up close to her, warm, smelling of woodsmoke. "I think you should come home with me," he murmured. "You don't have anywhere else to go."

"Thanks, but I'm sure I can find someplace to stay. I should go see Rima."

"Rima's dead. Zeb King told me she died earlier this evening. Looks like she was suffocated. Doc probably would have called it a heart attack."

Sophie didn't say anything. Everything had taken on a strange, macabre twist, and nothing made sense anymore. "I'll stay with Marge Averill."

"I'll give you a ride there."

"Don't bother. I'm sure she'll show up anytime

22

"So what are you going to do with your life?"
Marge Averill asked her one morning two weeks
later. "It's not that I don't love having you here,
and you're welcome to stay as long as you like, but
the rest of your family is nicely settled, and you're
still wandering around like a lost soul."

Sophie managed a wary smile. "They don't need
me anymore."

"No, they don't," Marge agreed tactlessly.
"Madelene Laflamme will take good care of Marty
and make sure she doesn't get into trouble. She
couldn't have found a better place to stay. I'm sure
she'll be fine."

"Yes," Sophie said. "She'll probably end up
marrying Patrick and having a dozen babies."

"Isn't she a little young?"

"Davis women are like that. We only fall in love
once, and no one else will do. At least Marty chose
wisely."

"It doesn't seem to me as if your mother has
spent her entire life faithful to one man," Marge
observed with some asperity.

now—she wouldn't let a melodrama like this pass her by."

"All right." He wasn't going to argue with her. He was probably glad he was going to get rid of her without a scene.

"I assume you're leaving," she said stiffly.

Silence. Then, "Do I have any reason to stay?"

She had no idea whether that was a rhetorical question or not. Was she supposed to ask him to stay? Tell him she'd fallen in love with his lying, treacherous face and wicked hands? Not to mention his mouth.

"I can't imagine why you'd want to."

Another silence. "Okay," he said, and she didn't know what he was agreeing with. "I'll go give Marge a call and make sure she's coming out here."

"If you want."

Silence. When she looked again he was gone.

She sat down on the end of the dock, putting her feet into the cool water. She'd lost her barn boots along the way, though she couldn't remember when, and the water felt wonderful. Maybe she should just slip into the lake, let the water wash the soot and sweat and sex from her body.

And maybe she didn't want to lose the last trace of him. She sat staring at the lake, telling herself what a fool she was.

"Actually she has. He died before she met my father, and she decided to make do. She's been making do ever since, but that's all."

"And what about you? What about your lost true love?"

"I don't have a lost true love."

"True enough. He's still here."

Sophie looked up sharply. "What are you talking about?"

"What do you think I'm talking about? Thomas Griffin's back in town. He was only gone for a couple of days, and then he came back. He bought the Whitten place, and he's been working on it."

"I hope he'll be happy."

"I don't think so. He's been snapping everyone's head off. I figure the fact that you won't talk to him might have something to do with it."

"There's nothing to say."

"Oh, I imagine there's quite a lot to say. I don't know what went on between you two, but I can imagine."

"Well, don't. Read a romance instead."

"That hot?" Marge said with a lascivious grin. "Lucky girl."

"I don't want to talk about it."

"All right, we won't talk about it. What are you going to do today? I've got to show a house later this morning, and I've got some office work to finish up. When are you going to decide what you want to do with the land? At least you were smart enough to insure the hell out of the place. You could probably pay off your mortgage and even build something smaller.''

''And do what?''

Marge shrugged. ''You'll figure it out. You've still got your freelance writing.''

''I want a home.''

''So find one. Make one. It was just a house, Sophie.''

And all her dreams. She rose, plastering a phony smile to her face. ''You know what they say—when the going gets tough, the tough go shopping. I need some new clothes. There isn't much in my style locally.''

''If you call that a style,'' Marge said with a sniff. ''You dress like an old lady.''

''I feel like an old lady,'' she said stubbornly.

''There's a Victoria's Secret in Burlington.''

''Go to work, Marge.''

The summer had vanished, and autumn had descended with a vengeance. The air was crisp and cool, with a freshly washed look to it. Leaves had come down in the wind, as well as a number of branches, and when Sophie drove back into town, just after seven, she could see the bright color tipping the trees surrounding the lake. The seasons were changing, and the nip in the air promised sharper and colder days to come.

And she had to figure out what the hell she was going to do. Her suddenly sane and vibrant mother was leaving for a trip to Paris, and she could go with her. Gracey had always wanted her to travel with her, and Sophie had always refused, too caught up in being responsible. Now there was nothing to be responsible for, but Gracey no longer seemed as eager to have her come along. She was off in Boston, planning her next trip, and for some reason she seemed to think Sophie was better off staying in Vermont. As if there was anything here left for her.

Even Marty didn't need her anymore. She was living under the strict maternal eye of Madelene Laflamme. Her hair was no longer fuchsia, her skirts were marginally longer, and her language had cleaned up considerably. She'd even given up cigarettes.

She was planning to stay there, helping out with the farm, and then go to UVM with Patrick. Everyone seemed to think it was a fine idea. Everyone except Sophie, who needed someone to need her.

She dumped her bags of clothing on the twin bed in Marge's guest room and headed for the shower. Her hair had been singed in the fire, but the salon owner, Tracy, had managed to salvage it with a shorter, feathery cut that suited Sophie's face but not her clothes.

She knew what she was going to do. She'd figured it out during the long drive to Burlington, and as the hours went on she'd known that she really had no choice. There was only one person left for whom she was responsible. And that was Sophie Davis.

She dried herself, smoothing gardenia-scented cream on her skin. She shaved her legs, then pulled on the scanty teal silk underwear. The black dress came next, clinging to her curves, showing much too much of her long legs. At least they were good legs, she had to admit it. Her butt was too big, but so was Jennifer Lopez's. Her boobs were too big, but he'd seemed to like them well enough. He'd wanted to see her in something slinky.

His time had come.

She even had high heels, though they weren't really made for the rocky Vermont terrain. At the last minute she chickened out, grabbing Marge's raincoat before she climbed back into her rental car and headed around the lake.

She drove first to what was left of the inn. The sun was just setting over the lake, and she pulled up in front of the ruins, staring at them. They weren't smoldering any longer—two weeks and three rainstorms had put out any lingering ember. The entire structure had collapsed in on itself. The only thing left standing was the walk-in cooler in the basement.

She looked out over the lake. It was a beautiful

view, and she missed her porch. Missed the kitchen and the pottery jars of flour and sugar. Missed the wallpaper she'd slaved over, missed the wood floors she'd refinished.

But most of all she missed Griffin. And she was tired of being a coward.

The driveway to the Whitten place was in worse shape than ever before. The rainstorms had taken their toll, and it looked as if some heavy equipment had been brought down there in the last few weeks. She pulled the car up beside the Jaguar, cursing. She'd been hoping she wouldn't have to do this, that Marge had been wrong, and he'd left, and she could find some other way to get on with her life.

But here he was. Hopefully alone.

The night was chilly, with the bite of fall in the air, and smoke was coming out of the chimney. A good smell, not like the gasoline-fueled stench of the inn.

Lights were on inside, making it look welcoming, but she had no illusions. Her future lay in there, for good or bad, but she wanted nothing more than to run away again.

Keeping the coat wrapped tightly around her, she climbed out of the car. One high-heeled shoe twisted underneath her, nearly spraining her ankle, and she kicked them off, cursing. Okay, barefoot was all right. Make it easier to run away if he didn't want her.

She knocked, but there was no answer. So he wasn't home. She could come back another day.

But she knew she wouldn't. The door wasn't locked, and she pushed it open, stepping into the warmth and light of the cottage.

She glanced at the rug, remembering exactly what she'd done there just a few weeks ago. She was out of her mind coming here—she'd done so well in ignoring him. But if she didn't face this, face him, then there was no getting on with her life. She crossed the room and sat down in the chair by the fire, keeping her coat wrapped tightly around her.

She heard his footsteps on the porch. She had no doubt that it was anyone but him—she'd know his step anywhere. He would see her car parked there, and be prepared to find her. That is, if he recognized the car she'd been forced to rent while her Subaru was being repaired.

He pushed the door open and stepped into the room, carrying an armload of firewood. He barely glanced at her, kicking the door shut behind him, closing out the chilly darkness, and dumped the logs on the stone hearth. He squatted by the fire and added a couple of logs, then tilted his head to glance at her, huddled in her borrowed raincoat.

"It's about time," he said in an even voice.

Somehow she found her voice. "You weren't here."

"I was gone for exactly two days. And stop look-

ing at me like I'm Jack the Ripper. I'm not a murderer, remember?''

He seemed almost lighthearted, which annoyed
her. How could he sound almost cheerful when she
was squirming with miserable uncertainty?

''I wouldn't think that would be something to
joke about.''

''I'm dead serious.''

He sat back on his heels, looking at her. She'd
forgotten just how gorgeous he was, with his gray-
streaked curls, the thin glasses perched on his nose,
the big strong hands and wicked mouth...

She was getting hot, and she wasn't about to dis-
pense with the raincoat.

''Why are you here? Just come to say good-bye,
or was there something you wanted?''

''I can leave...'' she said, starting to rise.

Mistake. It made him put his hands on her, just
for a brief moment, to shove her back into her chair.
She'd forgotten how powerful the feel of his hands
was.

''No, you can't,'' he said. ''Not until we figure
out what we're going to do.''

''What do you mean?''

''Are we going to keep fighting, or are we going
to go upstairs? We haven't tried a bed yet. It might
add a refreshing sense of adventure.''

''Do you think about anything besides sex?''

''It does tend to be foremost in my mind when I

look at you. When I don't look at you, when you're shut up somewhere refusing to see me, I tend to think about how annoying you are, what a total pain in the butt you can be, and how I can't stand not seeing you.''

''That's not enough.''

''You want me to tell you I'm madly in love with you, Sophie? Hey, I'm a lawyer—I can lie with the best of them.''

She blinked. There it was out in the open, under the harsh glare of light. Except that the light wasn't harsh at all, it was a soft glow from the fire and the old lamps.

''Then we've got a problem,'' she said softly.

''Do we?''

''Because I'm in love with you.''

He didn't look particularly happy to hear it. ''It's just sex, Sophie.''

''So why did you come back?''

He shrugged. ''Unfinished business? Lust? A latent sense of decency?''

''You said you're a lawyer. No such thing.''

''What do you want from me?''

''Why don't you tell me what you want from me?''

He hesitated. ''I want you.''

''Yes,'' she said, gently encouraging.

''I want you in my bed. I want you in my house. Hell, Sophie, I want you in my life. I want to take you upstairs to that nice big bed and make love to you, very slowly, and then I want to sleep with you, which is weird as hell because I don't like to sleep with the women I have sex with. I want to wake up with you in the morning, I want to fight with you in the afternoon, and I want to make love on any and every available surface in this place. And then I want to do it all over again. Come upstairs with me, Sophie. I'll keep you warm. I'll keep the darkness away.''

She was beginning to melt. ''We have nothing in common,'' she said.

''I know.''

''We'll fight all the time.''

''But then we'll make up.''

''True,'' she said. ''You're going to marry me.''

He blinked at that. ''Yeah,'' he said morosely, ''you're right.''

''And you're going to love me.'' She stood and dropped the raincoat in the chair behind her.

He rose, towering over her, and he put his big, strong hands on her shoulders and pulled her to him. ''God help me, you're right about that, too.''

And he kissed her.